M000197177

"'They make things big in America,' is a phrase from 'The Old Olive Tree,' a story worthy of Saroyan and one of twenty in Mike Maggio's vibrant collection, *Letters from Inside*. Maggio makes a big splash with this book, a most welcome yet quiet one, undulating ripples of deep and careful prose from the inside of the heart. Listen carefully as you read."
RAFAEL ALVAREZ, AUTHOR OF
BASILIO BOULLOSA STARS IN THE FOUNTAIN OF HIGHLANDTOWN

"*Letters from Inside* is a treasure chest of a book. Each story is different. A few are Kafkaesque. Sometimes Mike Maggio writes like a weaver or sculptor. Sometimes he is simply a magician when it comes to words. *Letters from Inside* is a collection of twenty stories that should be given a home on every bookshelf."
E. ETHELBERT MILLER, HOST OF ON THE MARGIN WPFW 89.3 FM

"Mike Maggio's latest collection of short stories displays his talent, once again, for voice, scenario, and characterization. What a delight it is to read these intricate portrayals—often reminiscent of folk tales with an ironic, frequently moral bite."
NATHAN LESLIE, AUTHOR OF *HURRY UP AND RELAX* AND
BEST SMALL FICTIONS SERIES EDITOR

ABOUT THE AUTHOR

Mike Maggio has published fiction, poetry, travel and reviews in many national and international publications including *Potomac Review, The L.A. Weekly, The Washington CityPaper, the Washington Independent Review of Books, the Jordan Times* and *Arabesques*. His novel, *The Wizard and the White House*, was released in 2014 by Little Feather Books, and his novella, *The Appointment*, was published by Vine Leaves Press in 2017. He is a graduate of George Mason University's MFA program and is the Northern Regional Vice-President of the Poetry Society of Virginia. Mike loves to hear from readers.

Visit the author: *www.mikemaggio.net*

.

LETTERS
FROM
INSIDE

The Best of Mike Maggio

MIKE MAGGIO

Vine Leaves Press
Melbourne, Vic, Australia

Letters from Inside
Copyright © 2019 Mike Maggio
All rights reserved.

Print Edition
ISBN: 978-1-925965-22-3
Published by Vine Leaves Press 2019
Melbourne, Victoria, Australia

No parts of this publication may be reproduced, stored in a retrieval system, or transmitted in any form or by any means, electronic, mechanical, photocopying, recording, or otherwise, without the prior written permission of the copyright owner.

This book is sold subject to the condition that it shall not, by way of trade or otherwise, be lent, resold, hired out, or otherwise circulated without the publisher's prior consent in any form of binding or cover other than that in which it is published and without a similar condition including this condition being imposed on the subsequent purchaser. Under no circumstances may any part of this book be photocopied for resale.

This is a work of fiction. Any similarity between the characters and situations within its pages and places or persons, living or dead, is unintentional and coincidental.

Cover design by Jessica Bell
Interior design by Amie McCracken

 A catalogue record for this book is available from the National Library of Australia

For my family: Amal, Fairuz, Yasmine and Karim,
for giving me the space

TABLE OF CONTENTS

Underneath the Griffin Tree 11

Key Bridge 27

The Good Civil Servant...45

The Departure..61

Letters from Inside 71

Book Burning...89

Metamorphosis II
(or The Sudden and Inexplicable Disappearance of David C. Roche).....103

The Herds are Charging Through the Room.....................................129

The Old Olive Tree..135

Atelier 145

Suddenly, There Was Harold 153

The Last Laugh..165

A Man and A Fish 183

A Sort of Santa Claus 195

The Keepers...217

About Being Caspar Crump 237

The Other 251

The Beasts 261

Prick..267

Crossing Pacific Avenue...275

The Men Have Come to Fix the Drain 287

UNDERNEATH THE GRIFFIN TREE

Wasn't just a few years ago I liked to lie under the Griffin tree. Least that's how it was known back then. A big ol' shady tree in the middle of a field where I'd go a-rompin' with the boys, givin' 'em of my sweetness, robbin' 'em of that last bit of innocence they pretended they no longer had. Oh, I'd get their number, right quick. Come along one o' them boys, all slick an' fine, an' I'd take just one look at him an' know just what he needed to complete his initiation into manhood.

Not that I'm a whore or nothing like that. No, sirree, I'm a church-goin' girl. My mama, bless her soul, brought me up right. An' Papa—well, Papa's another story, always beatin' up on Mama, but that's the way a man is, least that's what Mama always said, an' despite his shortcomin's, Papa done his best to raise me proper.

Still, I never saw no harm in using my God-given gifts to their fullest, pleasin' the boys an' havin' a good ol' time till the time come for me to settle on down an' bring home the babies.

An' that really is why they done called it the Griffin tree. After me, Sue Ella Griffin, though they always called me Sue Elle, dropping off the "a" as if it made me some sort of foreigner they was too damn afraid to come near. No, Sue Elle had a nice ring to it, far as they was concerned. It just slid off their tongues so fine an' so fast—Sue Elle, Sueelle—till it sounded just like "swell" as a cool breeze blew a sweet song through the leaves of the Griffin tree an' I slid open their tight zippers an' slipped my hand in onto their hot, hard, bundle o' joy.

Now that was all fine an' dandy, 'cause, those days, my mama an' papa knew nothing about what was going on, an' Lord help me had they heard even one hint.

"Sue Ella," my mama would call as I was 'bout ready to run out the door an' off to see who might be a-waitin' for me. "Where ya going', always runnin' off like some coyote caught with the goods."

"I'm goin' off to the crick, Mama," 'cause there was a crick ran right by that ol' tree, an' I wasn't 'bout to lie to Mama.

"Whatcha doin' down there all the time, girl? Must be somethin' real good fer you to be spendin' the whole summer."

"Oh, nothin' much, Mama. It's jus' nice an' quiet, an' I like to lie down an' listen to the crick go by."

"You be careful now, Sue Ella. I heard jus' the other day from ol' lady Hutchins 'bout some stranger come to town. Eyin' up all the girls an' lookin' for something he ain't got no right to. Up to no good, I reckon."

"Don't you worry, Mama. First I see of anyone I don't know, I'll come a-runnin' on home."

An' that's the day I met Willy.

Now Willy was a fine-bred boy, not one o' those hillbillies come down to town, gettin' all a-drunk an' lookin' to pitch a fight. No,

Willy was from the city, so he said, had nice, smooth skin an' a face to melt away the heart. His hair was long an' black an' always combed neatly an' his clothes was always pressed jus' right.

We met at Ben's Soda Fountain, 'cause when I went down to the crick that day an' found no one a-waitin', I hiked on over to town an', being that I worked up a thirst, made my way to Ben's an' ordered me some pop.

"What's a pretty little girl like you doin' all alone on a fine day like this," he called out to me, jus' like that, as I rocked back an' forth on my stool an' waited for Ben to bring me my soda.

He was sitting in one of them booths, fingering his hair like he was the Prince o' Wales an' I was s'pposed to bow down to him or somethin' like that. An' truly to God, I would a done jus' that or perhaps swooned at his feet but, seeing how Ben was around, I jus' kept my cool.

"I don' reckon I know you fer you to be talkin' to me like that," I said to him. "Don't you be runnin' your mouth off like that 'fore you know what you're getting into."

"Whoooee," he hollered, with a great big smile, standin' up an' walkin' on over to me. "You is feisty as a fox." An' he sat himself down on the stool 'side mine an' looked me straight in the eye. "Name's Willy. I'm new in town, an' I'm jus' tryin' to strike me up a friendship."

Now jus' about this time, Ben come along with my soda pop an' put it right down in front of me, an' he jus' stood there a-watchin' an' a-listenin' to all o' this, an' I knew if I didn't behave proper, my mama an' papa would soon enough know everything that had gone on.

"Now you listen to me," I said, acting quickly. "I don' care what your name is or what you're doin' here. You jus' min' your manners an' if you can't do that, then you just go on back to where you come from."

An' then I drank up an' paid my bill an' hightailed it right outta there, knowin' full well that a man like that was not jus' goin' to stand there an' let his tail wag between his legs, if you know what I'm sayin'.

An' so I headed straight for the Griffin tree an' sure 'nough, he followed right behind, though he was discreet about it an' kept his distance, an' I sure did 'preciate that 'cause my mama an' papa would have surely heard about it that very day.

Willy an' I became best o' buddies that summer, an' all the other boys, they soon heard about it, so they stopped comin' 'round, an' it was jus' me an' Willy lying beneath that Griffin tree, havin' a swell ol' time an' enjoyin' each other's sweetness as the days wore on an' the summer heat got even hotter.

An' Willy, he wasn't afraid to call me Sue Ella neither.

"Sue Ella," he would say, after we had done our business an' we was jus' lyin' there, looking up at the sunset or listenin' to the birds a-coo an' a-holler, "I'm gonna marry you one day. I'm gonna marry you an' put a baby in that belly o' your'n an' we gonna be happy as pie."

"Willy," I'd tell him, "stop talkin' nonsense. Before you marry me, you got to get a job, an' then we got to find a way to tell Ma an' Pa how I even come to know you. An' besides," I'd say, puttin' on the look o' the devil, jus' to get him all a-bothered, "who says I wanna marry you, anyhoot?"

"Don't you worry 'bout that," he'd answer me, all indignant an' stuff. "I'm gonna take care o' all of that, an' we're gonna marry, an' you'll see."

An' then he'd put his arm around me an' draw me close, an' before you know it, we'd be doin' it again, like we had never done it before.

Now this went on all summer, an' far as I was concerned, I couldn't a asked for anything more. But come August an' Willy, he's still talkin' up a storm o' nonsense: "Sue Ella, I'm gonna make you the happiest girl this neck o' the woods. Sue Ella, I'm gonna buy you the biggest ol' house, jus' you wait an' see." Sue Ella this, Sue Ella that. Till, soon enough, I was jus' about believin' that boy's crazy talk.

Then one hot August day, with the sun a-beatin' down an' the cicadas a-singin' their sad, foolish song, we was lying under the Griffin tree, gettin' all a-cozy, listenin' to the breeze blow an' watchin' the birds struttin' around near the edge of the crick, when suddenly I get an achin' in my belly, an' my head begin to spin, an' I get to feelin' this great, big pit in my stomach. Now Willy, he jus' sat there, playin' with the grass an' the leaves on the ground, like everything was fine, but soon enough he put his arm around me, makin' me think he was gonna try to comfort me or something, but instead he starts a-making it. Well, Lordee, I jus' pulled his arm off o' me right then an' there an' put it right back in his lap.

"Whatcha go an' do that for, Sue Ella?" he said. "I ain't done nothin' wrong to you, honey, now have I?"

"I jus' don't feel like doin' it t'day, ok?"

"C'mon, honey," he said, puttin' his arm right back where I had just removed it from.

Now maybe it's 'cause I was feelin' sick, an' maybe not, but something a-sudden got into me, an' 'fore I knew it, I slapped him one right upside the head.

"Whoooee," he hollered, rubbing his hand slowly on his cheek an' lookin' at me like I was crazy or somethin'. "You sure is actin' crazy, today. You got the rag on or somethin'?"

An' maybe I was crazy, what with school comin' up an' me bein' a senior an' wonderin' what I was gonna do with my life come next year.

"Willy," I said, "you've been talkin' up your nonsense all summer, about how we gonna be married, an' here it is August an' you still ain't got no job."

"Now, Sue Ella you know I been lookin'."

"Lookin'? How can you be lookin' fer work when everyday you're down here with me, an' every night, so I hear, you be carousin' with the boys in town."

"Now, Sue Ella," he said again, gettin' all defensive, "a man got a right to do what he want at night. I'n't so?"

"I ain't talkin' about whatcha gotta right to an' whatcha don't. I'm talkin' about all the promises you done made to me."

Now I've always been a strong girl. Everyone in town know they can't pull no fast one on me. Take my ball an' I'll chase you till the sun goes down. Throw a stone at me an' I'll whip your hide 'fore the day's through. But that day, I wasn't feelin' myself. Maybe it was a realization that I had been had, but suddenly I could no longer control myself an' I just started cryin'. An' I mean a-screamin' an' a-wailin' like when death strikes your closest kin or like when you've done something terrible an' you know you've got to face the wrath of the Lord.

"Sue Ella," he said, gettin' all sweet an' fingerin' my long, blonde hair. "I'll get a job. I promise."

"Willy," I cried, "you ain't kept none o' your promises so far, 'ceptin' one."

Now Willy, upon hearing those words, got all serious an' stuff.

"What is it, Sue Ella. What're you tryin' to tell me?"

An' here the tears came down even more, an' my voice began a-trembling, an' that awful pit in my stomach seemed to grow until I thought it would swallow me right then an' there. A summer breeze ran through the air an' stirred up the Griffin tree, an' I tried to concentrate on the sound of the leaves, hopin' that would help me forget my woes. An' then, lookin' at Willy, an' knowin' he was a-waitin' for an answer an' not knowin' what else to do or say, I jus' took his hand an' slowly placed it on my belly.

"Whatcha gonna do about it, Willy?" I said.

Well, poor Willy, he didn't know what to do. The look on his face went from happy to downright scared, like he had swallowed a wild berry an' found out it was poison.

"We'll think of somethin'?" he said, when he finally got back use of his tongue.

"Think of somethin'?" I said. "What kinda girl do you think I am? Think of somethin'? You better be thinkin' of nothin' else 'cept findin' a job an' gettin' married, if you know what's good fer you."

"Now, Sue Ella, there are ways. There are things that can be done."

"Things?"

Well, Lord strike me dead, I could barely control myself, an' before I knew it, I was all over him, a-poundin' my fists into him like there was no tomorrow an' poor Willy, he jus' barely got out of my grip when I began a-chasin' him 'round an' 'round the Griffin tree, spillin' out my guts like a lost child an' jus' achin' to get my hands on that no-good son-of-a-bitch.

Well, somehow, when it was all over, we were back in each other's arms again, all sweaty an' outta breath. Willy 'pologized again an' again, an' promised me he'd start looking for a job the very next morning. An' 'fore the day was through, we did it least three times, though Lord only knows why I ever agreed.

Course, I never did get to see Willy again. Guess he knew his time was up an' he'd better hightail it right outta town. But what ol' Willy didn't know was that I really wasn't pregnant. Least, not that day. But not long after, come time fer my monthly flow, an' I begin feelin' all crampy an' it refuses to come. So I wait a few days, an' it still don't come, an' all I could think of was Willy a-sittin' there under the Griffin tree with his tongue hangin' out like a mad raccoon an' tellin' me there was ways.

When I finally got to acceptin' that I had done wrong an' there was nothin' I could do about it 'ceptin' one. I kept thinkin' 'bout how that would sit with the Lord, an' I knew the Lord would not be happy with me for killin' a poor, ol' innocent child.

Then one Sunday, I was sittin' in church with my mama an' papa, listenin' to the preacher preach, tryin' to ignore Papa sleepin' off his Saturday night drink, lookin' at Mama with that sad look on her face an' a great big bruise jus' below the eye, an' thinkin' 'bout that baby a-growin' inside o' me an' not knowin' what to do about it. An', what with the heat an' everything, I suddenly began to feel green, even with the fans a-hummin' through the still church air, an' I looked up at my mama an' let out a sigh like the apocalypse was a-sittin' right there on the horizon.

"What's wrong child?" Mama whispered to me under her breath, already humiliated by Papa's behavior an' not wantin' me to add to it.

But before I could answer, I jumped out of my seat an' ran right out of that church, an' I reckon no one in that town never did see someone hightail it outta Sunday service fast as that, 'ceptin', perhaps, for the boys when they be makin' trouble an' the preacher chases them away in the name of the Lord.

Well the day went by, an' my mama an' papa said nothin' 'bout what had happened, but sure 'nough, come dinner time, an' we're sittin' 'round the table an' Papa's a-drinkin' his moonshine an' a-rubbin' his chin like he does when he's mullin' something over, when suddenly he looks straight at me an' says:

"Sue Ella. You been actin' strange these past few days. Somethin' eatin' at you?"

"No, Papa," I said.

"You worried, maybe, 'bout school startin'?"

"No, Papa. Things are jus' fine."

"I been hearing tales 'bout you, Sue Ella," Mama piped in then.

"I hope, fer your sake, they're nothin' but tales, you know what's good fer you."

"Whatcha mean, Mama?"

"You know what I'm talkin' 'bout, girl. Don't think I don't know what happened at Ben's a while back. Don't think I don't hear 'bout the boys followin' you all 'round town. I'm not deaf, Sue Ella. People are talkin' an' I'm a-hearing."

"You better watch it girl," Papa said then, standin' up an' leanin' over the table. "Else I'm gonna lock you in your room. An' you ain't never gonna come out 'ceptin' to eat. Understand?"

An' Papa, he banged his fist so hard on the table that it nearly tipped over, an' everything went a-flyin' an' landed all over him, an' I never did see Papa cuss up a storm like he did that day, an' poor Mama, she was beside herself with grief, what with worryin' over me an' tryin' to calm Papa down an' clean up the mess he had made all at the same time.

Well I realized that day that 'fore I had to face the wrath of the Lord, I'd have to face my mama an' papa's an', Lord forgive me, but they won out an' I decided right there an' then to do somethin' about gettin' rid o' that baby.

Over the next couple of days, I tried jus' about everything, short of goin' to a doctor, 'cause then surely my Mama an' Papa woulda found out. I ran around an' tuckered myself out. I jumped up an' down continuously for an hour straight. I tried strenuous exercise: bending at the waist, doin' sit-ups an' pull-ups an' all other kinds of nonsense. But that little ol' baby was tied in tight an' I reckon had no intention of lettin' loose.

Now just about this time, school began an' I got to see all my friends an' acquaintances once again, an' it was all we could do but talk about what we had done over the summer. Well, girls bein' girls, we discussed just about everything, 'specially in the locker room after gym class. So one day, while we was changin', after a rigorous workout on the track, I noticed ol' Mary Beth eyein' me up, like maybe I was beginnin' to show, an' she began runnin' her mouth 'bout how her cousin had gotten pregnant an' how she had dislodged that baby with nothin' but a plain, ol' metal hanger.

"Said it was easy as pie," Mary Beth said, like she knew what she was talkin' about. "Said she just shoved that little ol' thing right up an' everything jus' came a tumblin' out."

"You sure she ain't pulling the wool over your eye?" I asked, secretly wonderin' if, perhaps, there was one thing I hadn't tried. "'Cause if it's that easy, why does everyone spend so much money goin' to a doctor to have it done?"

"I do declare," Mary Beth answered. "You're just as skeptical as a mouse, Sue Ella Griffin. Perhaps you ought to try it an' see for yourself."

Well, I didn't pay Mary Beth no mind, nor the other girls who began laughing away like hyenas. Didn't give a damn 'bout what they knew an' what they didn't. But that night, when I was all alone in my room an' everyone was fast asleep, I got to thinkin' that this might be the only way I had left.

So I got up out of bed an' walked over to the closet an' fumbled around in the dark till I found one o' them wire hangers. Then I slowly tiptoed my way down the hallway, past Mama an' Papa's

21

room to the bathroom, petrifyin' every time that ol' wooden floor gave out a creak.

When I finally made it, I locked the door an' got all undressed. Then I got in the tub an', with nothin' but the moonlight as my guide, I slowly twisted that hanger apart an' when it was nice an' long an' straight, made a little hook at the end jus' like Mary Beth had described an' slowly entered it up between my legs.

Well, at first the pain was bearable, but soon enough, as I pushed it up, it starting aching so bad I couldn't take it, so I tried to remove it from inside but the more I pulled, the more it hurt till I thought surely I was gonna pull my insides out. An' sure 'nough the blood started comin' an' I didn't know what to do an' I soon let out a scream loud enough to wake up the dead.

The last thing I remember that night was my papa breaking down the door in his underwear an' my mama standin' in the doorway, shoutin' the Lord's name an' starin' in disbelief at the puddle of blood that had gathered down around my feet.

When I awoke, all I could see was white, an' Lord, for a moment, I thought I had died an' gone to heaven. The walls, the ceiling, the bed, the sheets—even the chair where Mama was sitting was white an' ghostly. A nurse was standing over me, taking my pulse, an' when she saw my eyes open, she smiled politely an' said I was going to be all right.

At first, I didn't know what was goin' on, but then it all came back to me.

"An' the baby?" I asked.

At these words, the nurse's face dropped like a stone in water, an' I could see, from the corner of my eye, Mama shiftin' nervously in her chair like she was convulsing inside. Instead of answering, the nurse silently finished taking my pulse, wrote the results on the chart that hung at the foot of my bed, an' left the room quickly as she could.

When she was gone, Mama pushed herself up outta that chair an' walked on over to me. She stood beside the bed an' stared at me without sayin' a word. Her eyes were red an' puffy, like she had been crying all night. Her hair was uncombed, an' her face was haggard an' freshly bruised. She was dressed in an ol' frock which, I reckon, she had thrown on quickly as the ambulance took me away. Her lips were trembling something terrible an' I could tell that she was trying to avoid looking at me.

Then, suddenly, she dropped down on the bed an' grabbed a-hold of me an' started to sob.

"Sue Ella," was all she could say. "Sue Ella." An' after a while: "Why?"

An' then she lifted me up carefully an' put her arms around me an' pressed my head tight against her bosom like she used to do when I was a child an' I had done something wrong an' she had finally decided to forgive me.

Mama held me tight like that for a long, long time, longer than she had ever done, quietly sobbing in fitful waves as though she was still tryin' hard to hold all her years of torment way inside.

Papa was not so kind. But then Papa wasn't a kind man. Only thought about work. An' when he wasn't workin', he was drinkin' his moonshine, or carousin' with the men folk, an' God only knows what kind of nonsense they got into, though I could well imagine cause some of them boys I was seeing that summer 'fore I met Willy was their own flesh an' blood.

When I first came home, Papa flat out refused to talk to me. Wouldn't even look at me, as if I had some disease that would turn him to salt were he to cast an eye on me.

As he had threatened, I was locked up in my room. My meals were brought to me three times a day an' whenever I needed to go to the bathroom, I knocked three times, waited five seconds, then knocked again. Then, my mother would come, unlock the room, an' escort me to the bathroom. When I was done, she locked me right up again. I don't believe she wanted to do this, 'cause the look in her eye, just before she closed the door, was drawn an' sad.

Then, a few weeks later, when I was fully recuperated, Papa came to see me. It was late at night, but my light was still on an' I reckon he knew I was still awake. He unlocked the door an' stood there, still an' impassable like a huge mountain. It's hard to say what he was feeling, but I knew from his eyes that he was drunk as hell. He said nothing. Jus' stared an' stared for the longest time. Then, he removed his belt an' gave me the worst beating I have ever received in my life.

When it was all over, an' I lay there a-whimpering, he quietly put his belt on an' said:

"Sue Ella. You've brought shame upon us. An' I reckon, I'm the one to blame."

Needless to say, I was taken out of school an' I was not permitted any visitors. An' I was only allowed out once, an' that was for the funeral. An' I was sure grateful to be allowed at least to give my baby a proper burial.

Not long after that, I was married. Forced to accept the only boy in town who would have me. Not that he's an angel. None of them are, Lord knows. But he's been kind to me, though he likes his moonshine, an' raises up holy hell when he's had too much. But then I guess I'd still be locked up, otherwise. Now, least I'm free, though I'm not as pretty as I used to be, an' I sometimes have to hide the black eyes an' the swollen cheeks with the make-up I buy from the five an' dime store whenever I can afford to.

We have two children, an' another one on the way. Doctor says I'm lucky I can still conceive. Guess that's a matter of opinion.

Sometimes, when the weather's nice, I take them little ones on down to the Griffin tree. We sit in the cool shade an' listen to the crick go by.

The big one likes to run around in circles. It's a game she plays, like she's chasin' someone, till, eventually, when she's all tuckered out, she drops down, looks sadly at me an' says: "He got away, Mama."

The younger one is jus' learnin' to crawl. Whenever a bird land on the grass, he gets up on his hands an' knees an' wiggles his ways towards it. Course, the bird flies away an' then that boy gets all excited, laughin' an' lookin' at me like he's the king o' Siam.

As for me, I like to gather wildflowers when I'm there. I pick them carefully, mixin' all different colors an' shapes an' trimmin' the stems so they're all the same size, till I have a right pretty bouquet. Then I take a long blade of grass an' tie it tight around the base of them flowers an' I place them under the Griffin tree, in the place where there is no longer any grass. When I'm finished, I gather up my kids an' slowly head on home, watchin' them chase each other innocently through the meadow, an' I look at the sun set, an' I thank the Lord that yet another day has gone by.

KEY BRIDGE

A most unusual thing happened on the morning of June 27th to M. as he was crossing the Key Bridge—unusual, perhaps, for anyone other than M., for he was not what one would call a typical bridge crosser in that part of town.

That morning—and it was a beautiful morning with the sun smiling in the sky, the sky a clear bright blue and the air light and breezy with not a trace of humidity—M., whose full name we never learned due to rules and regulations surrounding his privacy, was on his way to Georgetown, enjoying a casual walk across the bridge, observing people dressed in their weekday best, watching the bikers and cars as they inched their way across, when he stopped to look down at the Potomac, as people often do when they are walking across the Key Bridge. Down below, individuals in kayaks were paddling east and west and, just as M. looked down at the river, which was sparkling brightly in the morning sun—so bright, it was almost blinding—a bird—a seagull, perhaps, or maybe an osprey, he couldn't tell—flew right by him and dove straight down towards the water, no doubt to fetch its morning meal. M., who had always been fond of birds, watched intently, tracing each movement with a swing of his right hand, as it swooped down and then, just as quickly, flew back up and disappeared into the sky.

Now all of this happened so quickly—so unexpectedly—that it seemed that someone—M., perhaps—had thrown something into the water, some foreign object or something, even, suspicious, which, as we all know, is illegal and possibly perilous, as trash on the Potomac, or any other river for that matter, is unsightly and creates pollution, and suspicious objects have a habit of creating havoc, even destruction, if not caught in time. And so it was that M., as he leaned over the bridge and watched this wonderful scene from nature unfold, received a sudden tap on the shoulder and, turning around, was faced by a policeman in full uniform with a shiny gold badge which gleamed in the sunlight, a gun hung prominently at his right side, which did not glow as brilliantly as the badge but looked menacing instead, and a full array of bullets tucked neatly inside his belt, as well as all the other paraphernalia that your typical policeman carries with him in this day and age.

Now this policeman, whose name has been kept secret for reasons unknown, had been watching M. making his way idly across the bridge, weaving among bikes and pedestrians who were coming and going in either direction, and was taken aback when he observed, as he saw it, M. dumping something questionable into the river. And because it happened so fast that one could easily misperceive what was going on—after all, a seagull could easily be mistaken for a plastic bag filled with trash, and a man such as M., who was as anonymous and nondescript as his name, could easily be mistaken for a tramp or a hoodlum or some other unsavory type of individual—this conscientious policeman decided to stop M. to clarify just what he was doing on the Key Bridge on that early June morning.

Now we are not sure what ethnicity M. identified with or otherwise what his background was. He was too light to be black, though being African-American was not out of the question. Yet he was several shades too dark to be white. And it was too difficult to tell from his swarthy face if he was Mexican or Honduran or even Middle Eastern or, for that matter, if he were simply a well-tanned white man, for his head was fully covered in a beard and moustache and a thick shock of hair all of which obscured whatever features might otherwise have been observed. And though his hair did not resemble the hair of a black man, nor of a Mexican or a Middle Easterner, it neither resembled that of a white man—it was what might be described as in between. Nor could one tell, from M.'s name, what his ethnicity might be, for we are not sure if that was even his real name, and M., after all, can easily be construed into Maurice or Manuel or even Mohammed.

"Good morning, my man," the policeman said to M. He was nonchalant as he said this and, seemingly, quite friendly. Still, one often needs to discount friendliness in a policeman, especially when something unusual is happening on a bridge in the middle of the city.

"Good morning, officer," M. responded in a most courteous fashion, for he had been brought up to respect authority whose job it was to keep the peace and protect the citizenry.

"And where are we off to today?" the policeman asked, quite causally, as if he were just making conversation.

"Georgetown," M. answered. And then, just to be sure, he added: "Sir."

"I see," the policeman said. "And did you know that some bridges were not meant to be walked across?"

"Sir?" M. answered, quite surprised.

"Certain bridges," the policeman continued, "were meant to be passed under. Just like that boat, for example."

And he pointed to a small craft—an orange kayak with two individuals who were paddling their way west and were just about to pass under the bridge.

"Or that object," the policeman added, pointing to something that was floating in the water, something that, through the slant of light and the sparkling of water in the wake of the kayak, could not be distinguished though one knew immediately that it did not belong on the river. "The river is not a dumping ground," he added.

"The question," the good policeman continued, "is not where you are going. The question is what did you throw down into the water."

And then, suddenly, the policeman's countenance became stern.

"I saw you throw something. Just now. And if it wasn't trash or any other kind of pollutant, then what was it?"

"Sir?" M. repeated yet again, for it seemed the only thing to say.

By now, a crowd had gathered—a crowd of typical bridge crossers who daily made their way between Rosslyn and George-town—and M. began to feel uncomfortable, for the eyes and ears of the city were suddenly upon him and the automobile traffic, already choked to a near halt, stopped completely as drivers and passengers tried to discern what was going on, as drivers and passengers are wont to do whenever they come upon some sort of commotion.

"I saw it, officer," someone shouted. "I saw him throw something off the bridge."

"Yes," someone else added. "It was a bag. Filled with trash."

"No," another said. "It was a box. About this big." And he indicated the size of a rather large package with his hands.

And pretty soon, everyone was shouting, describing what they purported to have seen M. throw off the bridge: "an old toaster," an elderly lady reported, wiggling her cane in the air; "a backpack filled with something rotten—you could smell it a mile away," a homeless man explained; "a dead bird," a middle-aged woman said, "it's disgusting what people will do," she added, "killing innocent animals, he ought to be arrested."

And then:

"I heard something strange," a respectable-looking woman in a stylish pants suit said. "Like a ticking sound. Just before he tossed it over."

"Oh my God," someone screamed. "It's a bomb!"

And quickly, the word "bomb" reverberated across the bridge, and chaos ensued, for people began to run this way and that, and the bikers panicked, and the drivers tried to move their cars whichever way they could, though traffic was tied up and going nowhere, and this caused several minor fender-benders to occur, even as some abandoned their vehicles and ran in either direction so they could get off that bridge before it blew up and they were tossed like scrap paper into the waters of the Potomac.

Meanwhile, M. found himself suddenly in handcuffs, a most unpleasant experience which he had never before encountered, and the policeman called for backup, and soon enough there were a dozen or so police cars, a helicopter circling in the air, police boats plying the waters of the Potomac, an ambulance, a firetruck and various members of the bomb and SWAT teams, all of whom converged on, under, or around the Key Bridge that morning amidst the growing pandemonium. Naturally, all the news outlets showed up, and soon enough M.'s face, by now distraught and panicked, appeared on television screens across the nation with the headlines screaming: SUSPECT IN CUSTODY AS BOMB PLOT TO BLOW UP D.C. BRIDGE IS FOILED.

Now we don't know much about what happened to M. after his arrest, for the authorities felt a need to protect him from the public and the press. After all, he was the prime suspect and, moreover, was considered evidence, and evidence, in a crime scene, is like gold in a gold shop: without it, the shop would go out of business. Similarly, without evidence, the case—in this instance, the alleged crime that M. had allegedly committed—would go up in smoke. Crimes would never be solved if evidence and suspects were not protected and innocent people's lives would be compromised. And since there were no other forensics to be had, at least as of yet, M. was the sole clue in the investigation and was, therefore, kept under lock and key.

Still, we do know certain things about M. from the news outlets who have their ways of extracting information and presenting it on their pages and screens so that the public can stay informed. And what we did learn was this: that M. was of no fixed address (he had moved twice during the last year); that he had never been arrested or in any way suspected of any crime (except for one minor infraction which involved dropping a gum wrapper on the sidewalk); that he was not associated with any known terror group or any group that had pledged loyalty to an enemy of the United States; and that, overall, despite his unseemly appearance (the mugshot conveyed an especially menacing aspect to his demeanor, for he was not allowed to smile, making him look even more dangerous than he was purported to be, and his long hair, which by then had become most disheveled, combined to make him look like a most unseemly criminal)—despite all of this, he had no record.

Still, the media and the authorities managed to locate individuals who claimed to have known him, who offered that he was a strange individual who had possibly done this or that, who often kept to himself and, though he appeared to be harmless, sometimes espoused radical and bizarre views—views that did not fit in with the norms of society. Some said he was anti-American, for he would often complain about the government which, he claimed (according to them) was never on the side of the people. Others said he was always criticizing the police and how they treated certain groups of individuals. While a number of people, who refused to speak publicly, suggested that his views, while not exactly kosher, were harmless in nature and, at any rate, they insisted, were protected by the First Amendment. Yet, no one claimed he was violent, advocated violence or, in any way, condoned violence as a means to an end. And as far as terrorism was concerned, there were certainly no known connections or inclinations, as far as they could see, in that arena. Overall, quite a number of people expressed shock at his arrest and asserted what a quiet individual he was, in their eyes—someone who could not possibly have done what he was being accused of. Still, they expressed confidence in the authorities and the job they were doing in protecting the nation.

Meanwhile, M. was granted a court-appointed lawyer whose job it was to defend him against all and sundry accusations and who (through no fault of his own, for he was not the brightest of lawyers else he would have joined some respectable law firm) found it difficult to provide consistent answers to the media, for he had not done well in his public relations class and, besides, could not get the facts straight as given by M. (after all, if you cannot tell the difference between a seagull and an osprey then how could anyone, even his lawyer, believe any other part of his story?).

So, as M.'s lawyer attempted to gather the facts from his client so that he could present them clearly in a court of law, and as the news outlets continued to investigate M.'s life (it was soon discovered that he had once been involved in training homing pigeons which, as we all know, can be used to carry secret messages, even destructive materials like small bombs and other incendiary devices), the authorities continued with their investigation, gathering evidence, which they were not allowed to share, to back up the charges that had been filed against him: charges which included intent to pollute, intent to incite violence, criminal possession of a weapon in the first degree (though no weapon was ever found), and association with a terrorist group, though this latter charge, it seemed, would be most difficult to prove.

A few hours after M.'s arrest, a small object—what looked like a scrap of metal, a piece of tail pipe, perhaps—was discovered near Union Station. Someone—a commuter with a keen eye and a nervous disposition—saw it and, due to his diligence, a rapid response team quickly arrived to defuse what was believed to be a bomb though, as some speculated, it might just as soon have been a piece of debris broken off from an old run-down car. Still, it was assumed to be a pipe bomb, homemade as pipe bombs tend to be, whose purpose it was to incite fear and panic in the lives of people rather than to create a critical mass of destruction. The press spent quite a deal of time on this incident, describing, in detail, how it was found, how pipe bombs are made, the possible motives the perpetrator might have had, and how this all fit in with a pattern of terrorism that was plaguing the world. There was Paris. There was London. There was Brussels. And now, there was Washington D.C. It was even suggested that there was a possible connection to M. who was, at the time of the discovery, consulting with his court-appointed lawyer who seemed mostly concerned with the species of bird that M. claimed to have seen that fateful day. And, even more suspiciously, several pigeons were seen loitering near the scene which, naturally, given M.'s inclination for homing pigeons (a fact which had been leaked by the press) raised suspicions among the authorities and the news outlets. The birds were quickly captured and caged and brought to a crime lab to preserve as evidence. The suspected pipe bomb was bagged, labeled and catalogued and sent to the FBI for further processing. And the anxious commuter was questioned and released, though he was told that he might have to appear in court at some later date to testify.

Now terrorism, as the name implies, is a terrible thing. It kills innocent people, wreaks havoc on the morning or evening commute, disrupts commerce, and instills fear in the lives of men and women when they should, otherwise, be enjoying their daily life of toil. So it came as no surprise that life in the city quickly became transformed. Terrorism became the talk of the town, with some openly expressing their fear and others hiding their concern under a mock aura of smug humor. Commuters on the metro went about their commute as normal, though some would peek up suspiciously from time to time from their books and magazines while others would surreptitiously look about, eyeing their fellow passengers to determine who seemed suspicious, who had a dangerous look about them and who to definitely avoid sitting next to. Backpacks and other suspicious packages took on a new meaning, especially when left abandoned on a subway platform or a street corner. And police presence around the city intensified, leaving everyone at once feeling safer and less secure. And, though life was suddenly not the same, it went on as usual, as life usually does, and soon acquired a feeling of normality—the new normal, some called it—despite the pall of fear that hung over the city.

Meanwhile, the sight of pigeons which, despite their usual ubiquity, had until then gone nearly unnoticed, now instilled a sense of uneasiness and suspicion, and eventually, after enough of a clamor, an emergency law was passed forbidding citizens from feeding them, engaging them in any activity or, otherwise, encouraging them in any way. Pigeons were now considered a dangerous species—for how could one possibly know a wild one from a trained one, or one that merely carried disease and one that carried something much more sinister. Open season was declared, after intense lobbying by the NRA, gun sales went up and the pigeon population quickly diminished which some decried as cruel and unnecessary and others lauded, given the dangers posed by the current situation.

It wasn't long after these events—several weeks perhaps but certainly no more—that people began to forget. M's pitiful face was seen less and less on TV; life in the city slowly began to return to normal; the Key Bridge regained its reputation as a safe means of getting from one side of the Potomac to the other; police presence in the city began to subside; and even the pigeon population seemed to regain its footing. M., now accustomed to incarceration, would meet daily with his public defender to discuss his knowledge of bomb-making (none), his involvement in raising homing pigeons (it was just a passing hobby), and his inability to distinguish between a seagull and an osprey despite his interest in ornithology (a word that was not part of his general vocabulary). And when his lawyer wasn't there, pressing him with pressing questions, he would spend his time staring out of his cell and watching birds of many species coming and going (though not once did he see a seagull or an osprey or any other water-prone bird, and not one pigeon came to beckon at his iron-barred window).

Life, in general, seemed good, as good as can be when one is incarcerated, for M. did not have to worry about working or paying the rent or even where his next meal might come from. And he could spend his days in contemplation, all the while watching the birds traverse his tiny window and wondering about the vagaries of life: how a simple incident had led him to a life of imprisonment—a life he had never imagined. And yet, innocent though he was, he now somehow accepted it. It was, as his mother had often said when things went wrong, simply meant to be. Still, after a while, he became bored and jittery, as is only natural, and he would sigh and mumble to himself, mumbo jumbo that was so subdued that no one around could comprehend even one syllable, adding an additional layer of suspicion in everyone's mind and leading them to believe that he was invoking some strange and ominous sentiment that did not bode well for anyone.

Then, one day, the city woke up to a new and most disconcerting situation. It was an early Sunday morning—a day following a raucous night of drinking and partying as occurs nearly every weekend in Washington or any other city for that matter—when an explosion was reported on M Street, right in the heart of Georgetown. This explosion—a loud pop that jolted the still-inebriated and the hung-over out of their stupors—was quickly followed by several others, each happening in syncopated succession up and down M Street. The police were quickly called in but, before they had a chance to arrive, a number of other bursts occurred around town, blowing out storefront windows, damaging vehicles, and terrifying residents and out-of-towners alike. This, of course, brought terrorism to the forefront once again and, with it, M., who was sleeping peacefully in his cell at the time, and his now notorious homing pigeons. Suddenly M. was a news sensation yet again, and his face was once more splattered across newspapers and TV screens alike.

Naturally, M. was interrogated extensively following these incidents. What possible involvement did he have in these explosions? Who had he communicated with since his incarceration (via homing pigeon or any other means)? And what knowledge did he have, prior to his imprisonment, of plans to terrorize the city? Who were his accomplices? And what future plans did they have to disrupt life in the city?

Poor M. was distraught. Never had he imagined that his life would take a turn such as this. He tried his best to answer their questions—to answer truthfully—though the twists and turns in their logic led him to believe that they were trying to trick him. And no matter how he answered, the implications seemed to multiply for, though he was unaware, the authorities had been keeping a close eye on him in his cell and became suspicious each time he looked out his window and interacted with the birds that flew by. It was not so much the bird watching that concerned them but the way he used his right hand in concert with each of their movements, as if he had a secret code he used to communicate with them. For, as we all know, animals have an intelligence that is deeply underappreciated and can learn to obey their masters no matter what. Moreover, he was spotted one day placing something on the ledge of his window, something which some passing bird quickly retrieved and flew off with. This immediately raised suspicions and, eventually, M. was moved to a cell that had no egress to the outside world.

The answers to their questions and his every reaction, no matter how small, were duly recorded and placed in a database, and the world wide web was scoured for clues that the authorities hoped would lead to the perpetrators and to a complete resolution of this very cryptic enigma.

Meanwhile, investigations into the mysterious explosions went into full-swing. Forensic teams were dispersed throughout the city, samples were collected and examined and fragments of broken windows and damaged cars were gathered and sent to crime labs for analysis. The FBI and other authorities diligently investigated all angles, questioning witnesses and attempting to piece together a puzzle that was scattered throughout the city. And the news outlets, ever so willing to lend their expertise and assistance, explored the connections between home-grown terrorism and known international organizations, the various techniques that these sinister organizations used in their zealous criminal endeavors, and the availability of everyday ingredients that could be put together to cause explosions and other unpleasant incidents.

Then, almost serendipitously, the cause of the explosions was suddenly uncovered. After much deliberation and many man-hours of labor, the District of Columbia Water and Sewer Authority came forward with the conclusions of their own investigation and revealed that the mysterious blasts were caused by excessive amounts of underground methane which had accumulated over time and had caused manhole covers throughout the city to blow their tops. It was a near-natural phenomenon, they claimed, and their arguments were so convincing that the press and the authorities believed this to be a sound and logical conclusion. Still, as is always the case, while most grudgingly agreed that exploding manhole covers were to blame (for exploding manhole covers did not make for as dramatic a story as home-grown terrorism), there were those who differed and continued to argue that this was a clear case of radical extremism.

Eventually, however, as is often the case, the entire topic was dropped. The news media went on to other items of importance, the politicians, eager to move on, returned to their normal order of business, and the authorities disappeared like ants under a sideboard, causing the populace to instantly forget what had been front and foremost in their minds for so many months.

And M.—poor M., who was nearly forgotten once again and who, now that things had become clear, was returned to his previous cell—remained oblivious to the events that had transpired and, to keep himself occupied, began keeping a record of the different types birds that flew by his window, including the numbers, the colors, the shapes, and their sizes. He even took to drawing them on scraps of paper until, eventually, he had enough to fill up a small book. And every day, after each meal, he would place some crumbs on his windowsill to attract stray fowl so he could continue his newfound hobby as well as provide them with sustenance. It was his small way of thanking them for keeping him company.

Eventually, after all the brouhaha had died down and this odd and alarming incident had receded into the depths of the city's collective memory, and when the authorities could produce no credible evidence and could therefore no longer justify keeping him in prison, M. was unceremoniously released and thrown back onto the streets. All charges against him were dropped and his face, once so prominently displayed on billboards and TV screens and so easily recognized, soon blended in harmoniously with the passing crowds so that no one, upon coming in contact with him, could identify him or otherwise associate him with the unusual events that had thrown the city and the nation into a coast-to-coast tizzy. M. returned to his quiet, itinerant life, settling here and there and then moving on, and continued roaming about the city, crossing bridges and riding the metro, though he diligently avoided the Key Bridge and the Georgetown area. And while he never returned to training homing pigeons, he maintained his fascination with all flying things and eventually began leading unsuspecting tourists on birdwatching tours throughout the parks and plazas that are scattered throughout the city. Likewise, his court-appointed lawyer moved on to bigger and better things, eventually landing a job with a not-so-prominent non-for-profit organization.

Life in Washington D.C. returned to normal. People went about their daily business, toiling away in office buildings and other employment venues, visiting the parks and monuments that the city is so famous for, attending baseball and football games according to their inclination, and once again riding the metro without fear, though they still had to contend with track fires, inoperable train doors, non-working escalators, and all the other annoying inconveniences that the Washington Metro is so famous for. The local news outlets went back to reporting on topics of local interest (exploding manhole covers became a repetitive subject as did human interest stories concerning homeless eagles and other local feathered beasts). Even the pigeon population seemed to improve, once again giving the lonely and the poor a means of spending their time, feeding and otherwise interacting with these urban creatures.

And the Key Bridge? Well, it soon regained its status as a stately means of crossing the Potomac on foot or on wheels though, every once in a while, some unfortunate pedestrian would suddenly remember the events that had taken place that day and would go into a panic and faint or simply fall to the ground in a fit of convulsions. And so ambulances became almost as ubiquitous as pigeons, coming and going with their screeching sirens to attend to medical and other life-threatening non-emergencies. But such is life in the big city, and the people simply kept quiet and accepted it, though some, for sure, continued to complain.

THE GOOD CIVIL SERVANT

Mr. Maxwell worked mindlessly through the stacks of papers that cluttered his desk as he had done for the past forty years. He signed, he stamped, he forwarded, he filed. He kept track of the countless forms and documents that constantly appeared, never giving a moment's thought to the impact the quick movement of his pen or the sudden thump of his rubber stamp might have. He did his job, and he did it well, and he took complete satisfaction in that fact, working until five, not one second more, not one second less.

So now, in the last few minutes of his long, undistinguished career, he thumped out his last seal, inscribed his last official signature, and straightened up his desk, as he had always done before leaving the office, making sure everything was neat and in its proper place.

When the clock struck its fifth chord and the lingering echo had faded into the corridors, Mr. Maxwell picked up his worn briefcase and looked around the small office, but before he could register even the simplest of emotions related to his departure, he was interrupted by the sound of Mr. Roberts's voice which came droning over the P.A. system.

"Mr. Maxwell. Please come to my office."

He had had ten different superiors during his long tenure in the service, he now recalled as he locked his door and started down the long, dark corridor. Otherwise, everything remained unchanged. The same dusty chandeliers hung from the ceilings; the same dark portraits guarded the hallways. He knew every portrait, every chandelier, every inch of the marble floors so well he could go to Mr. Roberts's office with his eyes closed if he had to.

He tapped lightly on the door and waited for permission to enter.

Unlike his predecessors, Mr. Roberts was a mere speck behind the large oak desk where he sat. His demeanor projected no power, instilled no confidence but served merely as a symbol of authority. Had it not been for the fact that he regularly filled out reports on his subordinates, his orders might never have been obeyed.

Mr. Roberts reluctantly lifted his small, beady eyes from the documents he was reviewing and gazed vacantly at Mr. Maxwell. Another employee leaving, another position to be filled.

"Finished, Mr. Maxwell?"

"Yes, sir."

Mr. Maxwell had always addressed his superiors in this way, even Mr. Roberts who was twenty years his junior. A man should always show respect, no matter what; a man should always know his place.

"A job well done, Mr. Maxwell."

"Thank you, sir. A job well done is a job worth doing. That's my motto, sir."

Mr. Roberts compressed his weary eyes as if to put Mr. Maxwell in focus.

"As you know, Mr. Maxwell, it's against regulations—a party, that is—you understand."

"Yes, sir. I'm quite familiar with the regulations."

"We did, however, take a collection."

Mr. Roberts opened the side drawer of his imposing desk and withdrew a neatly wrapped box.

"It's a small token."

"Thank you, sir."

Mr. Maxwell propped his briefcase up on his knee, popped open the two rickety locks, and placed the gift inside.

"You may have a seat, Mr. Maxwell."

"Thank you, sir."

"Very well, Mr. Maxwell, let's get through the formalities," Mr. Roberts said, placing a checklist in front of him.

"Office key...key to the men's room... key to the supply room... rubber stamp...stamp pad...master file..."

Mr. Maxwell had carefully arranged the supplies he had been allocated in his briefcase and now handed them one by one to Mr. Roberts who promptly ticked the appropriate box on his list.

"Very well, Mr. Maxwell."

"You forgot the letter opener, beggin' your pardon, sir."

"Ah, yes," Mr. Roberts said, clearing his throat. "The letter opener."

"And the brown cardboard file with the lace ties."

"Anything else, Mr. Maxwell?"

"No, sir."

Mr. Roberts placed the items and the checklist in a large brown envelope, carefully sealed it, and wrote Mr. Maxwell's name on the front.

"Everything official, Mr. Maxwell."

"Yes, sir."

"You will, of course, receive your monthly pension."

"Yes, sir."

"Have I forgotten anything?"

"No, sir."

"Very well, Mr. Maxwell, you may leave."

"Yes, sir. Thank you, sir."

Mr. Maxwell picked up his briefcase, walked across the room and briefly hesitated at the door.

"Goodbye, sir."

"Goodbye, Mr. Maxwell."

Mr. Maxwell quietly closed the door behind him and headed down the deserted corridor toward the stairwell. He never took the elevator down, in order to save electricity, in fact, had only begun riding up in the last five years, and now, as he walked down the six flights of stairs, he tried to remember whether he had ever initiated conversation with a superior as he had just done with Mr. Roberts. He mulled over this question until he reached the main lobby where he said good night to the evening guard and left the building for the last time, climbing down the high tier of stone steps that fronted the building.

The district where he worked or, as he now reminded himself, used to work—it was difficult for him to shift to this new grammatical concept—in this district were located all the hallowed halls of government. Here, the massive, stone-cut buildings loomed with their impressive columns, their seemingly infinite rows of windows, like so many eyes, and their foreboding portals which swallowed thousands of workers and visitors each day.

Mr. Maxwell lingered in the empty plaza, contemplating his days at the service, trying to accustom himself to the idea that he was now retired. The realization, however, forged a pit in his stomach, and he immediately set off on his last journey home.

He walked, as usual, along the same streets he had taken for forty years, twice a day, five days a week, fifty weeks a year. Give or take a few holidays, and the two days he had been sick, this worked out to about twenty thousand trips back and forth. Life is a series of repetitions, he thought, that add up to complete one's life, and at twenty minutes each way—but the calculations became too complicated, and he gave up.

At last, Mr. Maxwell reached his building. He unlocked the security gate, climbed the one flight of stairs, and opened the door to the small apartment he had occupied most of his working life. It was his government career that had enabled him to afford this place, to make his mother, in her last years, more comfortable than she had ever been. And while the rooms were not quite as big as she would have liked and the furniture not quite suitable to her tastes, it was more than he would have been able to provide had his uncle not used his influence to obtain him a civil service position.

He reached for the light switch, released his briefcase in his usual absent-minded manner, and looked in surprise when he heard it crash against the hardwood floor. Glancing around the

Mike Maggio

vestibule, he noticed that the chair where he normally placed his briefcase was not in its place. In fact, it was nowhere to be seen.

Mr. Maxwell entered the living room, switched on the ceiling light, and discovered that the room was empty. The same was true of the bedroom and the kitchen. Indeed, every piece of furniture, every moveable appliance, every wall-hanging he had inherited or purchased over the years had disappeared, except for an old television set which now sat centered on the floor against the living room wall.

Mr. Maxwell's first thought was that he had been evicted, although he had been a model tenant, had always paid his rent on time and had lived a quiet, unnoticeable life that would please any landlord or neighbor. Still, thinking the worst, he reached for the telephone to call the superintendent, but that, too, was gone.

Locking his door, he rushed upstairs to the superintendent's apartment only to find, after knocking several times, that no one was in—a rather unusual thing for that time of day.

His next thought was that, perhaps, he had been burglarized, that he should go to the local police station and file a report, but when he arrived downstairs, he was confronted with a jammed security gate, and no matter how he tried jiggling the key, it would not open.

Now Mr. Maxwell was a level-headed man, prone neither to emotional outbursts nor irrational impulses. Throughout all the crises in his life, he had reacted with utmost restraint. When his mother took ill, he calmly arranged his life so that she could be cared for without having to miss a single day's work. And when, at the end, she accused him of being self-centered and, as she had

50

termed it, slow with the dollar (despite the fact that he had taken her to the best doctors and had hired a day nurse to care for her in his absence), he attributed her callousness to senility and the crankiness that besets the aged and the infirmed, and he tried to shrug it off as best he could. Even at her funeral, a small, poorly attended affair, he had not shed a tear or expressed an iota of self-pity, despite the fact that he had suddenly found himself utterly alone.

So now, as he returned to his apartment and his eyes swept through the bare rooms, he discovered that there was, at least, food in the cupboard, and he calmly decided to fix himself something to eat, watch TV, go to bed—he'd have to sleep on the floor—and deal with the situation in the morning.

The next day, Mr. Maxwell was awakened by a loud banging on his apartment door and a sharp pain in his back, both of which seemed to manifest themselves at the very same moment. He jumped up from the hard wooden floor, limped, half-asleep, to the vestibule and opened the door to two plain-suited gentlemen.

"Jonathan Freeman Maxwell?"

"Yes."

"We've been informed of the disturbance."

"Disturbance? Oh yes. Disturbance. Won't you come in."

"I'm afraid you'll have to come with us."

"Why, yes, of course. Wouldn't you like to come in and have a look?"

"That won't be necessary, Mr. Maxwell. Please hurry. We don't want to be late for our appointment."

Mr. Maxwell hobbled back to his bedroom, puzzled at the tone of their voices and the curious way they were conducting their investigation, but he assumed they knew best how to perform their duties and, relieved that something, at least, was being done, he readied himself for his visit with the authorities.

When he was fully washed, shaved, and dressed in his navy blue suit, he returned to the two men who were waiting silently in the vestibule.

"Ready, Mr. Maxwell?"

The news had spread quickly for, as he opened the door, he saw that most of the tenants had gathered in the hallway, and those who were not quite ready to appear in public peered curiously through their narrowly opened doors. Even the landlord and his family had come down and looked on as if witnessing some odd and not quite respectable event. It reminded him of the day his mother's body had been removed, how the neighbors had all gathered and watched quietly and solemnly, as if he had been to blame.

He felt an inexplicable sense of shame, and he noticed that not one of his neighbors was smiling, not even little Sarah, whom he had often taken care of and who now stood barefoot, clutching her mother's hand and glaring at him as if he were a criminal.

With eyes turned to the floor and grasping his briefcase with both hands, Mr. Maxwell walked through the hall, down the stairs, and out the building, flanked by the two men, who directed him into a car that was parked in front.

As they pulled into the street, Mr. Maxwell began to wonder about everything that had happened since he had left his office the day before. If his empty apartment had been a mystery, the strange events that were happening to him this morning were even more so. Who were these two men anyhow? he now asked himself. And why were they treating him as if he had done something wrong? He did, indeed, feel like a criminal, he now realized, and it was no wonder that little Sarah, whom he had loved and cherished as his own daughter, had looked at him the way she had.

"Excuse me," he said at last, breaking the silence, "may I ask where you're taking me?"

"Don't worry, Mr. Maxwell," one of the men responded. "Everything will be rectified. That's why we were sent. These situations always get rectified. They just take a little time."

Saying that, they drove without another word.

At last, they entered the government district, drove past his former office building, and finally pulled up to a huge, stone facade which Mr. Maxwell had never before noticed.

The two men escorted him up the steep flight of steps. The large marble foyer they entered was packed with old men who, aided by canes and wheelchairs, seemed lost in the labyrinth of hallways. Young men in blue suits with piles of charts darted back and forth. Names were called, voices were raised. Mr. Maxwell could hardly stand the din that pervaded the atmosphere or the peculiar smell that filled the air, an odor that reminded him of death and that soon began to make him feel dizzy.

The two men, at last, delivered him to an empty room, motioned for him to have a seat and left, closing the door behind them and leaving him alone and in utter silence.

It was a large, wood-paneled chamber, much like a court room, filled with long, worn-out benches. He took a seat in the first row, relieved at the sudden quiet that surrounded him. A few minutes later, a side door opened, a clerk entered, handed him a stack of papers, and disappeared.

Mr. Maxwell glanced nervously through the forms, becoming increasingly convinced that something was wrong. There was a health questionnaire, a financial questionnaire, a form labeled "Needs Analysis" and another on which were printed the words "IMPLEMENTATION SCHEDULE." All in all, there were about twenty pages and, no sooner had he looked through them, the same clerk returned and told him he could step into the office. Mr. Maxwell followed him inside and sat in the indicated chair.

"You must be Mr. Maxwell."

"Yes, that's correct."

"A very good morning to you, Mr. Maxwell. Now let's see, you're here to begin the rectification process, is that correct?"

"Beggin' your pardon, I think there's been some mistake."

"Mistake?"

"Yes, mistake."

"That's hardly possible, Mr. Maxwell. Not in this office. Every work request is carefully checked before it's acted on. You see," he continued, holding up a form for Mr. Maxwell's benefit, "it says right here 'Mr. Jonathan Freeman Maxwell—rectification.' Isn't that so?"

"Yes, it does."

"Well, then there can't have been a mistake, can there?"

"But I thought I was being taken to the police department."

"Police department?"

The clerk removed his horn-rimmed glasses and scrutinized Mr. Maxwell curiously through his squinted eyes.

"No, Mr. Maxwell, this is the Bureau of Qualified Assistance."

"Bureau of Qualified Assistance?"

"Yes. Bureau of Qualified Assistance."

"But I need to report a burglary."

"A burglary, Mr. Maxwell?"

"Yes. My apartment."

"I'm sorry Mr. Maxwell, there has been no burglary."

Mr. Maxwell's palms began to sweat. He pulled a handkerchief out of his breast pocket and nervously wiped his hands.

"But everything is gone," he said at last.

"Mr. Maxwell," the clerk said impatiently, "how long did you work for the service?"

"Forty years."

"And were you a good employee?"

"Well, I like to think so. A job well done—"

"Is a job worth doing?" The clerk looked briefly at the file before him. "Yes, that's correct, isn't it, Mr. Maxwell?"

Mr. Maxwell wiped his face.

"A very good motto, I'd like to add. And since you were such an efficient worker, you should be aware that the proper use of language also constitutes efficiency. And burglary, Mr. Maxwell, is not the correct word."

"Well—" he began.

"Your belongings, Mr. Maxwell, were not stolen. They have been secured."

"Secured?"

"We have to take an inventory. You are now retired. You are about to receive a government pension. We want to make sure you get the right amount. Don't want you to be a burden to society, you know. There are many needy people out there. Homeless families. Hungry children. Much as we'd like to help everyone, there's not enough to go around."

The clerk returned his large glasses to his tiny face and leaned forward with a big smile.

"Mr. Maxwell, we need you to assist us in helping you."

"I see."

In fact, Mr. Maxwell did not see, but he was, at that moment, at a loss for words. True, he now had some inkling as to what had become of his belongings. But why they had been taken in the first place and why he had been brought here was still beyond his comprehension. And what kind of help they were offering him when he desired no assistance, except for the pension that he had earned, that he deserved, was still a mystery.

"Now Mr. Maxwell," the clerk continued, shuffling through the papers on his desk, "I believe we have all the information we need. According to our records, you have a total of twenty-seven thousand, two hundred and fifty dollars and sixty-two cents in savings. Is that correct?"

"Yes."

"Fine. That and the possessions we have secured then constitute all of your belongings."

"Why, yes."

"Unless, that is, you have something you're hiding from us."

Mr. Maxwell shrank back in his chair.

"No, that's everything. Well, except for my briefcase."

"Your briefcase?"

"Yes, I have it right here."

"May I have a look at it?"

Mr. Maxwell handed him the briefcase his mother had given him to mark the start of his career. The clerk examined it thoroughly, inside and out, writing notes in the file before him."

"May I ask what's in this box, Mr. Maxwell?"

"I don't know."

"You don't know? You carry something around and you don't know what it is?"

"It's a gift."

"A gift, Mr. Maxwell? You can't be accepting gifts, you know. You are, after all, on a government pension now."

"Mr. Roberts said it was just a small token," he said hesitantly. "It can't be worth very much."

The clerk turned the package over in his hands, made a note of it and placed it back in the briefcase.

"Very well, Mr. Maxwell. You may take your briefcase."

Mr. Maxwell took the briefcase and placed it on the floor beside his chair.

The clerk pulled out the envelope containing the items Mr. Maxwell had surrendered to Mr. Roberts. He opened it up and looked at the checklist.

"According to this, you have returned all the work supplies you were allotted in order to carry out your duties."

"That's correct."

"Very well, Mr. Maxwell. Now, according to our analysis, you will be given five hundred dollars a month in pension. That, plus your savings and the interest it incurs, should be sufficient for your needs. In addition, you will have a lifetime medical plan. You will be allowed one free doctor's visit per year plus one emergency hospitalization not to exceed seven days. That's a very generous plan, Mr. Maxwell. I understand you only missed work twice in all your years of employment."

"That's correct."

"Well, I expect you to have a very healthy retirement as well."

"Thank you."

"As for your apartment, you will be allowed to return there today. Your possessions allowance will be delivered next week. We will be returning your kitchen table and one chair, a sofa for the living room, one end table and a living room lamp, one night table and lamp for your bedroom. All of that plus the television we left you for your entertainment needs should be sufficient. The rest will be auctioned off."

"Auctioned off?"

"To help defray the costs."

"But those are my possessions. I spent my life working to—"

"Now, Mr. Maxwell, you do want to be cooperative, don't you?"

"But you have no right."

"Am I to understand then that you don't want any assistance?"

"Well, no."

Mr. Maxwell's heart was beating fast. His eyelids were fluttering. His legs were shaking so much he thought the chair would no longer hold him. He wanted to know what his rights were, wanted to know if he could consult a lawyer, but could not formulate these thoughts into sentences.

"What about the bed?" he said at last.

"The bed?"

"The bed," he repeated.

The clerk examined his papers thoroughly.

"I'm sorry, Mr. Maxwell, that would be above and beyond your allowance. You can, however, substitute the bed for the sofa if you'd like."

Mr. Maxwell tried holding his head up with his hand but, having nothing to rest his arm on, was forced instead to lean forward on the clerk's desk.

"I understand, Mr. Maxwell. These adjustments can be trying. Give yourself a few days. Then, if you have any questions, just give me a call. That's what I'm here for. At any rate, you'll need to fill out those forms and return them to me next week. That'll make everything official. Is Monday time enough?"

"Yes."

"Very well. See you then. And I do wish you the best in your retirement."

"Thank you."

"Thank *you*, Mr. Maxwell. Goodbye."

Mr. Maxwell made his way through the building and out the door, feeling very old and tired. He had been self-sufficient all his life, needing not even a wife to cook his meals or iron his clothes. Now, like so many others, he had to rely not on another person but on the government for his needs.

Of course, he could not have a bed! he now scolded himself. Who was he, one of the thousands of civil servants, to demand such a privilege when there were so many needy people?

When Mr. Maxwell reached his apartment, he sat on the floor in the living room and carefully filled out each form the clerk had given him. It seemed somewhat unnecessary to him, but it would be the last official act he would perform.

When he finished, he placed the forms in his briefcase and came upon the package Mr. Roberts had given him. He took it out, unwrapped it, and withdrew a small plaque, smiling contentedly at the inscription: "A Job Well Done Is A Job Worth Doing."

Mr. Maxwell hung the plaque on the wall where the picture of his mother had been. Then he switched on the TV.

THE DEPARTURE

When Walter Feebish said that he could not afford to die, he meant it. Literally. After all, there were the funeral expenses to be paid—the hall rental, the flowers, the casket, and the undertaker who, let's face it, had to make a living like anyone else. Then there was the organist, who would provide the appropriate background, and the singer, both of whom would need to be paid. And there were other incidentals as well—the chaplain, the notice to be sent to the local newspapers, memorial cards with their comforting pictures and prayers, the suit and tie he would need to be buried in, a new pair of shoes, and thank you cards for those who had taken the time to attend. And, of course, the tombstone.

And then there was the cemetery plot. A costly piece of property, upwards of $1000, where he would rest for the remainder of eternity, and the yearly maintenance fee. Normally, these charges would be paid by the next of kin but, in his case, there weren't any.

All of these would add up to a sum he just did not have. He could, of course, purchase it all on credit, but he wasn't sure there would be enough time to pay it all off, especially the maintenance fee which would most likely have to be paid in advance. And Walter did not want to ruin his perfect credit rating, even though he would no longer be around to defend it.

So Walter Feebish told his doctor that, under no circumstances, was he to be allowed to die. He should remain on life-support, if it came to that, or whatever it took, for at least his insurance would cover those expenses.

Walter's doctor, a smidgen of a man, who never took the time to listen to his patients, whose white smock always sported a dash of blood or a spot of pus, who was constantly worrying about the next incurable patient, for his practice was slowly dwindling away, simply nodded as Walter mumbled on incoherently, and said, in his usual way: "Everything is going to be just fine," though he knew quite well that Walter was terminal, though he knew that, just as sure as his stethoscope rested against his chest each day, Walter would not last for more than a week or two.

"Just rest now, Mr. Feebish. The nurse will give you something to calm you down."

And with that, he picked up his black bag—an antique leather case he toted around each day though it was no longer in vogue—and lumbered sadly out of the room, leaving Walter in a state between life and death, between certainty and uncertainty, in a world where exactitude had suddenly become the norm.

But Walter would not rest, could not with so much on his mind. Despite the sedative the nurse dutifully gave him. Despite the pain killers. Despite all the drugs and palliatives they administered to make him feel comfortable, to let him wander off freely into the land of Lethe, Walter could just not get his mind off his predicament. How was he going to arrange his funeral? Who was he going to invite and who would come? And if he did not have a funeral, how would anyone know that he had died in the first place?

Walter's thoughts rambled on in this way, continuously and circuitously, depriving him of his rest, rest which he so desperately needed, when there appeared before him a man of uncertain form, wearing a black tie and a white shirt, though Walter found it hard to distinguish between the two, and carrying in his hand a portfolio of dubious proportions, what seemed to Walter through the haze of medication to be a collection of somber-looking brochures.

"Mr. Feebish," the man's voice came, as if out of nowhere. "Sorry to disturb you, but I've come on a most important mission."

Walter stared incomprehensibly at the man through his glazed vision and wondered just how important a mission it could possibly be seeing as he apparently did not have much time to live. And so he mustered up all the attention he could gather and opened his eyes as wide as he could to better listen.

"I understand," the man continued, "how difficult these times can be. How utterly frustrating death can sometimes seem. That's why we're here to help you. To assist you with your decisions as you enter the final days—the next phase—of your life."

Walter attempted a nod to let the man know he was listening, parted his lips as if to speak, raised his head feebly, then let it drop back down suddenly onto the pillow.

"Let me introduce myself," the man persisted. "Percival

Pleasant. Of Pleasant Days Ahead Planning and Comfort Services. You can call me Pleasant. No need for formalities at this point, Mr. Feebish. Your name is Feebish, isn't it? Walter Feebish? Dr. Stringfellow's patient? Scheduled to depart on—"

The man checked his chart, then looked back at Walter with concern in his eye.

"You are not scheduled, Mr. Feebish? Is this correct? You refuse to move on for unspecified reasons?"

A tinge of guilt inched its way up from the pit of Walter's consciousness, curled up and around his weakened spine and lingered on his wizened face which briefly turned a light shade of red.

"You are, you know," Mr. Pleasant continued, "holding up the line. Keeping things from moving smoothly. There's a kink in the system, Mr. Feebish, and you are responsible for it."

Pleasant looked reproachfully at him, scowled slightly, or at least that's what Walter perceived as he fumbled with his focus and tried as hard as he could to concentrate.

"Now I know these things are never easy but—how shall I say it—we are all moving cogs. Interconnected circuits. And when one circuit stops working, the rest of the system breaks down. Unless, of course, it's repaired. Or replaced. Or—removed. Your car is broken down, Mr. Feebish. Warranty is up. It needs to be towed away."

Walter had never thought of it that way, had always fancied himself an individual whose existence had no effect on the next person or the last. Attempting a smile, he remembered all the cars he had owned throughout his life, all the breakdowns—that time his Pontiac had been totaled by an eighteen-wheeler—the flat tires, the overheated radiators, the failed transmissions, and all the times he had had to be towed.

"There," Pleasant continued. "I see that you're beginning to see. Now, let's get down to business. That is, after all, what life is all about."

His eye gleamed, pleasantly, and a kind smile crossed his face.

"Now, Mr. Feebish, Let's not waste time. We need to plan for your upcoming departure. The sooner we get to work, the better. Before it's too late."

Mr. Pleasant arranged his brochures and began to explain the various services his company had to offer, detailing the amenities each one contained—one plan offered memorial bumper stickers, another came with a solar-powered digital tombstone ("environmentally friendly," Pleasant emphasized with a beam in his eye) which flashed predetermined messages, day and night, and was guaranteed for at least two hundred years. One even came with a memorial Facebook page.

"It's our latest offering, Mr. Feebish. We will encapsulate your life, from birth to departure, annotate each and every life event and store it digitally for all eternity to see. Historic accuracy is guaranteed and future generations will be able to view, comment, and share. And, Mr. Feebish, even you, after you are gone, will be able to post updates using our latest technology. That way, your page will always be kept up to date."

Walter was indeed impressed, even, one might say, swayed.

"Now these are all guaranteed, Mr. Feebish. Money back, if not satisfied. And, in case you're wondering, we are licensed by the

State. Everything legitimate and up-front. We are, Mr. Feebish, here to help you…in your time of need."

But for Walter, it wasn't help with the planning that he needed. It was a question of pride. After all, he was alone. He had no wife—never had—no children, and all of his relatives were gone. As for friends, he could count them on one hand. There were plenty of acquaintances and colleagues, of course, but which of them would come? What if nobody came? How humiliating it would be if he planned an elaborate funeral and no one showed up. No, there was no need for fancy funerals. No need for plaques and tombstones and memorials and the like. All he wanted was something plain and simple. Something inconspicuous, just like his life had been. Something he could afford.

"Now, Mr. Feebish," Pleasant said, as if reading his mind. "I've had many clients like you before. Their loved ones are gone. There's no one left to mourn. To grieve. To testify to all your accomplishments. At Pleasant Days Ahead, we are ready for each and every circumstance. So we will make sure that your funeral is well-attended. In fact, attendance will be maximized. Guaranteed or your money back. Twenty, thirty people, shall we say? You tell us how many. And we will even screen them for you to make sure they meet your specifications. It's part of the deal."

Pleasant's eyes twinkled, kindly one might say, and he leveraged a smile, just a slight curl so as not to appear too forward, as he let Walter Feebish digest all that had been said.

But Walter was not convinced. He did not need a fancy grave. He did not need all those bells and whistles. He did not own a computer, never had, so what would he want with Facebook?

And a digital tombstone? For what? Who would be there to see it? As for attendance—well, that did hold some appeal but, in the end, he would still be alone. It would be like a party where, after everyone had wined and dined, danced and laughed, parted and gone, there would be nothing remaining but silence. In the end, he would still be left by himself once they had all taken their leave.

No, he did not want a fancy funeral. He did not want anything but to be left alone, and the more that Pleasant talked, the more adamant Walter became. Besides, he just did not have the money.

"Now, now, Mr. Feebish," Pleasant said reprovingly, "there's no need to worry. Finances are finances. These things have a way of taking care of themselves. One never knows what tomorrow might bring. Today we're poor. Tomorrow rich. All you need to do is decide, sign the contract, and leave the rest to us. No need to worry about money at a time like this. If you can't pay, society will. It's guaranteed."

But Walter would have nothing of it. He just could not afford to die and that was that. Hadn't he made that clear? No need for discussion. No need to argue. No need for convincing. If he could not afford it, he would not buy it. That's the way he had lived and that's the way he would die.

"I see," Pleasant said at last. "You're a hard one to please. A hard one to bargain with. And I truly respect that. I really do. But the truth is, there isn't much time left and something has to be done. After all, Mr. Feebish, you don't want to be a burden, do you? I mean, when the time comes—and it will come, I assure you— something has to be done. You can't just stay here. I mean, it just wouldn't be very pleasant to say the least, would it now?"

Well, he did have a point, Walter admitted. And he was not one to create problems. To be a nuisance. A blemish on society.

Walter fidgeted under his covers, tried to move this way and that, to comfort his body and his soul, to hide his stubbornness and his shame, but each time he looked back up, he was faced with the same vacuous specter staring persistently at him from the side of his bed.

"Well, Mr. Feebish," Pleasant said at last, after he had left Walter to his thoughts for some time. "I see you're a man of principle. An admirable quality. One which we shall note for posterity. I do have one last option for you. One which I believe you can afford, given your current circumstances."

Pleasant began to explain, but for all that Walter tried, he could no longer make out a word, could no longer concentrate, could no longer focus on the flimsy form that appeared beside him, whose voice seemed to come and go. Walter's mind began to wander, his hearing modulated in such a way that whatever Pleasant said seemed a mere wash of words. His vision softened and dimmed so that what was left of Percival Pleasant was a mere speck of light in an increasingly murky room.

The first thing Walter perceived—later, when Percival Pleasant was less than a memory, later, when the hospital monitors no longer sounded, when the comings and goings of doctors and nurses no longer seemed to take place—was a monotonous jangle, like train against track, was a distant whistle which continually diminished, was a rush of cool wind which tenderly brushed against his face. He was sitting, or maybe lying, he couldn't tell, but his body swayed gently back and forth to the motion, as everything quietly faded, even his concerns, and, for the first time he could remember, Walter Feebish felt his body gradually relax.

LETTERS FROM INSIDE

April 10

Dear Mary,

Sorry for the break in communication. As you can imagine, the circumstances here aren't the best. Besides, it's always the same routine and there isn't much to write about—get up in the morning, breakfast at seven, morning activity (woodcarving, leather work, etc., sometimes they let us out on the grounds, especially now that the weather is improving, but this depends on how many merit points you've earned). In the afternoon, I see Dr. Schwartz. By the end of the day, I'm really drained.

But then you haven't written for more than a year, as I recall.

They say I'm improving, Mary. They say maybe in another twelve months or so I can go home, go back to work, begin my life all over again. How long have I been here now? Five, six years? Do you remember? Except for the turning of the seasons, you'd never recognize that time was passing in this place.

I think of you often—your little apartment overlooking the

ocean, those lunches we used to have over in Venice—the Rose Cafe, wasn't it?—the museums downtown, the galleries—are they still there? It all seems like a fairy tale, a dream where I wander like a ghost—no substance, no reality. How I long to be free, to see the world again, especially you if you're willing to risk it. Or is that why you've stopped writing?

Funny how easily we took freedom for granted. I know we constantly talked about it, theorized, pretended—yes, pretended—to be its stalwart defenders, but did we ever appreciate it? Did we ever know what it meant? Who would have thought it would come to this, Mary? And right under our very eyes. But I'd better not speak like this, not now, not when I'm on the verge of recovery.

Outside my window, I can hear the birds singing. I wish you could hear them, Mary. They sound so beautiful. They must be nightingales. When was the last time you listened to a nightingale, Mary, tried to understand its message? Do you remember that scene in Romeo and Juliet, or is that still forbidden? Mary, it's as if they come especially for me. Every once in a while, one enters through the bars and perches on my windowsill, examining me, my surroundings, like a curious spectator at a zoo or a freak show. Then just as suddenly, he flies off, leaving me alone to my confinement.

Did you notice I used "he?"

But I'm good now, Mary, I really am. I want to be cured. Not like in the beginning when I resisted, defied them every chance I could. Though I think they still restrain me sometimes. It's all a fog to me, as if I'm on a cloud, floating helplessly, at the mercy of the winds, and the winds have no mercy, believe me. Yet I remember struggling, screaming, pleading with them, begging them to believe me. I told this to Dr. Schwartz today. Silly of me, really. The response was predictable—still paranoid, part of my condition.

This letter has gone on too long. The shorter the better. Trust me. Remember that when you write. Anyhow, it's time I went to sleep. They're good about that here. When I'm in my room, locked away from the world, I'm free to do as I please. Not exactly the way I thought my life would ever be, but one learns to savor these rare moments of freedom. Yes, freedom. Because no matter what the circumstances, there is always an element of freedom. I've learned that. You just have to recognize it, seize it, enjoy it to the fullest and let it compensate for everything else.

Mary, it's been so long. Don't get me wrong. I'm not blaming you. I understand if it's become a problem. It's just that things are difficult enough here, and worrying about you makes it even more so. Please write.

Jack

April 14

Dear Mary,

I forgot to tell you something when I wrote the other day. Dr. Schwartz says I'm full of denial. That the reason I don't know why I'm here is that I've disavowed my crime.

I asked her point-blank what my crime was. She said she didn't know, it really wasn't her business, and even if she did, she wouldn't tell me, that it was something I'd have to find for myself. It's part of the healing process, she said.

Why is it I remember things from my childhood as vividly as if they happened yesterday?

Mary, what did I do? Why can't I remember? I trust your judgment. You know me better than anyone. Of course, there's Danny, but how much can he have learned about me in a place like this, even if we've known each other since the day I arrived. You know, Mary, he'd been here once before, and I remember he told me, one day, in the beginning, when I first arrived, he said trust only what your eyes see, and then only after you've analyzed it thoroughly. Disregard everything else as a trick on your existence.

Anyhow, I had to tell you this before I forgot.

How are all our friends? How's Bob? Is he still seeing that actress? What about Sharon? Tell them all I said hello. God, I can't believe it's been five years. Five years!

Jack

May 21

Dear Mary,

Something rather strange has happened. Danny hasn't shown up to woodcarving class. It's been three days now.

Last week, he had a visitor. That's strange enough around here. They rarely allow visitors, and then only under certain circumstances—you're terminally ill and about to die, or you're nearly cured and about to be released. Then they allow frequent visits to help in the readjustment.

But Danny was neither of these, and this visitor—they said it was his brother, but when Danny went to the reception cell, he didn't recognize him, said he had never seen him before. Well, whoever it was, he smuggled in a small radio, about the size of a credit card, he said. The next day, we're outside on the grounds, working in the flower patch, and he pulls me over, whispers to me, says we're at war. He says the cities are being destroyed, he says the security forces are slaughtering the people like rats.

Mary, believe me, I tried not to listen. I thought to myself he's crazy, suffers from delusions. How can you believe someone like that? Besides, I don't want to get involved anymore. I just want out. But he kept talking, wouldn't shut up. He said he hadn't wanted to take the radio, but the man insisted, assured him no one would ever know. When he got to his room, he hid it under his bed, swore he would never listen to it. Then as the night wore on, it started to gnaw at him, the thought that an opportunity had come to see what was really happening in the world—not what they tell you Mary, not what they want you to know.

And now he's disappeared. I mentioned it to Dr. Schwartz today, thought for sure she would have seen him—three days, Mary, three days he hasn't shown up—and she dismissed it as my paranoia again, never told me whether he had come to his appointments or not.

Mary, I'm afraid. I don't trust anyone here. Especially her.

Jack

July 10

Dear Mary,

They found Danny this morning. After all this time. Dead. Impaled on one of the fence posts that hold up the barbed wire. Except it's not plain barbed wire. It's got lasers at the top, or so I hear. As if they want to encourage you to try, bloody yourself up, get your hopes high, so that just when you think you're going to make it—poof.

And that's what they said about him. An escapee. Did it to himself. But Mary, I know it's not true. Danny had no intention of escaping. If he had, I would have known about it, believe me. And besides, he was impaled, at least that's what everyone is saying.

Mary, do you think they killed him? To make an example of him? I know I'm not supposed to talk like this anymore, but I can't help it. I can't stop wondering what they may have done to him. And to think we've let this happen. But I will not fight them anymore. Even if he was my friend. I want out. I want my freedom. Even if it has to be on their terms.

What's it like, Mary? What's it like to be out there? I've forgotten. The pleasure of picking up a newspaper, a book. To read a poem, a story. To feel the paper brush against your skin, to hear the crisp sound of the pages as they turn. Even those slick advertisements we used to denounce seem so attractive now. Or to go to a restaurant, to dine, to indulge in a bottle of wine. What's the latest in cuisines, Mary? What do the restaurants look like nowadays? I'm starving, Mary, and you're my only source, the only one ever willing to risk writing to me. Why don't you answer? Why do I wait and receive no letter?

Jack

September 5

Dear Mary,

A new phase in my incarceration has begun.

The warden came to see me today. Imagine. As if I'm that important. Do you think it's a test? Do they always start this way? After all, they keep saying I'll be going home soon. Do they want to trick me? Make me slip when I least expect it? Put me at ease, or perhaps frighten me, so that either way my defenses will be down and they'll get inside of me, find out that I really despise them?

Mary, what should I do? How should I behave? Should I go along with him, and if I do, how will I maintain my guard? And if I don't, what will he do to me, what happens to my release? Will they cancel it? Will they keep me here forever?

There was a time I learned to accept my situation. Being locked up, dealing with Dr. Schwartz. Things went along smoothly, things never changed. Somehow, I've got to figure out how to deal with this turn in events.

Jack

September 8

Mary—

Dr. Schwartz is an agent. I'm convinced of this now. She works with them, she informs them of everything I say. I know this as clearly as day from night. I'm not surprised, of course. But I thought she followed, however minimally, her oath of confidentiality. Don't they still take an oath like that? Or have things changed that much?

I tested her, Mary, I fished with her, so to speak. I told her Danny was alive, that I had seen him. She said I was deluding, of course. We all know he's dead, she insisted—but it was the way she said it that got me, the stony look in her eyes, the cold, flat tone of her words, as if it were not true, yet still essential that I believe it.

Well today I was called into the warden's office again. There were a few preliminaries, a few niceties, the kind of behavior you don't expect in this context. And every so often, he mentioned Danny—wasn't it a shame about him, he would have been a free man if only, etc. etc. Then he set his eyes on me—hard powerful eyes that seemed to bore through me. You'd better be careful if you know what's good for you, he said to me at last, his voice suddenly callous. And then he dismissed me.

How do you suppose I'll have to pay for this mistake?

Jack

Sept 15

Dear Mary,

Last night I had a horrible nightmare. I dreamed that they took me from my room—the warden and two guards. They led me away, through long, narrow corridors that seemed to go on and on. They were dark and creepy, and the lights flickered every so often as if the electrical system were being overburdened. We were in a maze of tunnels that twisted and turned and seemed to be leading us down, deep down. I could hear groans and screams and the sounds of men laughing.

Eventually, we came to an iron door that the warden unlocked with a set of heavy keys—the sound as he forced it open rushed through me like a knife—you know how metal sounds when it grates against stone. I wanted to cover my ears but I couldn't. My hands were tied behind my back.

It was dark inside, but I could hear someone breathing rapidly, as if resting after a long, strenuous ordeal. Soon, my eyes began to adjust and through the darkness I could make out a figure standing in the shadows. It was Danny. He was alive, except he was somehow different, not the Danny I had known. He had turned into some kind of vengeful monster. In his hand was a blowtorch. It was unlit, but I immediately detected the smell of burned flesh, and then I noticed a man strapped to a table, naked, his body blackened with burns.

Danny turned to me. He smiled—a wild, insane smile, filled

with sadness and fear, as if he had gone to hell and returned with the knowledge of survival. Suddenly, he lit the torch and applied it to the man's body and, as he did so, he grinned at me. The incongruity jolted me, but it was purposeful, as if he wanted me to understand the horror his life had become. The man made no sound, though his body was shivering like he was freezing instead of being burned alive. The warden and the two guards laughed, as if the scene had suddenly turned comic, and the sounds reverberated violently through the dingy chamber.

I woke up in a sweat. It was morning. I could hear the birds outside, and the light was filtering in gently through the trees. But I couldn't move. I felt groggy, mentally and emotionally drained, my eyes were heavy. It was as if, despite what my senses were telling me, I was still there in that room with Danny.

Later that morning, I was invited to the warden's office. Again. This time I was treated like a king. They offered me breakfast—eggs benedict, gourmet coffee, fresh orange juice—none of that artificial stuff they feed us every day.

I ate heartily. I didn't want to, but it's been so long. You remember how food has always been my weakness. While I ate, the warden watched me, relishing each bite I took as if he were eating for the first time. He made small talk, like we were two friends meeting at a restaurant—two free men, associating by choice, not by edict. How did I feel this morning? I didn't look well. Perhaps I hadn't slept during the night.

What frightens me Mary is that this encounter was more a dream than my nightmare was. What do you suppose is happening to me? I refuse to discuss this with Dr. Schwartz. I refuse to discuss anything with her anymore. The problem is what to do during our sessions. Silence will indict me. And since she knows what's going on, I can't escape not talking about it. I've got to learn to play their game, only I'm not sure what it is.

Jack

September 20

Dear Mary,

Dr. Schwartz has asked me to keep a dream journal. Do you think it's just a coincidence? I know it's a common practice in therapy, but the timing is uncanny. Moreover, she's been skirting around the subject for two days now—as if she knows something.

She asked me about Danny again—not directly. She asked me if I had had any other hallucinations. Of course, she was referring to my little lie—I refuse to tell her about that dream I had. Yet, it's as if she knows.

Mary, do you think it's possible for them to induce dreaming? Do you remember the LSD experiments back in the '60s? Could they have refined it, developed it to a point where they can make you see what they want?

Now that I have to keep a journal, my dreams have become vivid—vibrant as if I'm living them. But I don't write about them. Not exactly. I tone them down, sometimes I even make them up. But somehow, I think she knows.

Jack

September 29

Dear Mary,

The warden can be a kind man. I learned this during a medical emergency that took place today. We were out on the grounds. It was a crisp, fall day, the kind that can only take place in this part of the country. The Northeast, Mary. There's nothing like the Northeast, especially in the Fall. Clear blue skies, dotted with clouds, the leaves crimson and gold, the smell of nature in its last glorious burst of life.

Anyhow, we were out tending the grounds when suddenly Mark—I don't believe I've told you about him, he's former CIA, relatively new here, from what I gathered from our short conversations, they picked him up planting bombs at government installations—anyhow, he had a fit—he's an epileptic. The warden happened to be out on an inspection when this occurred, and he immediately ran over and assisted him. He's a medical doctor by training, and he treated Mark with such skill and care, looking at me and smiling in a kindly way.

Things have calmed down, Mary. No more visits to the warden, no problems with Dr. Schwartz. It's as if they've let everything pass. As if it were all a test. Perhaps I'm learning to play the game.

Mary, I'm not going to ask you to write anymore. In fact, I've stopped waiting for your letters. I ask only one thing—please let me continue this correspondence. Leave me at least that.

Jack

November 10

Dear Mary,

My dreams continue to get stranger. Last night I dreamed I was writing to you. It was as if I really were. And what I was writing about was this very same thing—that I dreamed I was writing to you about this dream. And here I am writing to you—except I feel like I'm dreaming. A sort of double déjà vu.

Mark came back from the infirmary today—this was in the dream too. He lost his tongue. They said they were too late in getting to him. How did I know that would happen?

Jack

November 22

Mary,

Dr. Schwartz knows about you. Don't ask me how, but she does. Everything. Your friends, what organizations you belong to, where you work. She even described every detail of your apartment.

I remained silent during our session today. This is my new tactic. Don't say a word. Avoid all encounters, all confrontations.

But she looked at me with her miserable brown eyes and started to spew off all this information about you. She must have seen my reaction—my eyes must have reflected the hatred I feel for her—because she stopped suddenly and came over to me, shoved her severe little face in mine.

You think you can hide things from me? she said. You think I don't know everything about you—what you like and don't like, your sexual habits, the way you like to fold your shirts in threes?

She stood up and walked triumphantly over to her desk—that's the only way I can describe it, as if she had conquered me by telling me this information. Then she opened the drawer and pulled out a photo album.

You know what these are? she said. She opened it up and showed it to me. And inside were pictures of me—all sorts, Mary you can't believe it. There I was skinny-dipping at Jones Beach, dining, dancing, speaking with my associates at the party and—at the very end—you.

We know who she is, she said, because you're the one who told us. And she picked up my file and proceeded to tell me when I had told her all these things about you—she quoted specific sessions and told me what I had said in each one.

You want her to remain untouched? she said finally. Cooperate. It's as simple as that.

But what am I supposed to cooperate with?

Mary, you've got to run away, go into hiding. Please, Mary, I'm begging you.

November 24

Dear Mary,

Thanksgiving. I have some visitors. Even as I write these words, they are watching me.

Danny has been here for about two hours. He's been sitting with his blowtorch and his horrid grin, staring at me in silence. It's as if he wants to tell me something but can't. As if he wants to congratulate me. Don't ask me how I know that. It's just a feeling. I don't know why he has the blowtorch or what he intends to do with it. I've been trying to remain calm.

Dr. Schwartz arrived about half an hour ago and immediately asked what the problem was. No one answered. She looked coldly from me to the warden, as if we were responsible for ruining her holiday, then glanced over towards where Danny was sitting, without acknowledging him, as if he were some kind of ghost whose presence she was aware of but refused to confirm.

Suddenly, the warden asked me how I felt about my impending release. I told him I wasn't aware of it, but that when it was granted, I was ready to return to society to lead a productive life. He seemed pleased with this, but Dr. Schwartz immediately objected. She insisted I wasn't ready. The warden brushed her off, as if she were a fly on his lapel, and pulled out a picture from his jacket pocket as evidence of my cure. It was grainy and unfocused, but it seemed to be of a woman, naked, with large black blotches all over her disfigured body, the bare bone just evident. On the bottom was the initial "M."

But I had no time to react because Danny, who had remained silent up to this point, walked over and took it from the warden to examine. Then he turned to me.

Nice job, he said, smiling at me, a big, proud smile, the smile of a master pleased with the work of his apprentice, then went back to inspecting the tip of his blowtorch as if it were a gun that had just been shot.

Now I'm writing this letter. I don't know why or how I came to be doing this. It's part of the process, Dr. Schwartz says. My farewell to malady. What does she mean? They're all waiting around silently—Danny with his torch, Dr. Schwartz with her cold, expressionless face, the warden with his kind smile which makes me feel unsettled. It's as if they want me to write to you, as if this is the reason they have come.

Because I am writing, and they are watching. Because they are allowing me to.

Mary, what have I done? Mary, please, you've got to answer me. Tell me you're alive. Tell me you're ok. Tell me why they're here, why they've been standing around, staring at me for so long. Tell me, Mary, why suddenly they're now gone, vanished, like ghosts, as if they had never been here at all. Have I gone mad? Have they managed to take total possession of my thoughts? Mary, tell me why I now find a big fat turkey on my table with all the trimmings, why there's music, why they have tapped into all my weaknesses, why now I discover, on a bone China plate, under a polished silver server, a tongue, freshly cut, steeping in blood, and beside it a picture I took of you when we were in college. Tell me why I find myself suddenly immune, as if it doesn't matter, why I find myself instead preparing to dine, carving the turkey, laying each slice neatly on the gold-trimmed plate they have provided me, serving myself mashed potatoes, candied yams, arranging the cranberry sauce neatly on the dish. And the wine, Mary. They have provided me wine. Pinot noir. My favorite. I pour it, savor its aroma, let it linger on my palate, and completely forget about you. As if I no longer have any feelings. As if they have torched them away, carefully excised them and left me numb and helpless as only they can do.

Lobotomy, Mary? Remember? *One Flew Over the Cuckoo's Nest*? Only this isn't physical, Mary. This is much more sophisticated. We are, after all, at the dawn of a new millennium.

And now, as I get ready to enjoy my first real Thanksgiving dinner in five years, one I have apparently earned, I pick up the radio from which come strains of Tchaikovsky's "1812 Overture"—oh, how glorious, Mary, complete with canons and fireworks—a tiny radio I never had but which has been prominently placed on my table—a small radio, like the one Danny was given a few months ago—with rich, magnificent sound. And I find myself changing the station, searching for the BBC or some other independent source of information, and I am at last in heaven. I am at last, for a while at least, enjoying life as I imagine I will upon my release.

I'm sorry, Mary. Please forgive me. I want to enjoy this moment. I want to relish every nuance, every second.

Jack

December 2

I'm crying, Mary. I'm crying and I can't stop. Mary, they've broken me. I thought I could play their game, but you can't, Mary. Or maybe you can, but you can never win.

Mary, they've ripped out my tongue. After all I did for them. Why? I couldn't have told anyone even if I wanted to. Don't they realize that? Why don't they let me be? Or kill me, get it all over with? But this is prison, Mary. This is, after all, punishment. For going against them, for defying them. No, death would be too easy. Too quick. Too merciful, even if they tortured me until the last weak breath left my body.

I was a fool to think they would ever release me. Instead, today, I am scheduled for amputation. An "operation," they call it. A "slight correction." Only it will be my left hand. The one I write with. The one I used to draft all those treatises to expose them, to draft all these letters to you. Not so slight, after all, is it?

Mary, I don't know what to say and have so little time to say it. Forgive me? You were a willing partner, after all. Wish you well? Hardly. After all, we do what we must to survive. Do you detect a little Darwin in me? Does that surprise you? I mean we all have our weaknesses and fall so easily into them, allow them be exploited. When push comes to shove, as they say.

Mary, I know you will never read this. As I know you've never read any of my letters. It's the way things are. I know that. So believe me when I tell you I was only doing what I thought was right.

Jack

BOOK BURNING

TODAY AT 3 read the sign on the neatly trimmed lawn in front of the Middleton Municipal Library.

Ruth Cummings, mother of three and steadfast pillar of the Middleton community, had completely forgotten, but now as she returned from her Saturday afternoon shopping, her bulging grocery cart in tow, and stumbled upon the prominently posted sign, she let out a sigh of guilt and glanced up at the library grounds where she witnessed the preparations in full swing.

Never one to waste a moment of God's precious time, Ruth quickly checked her watch. 2:15. She had forty-five minutes to make it home and gather the books she had accumulated over the past year—horrid books: fiction, non-fiction, even poetry; books about sex and drugs; books morally corrupt; books she had collected while shopping—some purchased, some surreptitiously taken (it was, after all, a civic duty); books she would be embarrassed to have read—she had only had to scan one or two pages and scour the jacket to determine what the content would be—books she decided were simply not fitting for any God-fearing individual.

Ruth Cummings, longtime member of the Hallelujah Auxiliary, which was responsible for organizing today's festivities, who had barely missed a scheduled meeting and who now marveled at how evil could so easily burrow its sinuous way into the heart of even the firmest believer, turned the corner, her face flush with sudden fervor. As she walked proudly down the sleepy street where not even the slightest crack was allowed to remain, she spotted, from the corner of her eye, Dr. Morton Pierce, her reclusive and rather questionable neighbor, relaxing nonchalantly on his front porch, and decided to assuage her burning guilt by urging him to attend today's vital civic event.

Spread comfortably on his plush, chaise lounge and dressed rather improperly in cut-off shorts (did he not have any sense of decency? Ruth wondered, turning her eyes swiftly away), Dr. Pierce sat, buried in his newspaper, which he quickly folded in two and placed under his arm as Ruth marched straightway up to him without as much as a nod or a knock.

"Good afternoon, Dr. Pierce," she announced in her strident voice.

"Good afternoon to you, Mrs. Cummings," Dr. Pierce responded politely.

Like others in the tight-knit Middleton community, Ruth had tried to befriend Dr. Pierce ever since he moved to town to take over a professorship at the local college, but he had always managed to maintain his distance, refusing invitations to church events and other important civic affairs. Middle-aged and single, he preferred to keep to himself, and his neighbors soon learned to begrudge his aloofness by limiting their interactions with him to the daily niceties of life.

"It's a lovely spring day, don't you think, Mrs. Cummings?" Dr. Pierce added, trying to mask his annoyance at her surprise visit.

"Yes, indeed," she answered. "And most appreciated after the long winter we had. Are you coming to the book burning today, Dr. Pierce?" she asked, coming abruptly to the point.

Dr. Pierce's face stiffened momentarily.

"I don't think so, Mrs. Cummings," he said, forcing a smile.

"A pity. We'd love to see someone of your stature there. It's always such a stirring event, praise the Lord."

"Yes," he responded, clearing his throat. "I'm sure it is."

"A pity," she repeated. "Well, good day, Dr. Pierce."

"Good day, Mrs. Cummings."

Ruth Cummings about-faced in her tall, stiff manner and strode down Dr. Pierce's bushy walkway, frustrated by his cocky disdain, but satisfied she had at least done her duty. He was, after all, she comforted herself, slightly eccentric, just a bit off what she would call normal, though she couldn't clearly say why. It was something in the way he talked—a turn of phrase here, a touch of affectation there, and—well a man his age—she didn't want to jump to conclusions, but, after all, he wasn't married, and all things being equal, a man is a man. She just didn't want to think about the possibilities, especially in this day and age. Yet, as far as she had heard, he was well-respected at the college, and the students seemed to like him, though there were one or two off-color rumors about his behavior, but God be her witness, she would be the last to pass judgment. At least now he was aware that the book burning was taking place. The rest was between him and his conscience.

Lost in thought, Dr. Morton Pierce paced nervously about his spacious living room as a warm breeze blew through the window and brushed against his ruddy face. Ruth Cummings's unannounced appearance had caught him by surprise, and news of the book burning had left a rather unwelcome taste in his mouth. Neither could have come at a worse time—Mrs. Cummings's visit, while he was reading the latest edition of *The New York Times*, a paper poorly regarded in this very conservative town, or today's alarming event, which was about to occur as his latest book, *Sex and Sensuality*, was causing a stir across the country.

How ironic, he thought, leaning his bare elbow on the cool mantel of the fireplace, that his best work had been produced in such a rigid environment. It was a bittersweet victory of sorts, a vindication of the two worst years he had spent in his academic life—his course on Human Sexuality had been censured, the book list had been subject to review, and he was convinced that some of the students had been sent specifically to spy on him. With Bible in hand, they challenged his views, then had the audacity to dispute the grades he had fairly given them.

Of course, he conceded, the position had come at the right time. Unemployed and in need of money, he had been desperate for work. Maybe now he would be able to leave Middleton. Perhaps, he thought hopefully, he would be offered a better-paying job at a reputable university.

Picking up a copy of his book from the mahogany coffee table, Dr. Pierce examined the jacket with a smile. Had he lived somewhere else, he would have placed it prominently on his bookshelf, but here it was something best left out of sight, even though he rarely had visitors.

Dr. Pierce gazed across the quiet dining room, past the large vase of colorful irises on his table, through the box window that over-looked his herb garden. Though the town library was obscured by the copse of trees that bordered his property, he could hear the day's activities starting to build. He dried the perspiration on his face with a handkerchief, poured himself a Scotch and glanced at the book in his hand, wondering if it wouldn't be better for him to pack up and leave town, at least for a couple of days.

Dr. Pierce savored the feel of the book as one relishes the texture of a well-aged wine. Then, he placed it in the center of the mantelpiece and stepped back to see how it looked. Satisfied, he took the newspaper and his drink and stepped back out onto the front porch.

Ruth stared blankly out the passenger window as her husband Jacob drove the van into the municipal parking lot. Having returned home to find her family anxiously awaiting her, she could not help but question the depth of her conviction. How could she have forgotten? she chided herself, feeling as guilty as a child who, having brazenly challenged the Sunday school teacher, was left to wallow in her own sense of shame. Though she had never considered herself overly zealous, she regarded the book burning as a personal and moral obligation. Now she wondered whether her forgetfulness was a sign of some deeper, spiritual crisis.

"Daddy, Daddy, look at the man on stilts!" her daughter, Mary, cried, startling her back to reality.

"Cool," Johnny, her eldest son, exclaimed, pointing to the huge bonfire.

"Can we go, can we go," Jamie, the youngest, begged in excitement.

"Ok," Jacob responded. "But don't go too far. And stay together."

Ruth fidgeted with her seat belt as the children ran off into the crowd, past the stage where the church choir was performing, and straight to the fire pit where they eagerly watched the roaring blaze.

As Jacob and Ruth began unloading their books from the van, Marge Bainbridge came scurrying up from out of the crowd.

"Ruth, you've got to come right away. The Hallelujah Auxiliary is about to make a surprise announcement. Quickly!"

"An announcement about what?" Ruth asked, relieved to see her friend.

"I don't know. C'mon, let's go see."

"It's ok," Jacob called. "You ladies run off. I'll take care of these boxes and catch up with you later."

"See you later," Marge sang, as she dragged Ruth away.

"Marge," Ruth exclaimed to her childhood friend as they rushed up the stone steps and into the library, "I've got to talk to you."

"Why what is it, Ruth, darling," Marge responded, suddenly noticing the unsettled look in Ruth's eyes.

Ruth grabbed Marge's arm and stopped her in the hallway.

"It's about the book burning," she said, not quite sure how to begin.

Marge eyed her anxiously for a moment then broke out into laughter.

"Why Ruth Cummings, you silly thing. You nearly frightened

me to death. Why I thought you were going to tell me something just awful. Now I see you're just excited over today's event just like everyone else is."

"Marge, you don't understand," Ruth said, nearly blushing in embarrassment.

"Course I do, honey. But you know what. If we don't hurry, we'll miss the meeting and the burning. Lord have mercy, I just can't imagine what the Hallelujah Auxiliary is up to. Constance Applebee informed me about it early this morning but she just wouldn't reveal a thing. Only that an emergency meeting had been called. You know how she is, all tight-lipped and proper, God forgive me. But she finally admitted, after a good prodding of course, that there was likely to be a sudden, unexpected change in the program. C'mon, let's don't be late," she said, pulling Ruth along.

Ruth followed Marge reluctantly into the crowded conference room as the meeting was called to order.

"Ladies, ladies," the chair said in a loud voice as a soft hush fell through the room. "Please quiet down. We've had some rather disturbing news, and we've got some urgent business to attend to even as today's glorious event begins."

"Really, Sister Faith," one member indignantly protested, "this is highly irregular. We planned this burning months ago, and now you take us away from it and want to make last minute changes besides. It's rather annoying, to say the least."

A hum of agreement spread through the room.

"Ladies, please," Sister Faith implored, trying to gain control of the meeting. "Do let us have some order here. Those who wish to leave are free to do so. But I assure you the business we have here today is extremely important and directly related to today's function."

"Sisters," Constance Applebee interjected impatiently, standing up and casting a stern look across the hall. "Let's hear what Sister Faith has to say. And we'll leave the rest to the Almighty."

"Yes," everyone agreed. "Let her speak."

The ladies of the Hallelujah Auxiliary took their seats again and waited anxiously for Sister Faith to state her business.

"Early this morning," Sister Faith began in her slow, plodding manner, "Brother James called me at home. Now, as you all know, Brother James monitors the papers each morning. Well, he was skimming through one of the more heinous ones when he came across a review of a book by one of our local professors—"

Ruth leaned unconsciously forward as the rest of the ladies clung to the air in silence.

"Dr. Morton Pierce," Sister Faith said at last.

At once, the room filled with gasps and sighs.

"Ladies, ladies. Please, let me finish. I'm appalled to say," she continued when everyone had settled down again, "that our own Dr. Pierce, whom we so graciously allowed to join our college and to settle in our fine community, and whom many of us have been, to say the least, suspicious of for quite some time, has written a most detestable treatise called"—here, Sister Faith winced in embarrassment—"well, I can't even say the name."

Again, a din of voices arose in the room.

"Ladies, I've called you here today so that, with God's help and guidance, we can decide how to deal with this most abhorrent situation."

"Let's seize every copy," one of the ladies shouted.

"Yes," another said. "We can burn them here today."

"Why don't we have him fired from the college?" Marge suggested. "That would send a strong message."

"Yes," everyone agreed.

"I say we run him out of town," Constance Applebee said.

Ruth sat quietly and listened to everyone's proposals when she had a sudden revelation: if forgetting today's book burning had been the work of the devil, her impulsive decision to pay a visit to Dr. Pierce was most certainly the work of God. Surely, He had guided her there for a purpose.

And then it struck her that maybe it wasn't enough to have just invited this horrid individual to today's event. Maybe he should have been forced to come. Indeed, maybe every citizen of Middleton should be required to attend. It was, after all, for their sakes that the book burning had originally been organized. By the same token, she reasoned, it was not enough just to burn his books. No, an example needed to be made: a lesson for the whole community that should begin not with the book but with the author himself.

Ruth Cummings stood up from her seat and, in a loud, clear voice worthy of the best of preachers, said: "Ladies. Let us think about this carefully and thoroughly. It is not enough to burn his books or to run him out of town. Dr. Pierce, if he is indeed worthy of that title, is a vile individual. I speak as one who knows him as well as anyone, as his neighbor, as one who, I am proud to say, visited him just this morning, imploring him to attend today's event. Yet, upon my invitation, he looked at with me with contempt, as if I had uttered the most ridiculous words or, worse, had rejected the word of God. Ladies, I'm afraid your suggestions do not go far enough. God has put us here to carry out His work, and we must do so precisely and thoroughly."

"What do you have in mind, Sister Ruth?" Sister Faith asked.

Ruth gazed upon the members of her congregation, her body shaking with renewed conviction, her sense of faith surging through her in sudden waves, her eyes burning with fervor, as if she were about to speak in tongues, as if, in Dr. Pierce, she had found a cause to pursue in God's name. For a moment, she felt like a saint, like Joan of Arc, ready to lead the troops into battle.

"We must treat vileness with vileness," she declared with the eloquence of a preacher. "Burning every copy of Dr. Pierce's book we can get our hands on and firing him from the college is not enough. Does not the Holy Bible implore us to smite God's enemies?"

The conference room broke out into a loud frenzy.

"Praise the Lord!" the ladies of the Hallelujah Auxiliary shouted. "Hallelujah!"

"Ladies, please," Sister Faith implored, trying to restore order to the meeting.

"We must root out evil," Ruth persisted. "We must cut it out as one would remove a cancer."

Fired up by Ruth's words, the ladies of the Hallelujah Auxiliary began to file out of the conference room as if they had been suddenly charged with a sacred duty they could not help but fulfill. So forceful was Ruth's argument and so powerfully was it delivered that not even the parish minister could have stopped them from carrying out their mission.

"Ladies, please," Sister Faith implored, "Calm down. Let us discuss Sister Ruth's suggestion rationally and then come to a decision. Ladies. Ladies. Please be seated. This is no time to be taking the law into your own hands. Ladies!"

"*Lady Chatterley's Lover*. Five copies. Seized from two local book stores and a branch of the Middleton Municipal Library."

The harshly amplified voice reverberated through the unusually warm spring air and abruptly awoke Dr. Pierce.

"*Lolita*. Seven copies. Confiscated from the college library, two book stores and a local citizen's house."

Disoriented, he blinked his eyes and shook his head, as if dispelling a bad dream. Then, recognizing his book on the porch table, he remembered Ruth Cummings's surprise visit and peered in the direction of the library. Just beyond the trees at the edge of his property, he could make out a black cloud of smoke rising up to the sky.

"*The Canterbury Tales*. Eight copies, including an anthology which contains other questionable material."

Dr. Pierce reached for his Scotch. Suddenly, he detected the faint sound of voices coming from the street.

"*Naked Lunch*. Ten copies, including five which were confiscated by the principal of our local high school."

Instinctively, he jumped up and ran into the house.

"Ladies and gentlemen, brother and sisters. I have just been handed thirty-three copies of a book by Dr. Morton Pierce. *Sex and Sensuality*. Seized this morning from our local bookstores as well as from the dorm rooms on our college campus."

Carrying as much as his hands could hold, Dr. Pierce rushed out of the house and jumped into his car, gunning the engine and taking off as quickly as he could.

"These are the works of Satan whose purpose it is to corrupt our children and lead them further into sin. Cast them into the fire. Let them burn as their authors will surely burn come God's judgment."

The blue smoke from Dr. Pierce's aging jalopy had barely cleared the air when a crowd of men and women arrived at his driveway. Like a virtuous general leading her troops into battle, Ruth Cummings preceded the angry mob, brandishing a torch in her right hand and marching forthrightly up to the foot of Dr. Pierce's verandah.

"Let us pray that those who promote depravity be recognized one day by our government as perpetrators of evil and that they be duly punished here on Earth as they will surely be punished by God."

"Dr. Pierce," Ruth called emphatically, her eyes burning with zeal, her renewed faith in God finely honed and ready to take aim. "You have betrayed our trust and confidence in you. Come out and surrender. You cannot escape God's wrath."

"Let us pray that the Lord guide us away from iniquity and lead us toward the straight and narrow path on which we were meant to travel."

"Come out!" the crowd demanded, waving their fists angrily in the air.

"Let us pray that evil be driven from our hearts and that, in its place, God's love and guidance will take root."

"Let him burn!" someone shouted, dousing the property with gasoline.

"Dr. Pierce," Ruth bellowed, raising her torch triumphantly in the air. "This is your last chance. Surrender or you will taste God's vengeance."

"Let us pray to God that, through his word, we will enter the Kingdom of Heaven."

"Let God's work be done!" Ruth shouted, tossing her torch high into the air. "Let the fire consume evil! Let all of God's enemies be defeated!"

"Praise be to God!" the crowd chanted, as the house burst into flames.

"Let us thank God for the bounty He has bestowed on us and for taking pity on our wretched plight. May our sins be forgiven and may we forever be bathed in the light of His mercy. Amen."

Dr. Pierce's house burst into flames, the thick, choking smoke combining with the rising black ashes of the burning books. Ruth Cummings and the ladies of the Hallelujah Auxiliary watched triumphantly, their faces illuminated by the blazing fire, as the book burning festivities came to a close.

METAMORPHOSIS II

(OR THE SUDDEN AND INEXPLICABLE DISAPPEARANCE OF DAVID C. ROCHE)

R. was drinking water from his favorite spot on the kitchen sink when he felt a fine spray cover his sleek brown body. Rubbing his tentacles together, he darted across the wet tiles and into a crack where he had often made his escape. He scrambled down the drainpipe, slipped through a narrow space in the wall and scurried through the darkness, exiting from a tiny crevice on the opposite side.

R.'s heart was beating fast, and he was beginning to feel sick when, suddenly, he found himself lying on his back with his little legs waving haphazardly in the air. His tentacles wiggled uncontrollably, and his body became weak. He struggled to turn over but was unsuccessful, and the more he tried, the sicker he felt.

R.'s mind became foggy and his body grew numb. He felt as if his hard, smooth skin were melting, as if, one by one, his legs were falling off, and he had the strangest sensation that his body was beginning to grow. He closed his eyes, hoping this would stop the world from spinning, and waited for what he surely thought would be death.

When he opened his eyes again, the world seemed a different place. The lamp on the table appeared smaller, and the couch, on which he loved to scramble, seemed as if it had shrunk. Indeed, the thought of scurrying along the soft upholstery no longer excited him. Even the ceiling—one of his favorite spots (for he loved to hang himself upside down, suspended by his sticky feet)—no longer had any appeal.

R. wondered at these changes when he suddenly realized that he was alive. Joyful, he let out a sound that shocked him as much as the sight of his body which he now observed from the slits of his blue eyes. His skin had turned white, and most of his legs had disappeared. Then, he touched his face and discovered that his beloved tentacles were no longer there. This alarmed him further, and he let out a loud, horrifying sound.

"Arnold, is that you?"

R. instinctively tensed his muscles but the reaction was not so much from fear of being discovered as it was from the realization that the sounds he heard, which before had seemed alien to him, now had a pattern he identified with, a meaning that he could somehow understand.

"Arnold?"

R. remained still, hidden behind the couch, until he heard the footsteps retreat. Then, slowly and with great difficulty, he turned over on his stomach, a feat that required complex maneuvering since he now had only four appendages to work with. Still, these served him well, especially the two at the upper extremity of his body, and he managed to flop, with some pain, into a position he was more accustomed to.

At last, he tried standing on all four limbs, but this seemed quite impractical, and R. feared that he would never be able to move about as quickly as he once had. So he propped himself against the back of the couch and pushed himself up, knocking a lamp over as he steadied himself on just two legs. Balancing himself, he took a few steps and discovered that he could move about more easily in this position. Testing out these new circumstances, he walked, ran, and jumped around the room, when there suddenly came a frightening sound, and R. lost his balance and fell.

"Arnold! There's a naked man in the living room!"

At that very moment, in another part of town, the household of Mr. David C. Roche was in a total state of confusion. The servants were searching the premises, the FBI was questioning members of the family, and the campaign staff—for Mr. Roche was a candidate for the United States Senate—were desperately trying to decide what to do about his appearance that morning at City Hall.

As his wife—the lovely Evelyn Dunworth Roche—explained to the FBI inspector, her husband had been sitting at the breakfast table, reviewing reports on the speech he had given the day before when, suddenly, the newspaper he was buried in dropped to the table, and, instantly, he was gone.

"Vanished—in thin air," she said, dramatically, to the agent.

He was a rotund, rather tiresome inspector with a shock of wavy hair and a pair of round spectacles on his plump, weary face.

"People don't just vanish," the inspector said, smoothing his thick, gray mustache with a stubby finger as he was wont to do when faced with such an exasperating client.

"Tell him about the—"

Mrs. Roche stopped her son short with a stern glance, but the inspector looked up from his notepad and fixed his eyes firmly on hers.

"Withholding information will only obstruct the investigation, Mrs. Roche."

"Well," she said, squirming in her chair. "You can imagine our disbelief. We all got up and ran over—and there—well you know it's quite embarrassing."

"Go on."

"There on the chair—"

"Was a big ugly cockroach," Christopher said, rushing to his mother's aid.

"I was shocked, of course."

"And I killed it," Christopher added proudly.

"Run along now, Christopher. The inspector and I have important things to discuss. We've never had this problem before," she resumed, turning to the inspector. "Naturally, we've called an exterminator. Do you have to write that in the report?"

"It's strictly confidential, Mrs. Roche."

"You know how these things are," she persisted, and she looked at him resentfully for his obvious lack of sensitivity. "The least thing could ruin my husband's career."

"I understand," he said with a perfunctory sigh as he continued writing in his notebook.

At that moment, Mr. Doug Fowler, the campaign chief, briskly entered the room and interrupted the proceedings of the inspector's interrogation.

"Mrs. Roche," he said. "May I have a minute with you?"

Mrs. Roche promptly excused herself, grateful to get away from the dreadful inspector who, as far as she was concerned, was probing too deeply into her personal affairs. It was bad enough her husband had disappeared, she thought to herself, but then to have such a punctilious inspector … yes, she thought, he was absolutely punctilious, and it was enough to ruin anyone's day.

"We have a statement for the press," Mr. Fowler said, closing the door for privacy.

Mrs. Roche nodded hesitantly, for despite her upbringing, she was not used to the delicacies of public relations, but she feigned experience and waited for him to continue.

Now Doug Fowler, as anyone on the campaign staff could proudly testify, possessed the unique talent of protecting his clients even under the worst circumstances. He did this without resorting to compromising statements and without having to commit his clients in one way or another. Despite his rather bovine approach to even the simplest of tasks, he could neutralize most any situation, using the most damaging evidence to his client's advantage, all in a way that was seemingly so honest and so benevolent that it would be difficult for anyone to question his credibility and intent.

"'This morning'" he read, "'after finishing up his breakfast, David Roche decided to go for a walk. He failed to inform anyone of his destination and, when he did not return, his family members became worried and notified the police. We have every reason to believe that Mr. Roche is safe since he never goes anywhere without his body guards, and we can assure you he will be at City Hall this morning.'"

Now Mr. Fowler was also a good judge of character, for Mrs. Roche was quite gullible and would believe almost anything she was told, even if the truth was staring her baldly between her tiny dull eyes.

"Why Mr. Fowler!" she exclaimed. "Then there's no problem after all. That's absolutely wonderful. Oh inspector!" she called, rushing away to convey the news to the good FBI agent.

Relieved to have gotten Mrs. Roche out of the way, Mr. Fowler calmly stepped outside and delivered his statement to the press.

"Given the rash of terrorist activity that's been plaguing this country, is it possible Mr. Roche has been kidnapped?"

"That's a very remote possibility," Mr. Fowler answered. "We are confident that Mr. Roche is off somewhere preparing his speech for today's rally."

"Does the Secret Service know where Mr. Roche is?"

"The Secret Service, as the name implies, is not in the habit of divulging information. If Mr. Roche does not want his whereabouts known, they are most certainly going to comply with his request."

"Isn't it unusual for Mr. Roche to deliberately not tell his family of his whereabouts?"

"Mr. Roche is very independent. That's exactly the point he's been making throughout this campaign. We can assure you that

Mr. Roche will not let the public down and that he is preparing for his victory. That's all the information we have at the moment."

R., meanwhile, had managed to escape from his house (for it was the place where he had been born, had grown up and where he had spent his entire entomological life,) and now, as he scuttered down the street, he realized that appearances make no difference in this world, for everyone stared at him in disgust, just as they had done before his mysterious metamorphosis. Nonetheless, it soon dawned on him as he compared himself to those around him, that he was lacking a basic necessity of life (or at least the life he had now assumed), and he suddenly remembered the word he had heard as he ran from the house.

Naked.

R. scurried around, searching frantically for something to cover himself with until his two legs were so numb that he feared they too would fall off, when at last, sifting through some trash in an empty lot, he found an old discarded robe that he wrapped tightly around his body.

Naked. He could hear the word clearly in his mind. He moved his lips, contorted his mouth to form it. It was difficult at first, but he slowly mastered it. Joyful at his newfound ability, he skipped merrily down the street, keeping a tight grip on his robe, and repeated the strange sound over and over.

And so with the instincts of a cockroach and the body of a man, R. wandered through the city, stopping to scavenge in his favorite types of places, hiding behind bushes and concealing himself behind trees, and secretly listening to conversations that he stumbled upon.

"Mommy, I'm hungry."

R. watched the little girl eat the sandwich her mother withdrew from a brown paper bag.

Encouraged by this simple act of discourse, R. approached an old woman sitting on a bench.

"Hungry," he said, mimicking the little girl.

"Oh you poor thing. You need food."

"Food."

"Here's some money."

"Money," R. repeated, putting the hard coins she handed him into his mouth.

"Money," she said. "For food."

"Money for food," he repeated.

R. scurried away, repeating the phrase over and over, then climbed into a large trash bin in search of something to eat.

"Excuse me, sir."

R. looked up from his rummaging, his face covered with grease and grime, and grinned.

"We're with Channel 2 News. We're doing a report on the homeless and we'd like to interview you."

In the meantime, all activity at the Roche household had come to a standstill so that the exterminator could perform his duties, for Mrs. Roche could concentrate on nothing except eliminating what she saw as *the* major obstacle to her husband's success.

"It's just astonishing," she repeated yet again, following him around to make sure he missed no potential haven for—well, she still couldn't get herself to say the word, not even to herself. "I just don't understand how this could've happened. Now you're sure you've sprayed everywhere?" she said yet again as the man gathered his sprays and nozzles and tubes.

"Yes, ma'am."

"Good," she said, handing him a fifty dollar bill. "This is for you. You can send me the bill. I trust you won't say a word of this to anyone."

"No ma'am. Thank you. And if you have any further trouble just give me a call."

"I hope that won't be necessary. Thank you. Goodbye."

Mrs. Roche closed the door and dropped onto the sofa, satisfied that she had overcome this latest hurdle in her quest, for she was going to be a senator's wife, and she would not let one—one … insect, there, she could say that—interfere with her plans. She breathed a deep sigh of relief but her expression of content immediately soured as the odor of insecticide filled her nostrils.

"Mrs. Roche."

Mrs. Roche, her face screwed up in disgust, could barely make out Mr. Fowler through the fog of disgust that enveloped her. Trying to restrain her emotions, she motioned for him to enter the room.

Mr. Fowler took a seat, hiding his contempt and hoping it would not show. After all, if it had not been for her, Roche's disappearance would never have gotten out, and he would not be faced with the enormous task of trying to cover everything up.

His biggest problem now was to figure out what particular quirk in her behavior he could tap into to get her to cooperate.

"This has been quite a shock," Mrs. Roche said, breaking the silence.

"I'm afraid I have something even more shocking."

Mr. Fowler calmly turned on the TV as Mrs. Roche focused her attention on the oversized screen.

"We asked our man on the street what he thought the major problem facing the homeless was. Here is his response: 'Hungry. Food.'"

Mrs. Roche glared incredulously at the TV.

"Is this some kind of joke, Mr. Fowler?"

"I'm afraid not, Mrs. Roche."

"Food. Money for food."

"Are there any other problems?"

"Naked."

"My Davy? Promoting charity? It just can't be."

"I'm afraid it's true. Your husband has apparently been wandering around the city and has been mistaken for a bum."

"Indeed! Really, this is quite embarrassing. You don't suppose anyone noticed?"

"The phones down at headquarters have been ringing off the hook."

Mrs. Roche was flabbergasted, and she wondered just what she had done to deserve all that had happened to her on this most noxious of days.

"Well, Mr. Fowler, what do you propose?"

"I'm afraid we'll have to pull out of the campaign. I've already canceled all your husband's appearances for today."

Mrs. Roche flinched. She stood up and looked out the window at the swarm of reporters camped outside.

"I'm sorry, Mr. Fowler, but I can't let you do that."

"Mrs. Roche. There's no alternative. Your husband is not fit to run. Look at him."

Mr. Fowler's words could not have been truer, for there on the screen was R., straddling a large trash bin, digging through the refuse and feeding voraciously on whatever scraps of food he could find.

"Mr. Fowler, my husband is going to be the next senator of this state no matter what."

"There is one other possibility," he said, waiting a few seconds to goad her curiosity. "We can announce that your husband's been kidnapped."

"Kidnapped?"

"We can say he's been brainwashed and that his appearance on TV was arranged by his captors. With all the terrorist activity that's been occurring, it would be quite plausible."

"My Davy kidnapped?"

"The public will eat it up."

"Mr. Fowler, you can't be serious?"

"Meanwhile, we'll launch a search for him. Just think of the publicity. He'll win by a landslide."

"I won't have it. Really, Mr. Fowler. I mean what would I tell the neighbors?"

"It's really quite fashionable, Mrs. Roche."

Mrs. Roche's heavy lips suddenly lifted.

"I mean just last week," Mr. Fowler continued, "the U.S.

Ambassador to Gabon was kidnapped. Just think of the company he'd be keeping."

"Ambassador," she muttered, imagining a tribe of savage, half-dressed natives abducting the poor, unsuspecting diplomat in the middle of the jungle. "And you really think it would help my husband get elected?"

"It's our only chance. He'd be a hero."

"A hero," she intoned, drifting off into dreams of cocktail parties with congressmen and senators and, yes, even the president who, of course, would be most charming towards her. It was all she could do to contain her joy.

"Very well, Mr. Fowler. We'll announce that my husband's been kidnapped. Only, I do hope they'll be gentle with him. I don't suppose you know how they're treating that Ambassador—where did you say?"

But just then, a large cockroach crawled unabashedly across the wall, and Mrs. Roche jumped out of her seat.

"There's another one," she screamed as she rushed to the telephone and began dialing. "This is totally unacceptable. Yes. Hello. This is Mrs. Roche. There's been another incident!"

"At approximately 9 a.m. this morning, Mr. Roche was kidnapped while walking in his garden. A group calling themselves United Front to Free the Homeless telephoned Campaign Headquarters shortly after and claimed responsibility for the act. So far, they have made no demands."

"Could this incident be related to Iran's support for international terrorism?"

"We are certainly not ruling out that possibility. The FBI is now looking into a possible connection with Iran and other rogue nations."

"Can you tell us what Mr. Roche meant by 'money for food'?" Does this mean he has changed his position on federal funding for the poor?"

"Mr. Roche is constantly assessing the situation so he can do what's best for the country. However, we do believe he was forced into making that statement."

"How do you think this affects Mr. Roche's chances of election?"

"I think we'll just have to wait and see. I'm sorry ladies and gentlemen. That's all for now."

During the next few days, R. turned up at the most unexpected places, creating a furor at each and every one. His appearance in the lobby of a posh restaurant on the fashionable west side caused such an outrage that the maître d' was forced to raise prices just to save face.

"Really, Muriel," one of the patrons remarked. "The clientele here has just degenerated."

"Why Cornelia, my dear, what did you expect? This place has become so affordable."

The maître d' eventually persuaded R. to leave by offering him a chateaubriand, done to perfection, left untouched by an indignant customer who had pompously paraded out of the restaurant upon R.'s appearance. R. devoured the chateaubriand on the spot and, after being escorted to the door, was told that, under no circumstances, was he to return. Five minutes later, the police arrived in full force, further offending the clientele.

R. next appeared at an upscale supermarket where he managed to consume a large quantity of products before being apprehended by a burly security guard who, unlike the maître d' at the restaurant, took from him everything he had managed to forage from the shelves.

"Get out and stay out," he said, heaving him out the door.

Once again, the authorities arrived too late.

Now R. was used to being mistreated, so it was no surprise when people suddenly began chasing him.

This first happened at the corner of First and Main. An elderly couple was walking their dog when the curious canine stopped to sniff at R.'s grimy foot. The dog spontaneously lifted his leg and released a warm stream that trickled down R.'s shin. R. followed the dog's lead, and the man and woman, who up to this point had done their best to ignore him, found this behavior much beyond their idea of tolerance.

"How dare you do that in front of my wife, you bum," the man shouted.

"Leave him alone, Harold," the woman muttered under her breath. "You never know what these people are liable to do."

But the man refused to listen and proceeded to chase R. down the street. A number of people joined in the pursuit, while the old woman, clutching onto her barking dog, shouted anxiously for help.

Eventually, R. bolted into a park and hid behind some bushes, but the smell of food soon attracted his attention and, obeying his instincts, he followed the aroma to its source.

"Hot dogs. Hot dogs."

"Hot dogs," R. repeated.

"How many?"

"Hungry."

The vendor smothered two hot dogs with sauerkraut and mustard and handed them to R.

"That'll be three fifty."

R. grabbed the hot dogs and quickly devoured them.

"Hungry. Food. Money for food."

"Yeah. Three fifty."

"Naked."

"Hey mac, what're you some kind of nut? Now that's three fifty you owe me."

"You bum."

"Hey look. All I want is my money, ok? Money. Do you understand? Money."

"Money," R. exclaimed, remembering the old woman on the bench. Reaching into his pocket, he pulled out the coins she had given him.

"Good. Now you owe me three dollars."

"Money. Money for food," R. repeated loudly, jumping up and down.

"Hey mac. I've had enough of you. Now get out of here before I call the police."

But R. continued to jump, and a curious crowd soon gathered around him and began to chant: "Money for food. Money for food."

For the first time in his life, R. felt appreciated. He walked proudly through the park repeating the phrase as the growing crowd marched behind him.

When they reached Main Street, they were suddenly confronted with an onrush of police, and the crowd began to disperse. R. used his instincts and weaved his way through the fleeing marchers, finally darting down a side street where he concealed himself in a darkened doorway.

"We'll be safe here," a stranger whispered.

"They represent the corporations. Money. Profits. Power."

R. listened, snatching the white bread, processed cheese and packaged meat his scraggly friend placed on the small kitchen table.

"They'll never do anything for us. You see how they chased us down the street?"

The stranger brought over two beers.

"No sir. People like that have to be eliminated."

Pushing his long, stringy hair out of his face, he sat down and joined R., who was eating ravenously.

"Food. Money for food," R. said.

"We need more than that," the stranger continued, placing his hand on R.'s arm. "We need jobs. We need better schools. We need decent housing."

"Housing," R. repeated, his mouth filled with food.

"Look at the squalor they force us to live in. The wallpaper's peeling. The toilet in the bathroom leaks. The heat don't work.

And do you think the landlord does anything about it? Of course not. And look at the furniture."

R. imagined himself crawling along the cracks in the wall, romping through the worn carpeting, searching for scraps of food as he had often done before his metamorphosis.

"And roaches?" his friend continued, pointing to a large cockroach meandering along the pipe that led to the ceiling.

"Roaches," R. beamed.

"I got roaches up the kazoo."

R. approached the little creature, which instantly darted away.

"Naked," he exclaimed, not knowing how else to express his happiness.

"Naked. Yeah. It's naked city. But we're gonna change that."

R. ran his eyes up to the ceiling and longed for the days when he could move around freely. He tried climbing up the pipe but settled, instead, for crawling around the apartment on his hands and knees.

"Nobody else is gonna do anything about it," the man continued. "We've got to take things into our own hands."

The man carefully placed a cardboard box on the table.

"See this package?"

"Package," R. repeated, spinning around in circles on the floor.

"There's this guy who wants to be senator. He supports the corporations. And he doesn't even try to hide it. Well this'll show him that there are people out here who aren't gonna stand for it."

R. stood up and gazed at the box.

"Finish eating my friend."

"Food," R. said as he resumed stuffing his mouth with bread and meat.

"Yeah. This'll get us food and much more."

When they finished eating, the man got up. R. followed him out the door and down the dark stairway, stopping outside to investigate the trash cans that lined the broken sidewalks.

"C'mon. Hurry up."

"Naked!"

"Clothing!"

"Naked!"

"Clothing!"

"Shit!"

"The demonstrators numbered in the hundreds and marched peacefully down Main Street. As authorities arrived, the crowd dispersed, and Roche once again disappeared. Several demonstrators were apprehended for questioning, but sources say so far nothing has been learned about the kidnapping."

Mr. Fowler spotted a roach scurrying across the room and angrily smashed it with his foot.

"Meanwhile, the candidate's wife made her first public appearance today. With tears in her eyes and a trembling voice, she appealed to the kidnappers to release her husband unharmed.

"'It's absolutely scandalous. You can't imagine what we're going through.'" Speaking to reporters from her home, Mrs. Roche said recent events had left her with what she described as a creepy feeling and that, ever since her husband's abduction, her house had been crawling with vermin."

"Christ!"

Picturing Mrs. Roche in his mind, Mr. Fowler smacked the newspaper he was holding against the wall and claimed another victim.

"A campaign aide later explained that the statement was not a reference to reporters but rather to a steady stream of onlookers who had been gathering in front of the Roche residence since the disappearance of the missing candidate. And a CBS news instant poll revealed that, "Ever since his disappearance, David Roche has jumped ahead of his opponent by ten percentage points in the hotly contested senate race. The poll also indicated that Roche's leap was due to voter sympathy and not to the sudden change in his campaign platform. Fifty-six percent of those polled said they opposed Roche's recent change of heart toward the poor but an overwhelming majority said they would vote for him anyway. In man-on-the-street interviews, those who opposed Roche's recent political turnaround said they would vote for him in order to combat foreign terrorists who were trying to influence American politics. The poll had a margin of error of plus or minus three percentage points.

"Coming up next ..."

Mr. Fowler switched off the radio, satisfied at the forecasts for his client. He had overcome all the obstacles. It was a real coup, outstripping everything he had done in his entire career. Then he remembered that Roche was still missing. He pounded his fist on the chair, triggering another rush of roaches, and stomped on them viciously as the door opened and Mrs. Roche marched in followed by a troop of servants.

"Move all the furniture. Remove the carpets. Make sure you spray everywhere."

"Beggin' your pardon ma'am, but the more we spray, the more they keep coming out."

"Then use your feet, your hands. I don't care what you do."

"Yes, ma'am."

Mr. Fowler watched incredulously as the servants set to work executing Mrs. Roche's latest attack against the little brown beasts, as she had now taken to calling them.

"Mrs. Roche," he protested, trailing her around the room.

"Make sure you spray under that painting. Not now, Mr. Fowler. And be careful!"

"Mrs. Roche."

"Get all the corners."

"Mrs. Roche!"

"Mr. Fowler! I've had enough!"

She stopped dead in her tracks and stared vengefully at him as if he had suddenly joined the ranks of the enemy.

"I don't want to hear anymore. Not unless you can tell me how to get rid of these little brown beasts."

"I can't believe you're more concerned about roaches—"

"Don't say that word!"

"—than you are about your own husband."

"Mr. Fowler. I've got a problem here—"

"You've got a problem? I can't believe it! Don't you realize what's going on? We're going to win the election!"

"Why Mr. Fowler. Why didn't you say that in the first place? Why that's wonderful news!"

Mrs. Roche spun around in joy, her face filled with rapture.

"I don't believe you understand, Mrs. Roche. Tomorrow is the election."

"Yes, Mr. Fowler, I understand."

"What do we do if we don't find your husband?"

The reality of Mr. Fowler's statement hit her almost as pointedly as the spray the servants were deploying, and Mrs. Roche's lips began to tremble.

"We've got to find him Mr. Fowler. We've just got to."

She sat down in one of the remaining chairs and tried to get a hold of herself. Just then, an explosion shook the house, causing the servants to panic and an army of cockroaches to appear. Mrs. Roche shrieked and rushed frantically out the front door.

Outside, the smoke was thick. The lawn was covered with rubble, and people were running in all directions. Lights were flashing as cameras rolled and, in the middle of it all was R., surrounded by reporters.

"Mr. Roche can you tell us something about your kidnappers?"

"Naked."

"How about your proposal for aid to the poor?"

"Package."

"Could you be more explicit?"

"Jobs. Schools. Housing."

"Do you have anything to say about the explosion that just occurred? Who do you think is behind it, sir?"

"Money. Profits."

"Davy!" Mrs. Roche ran toward him, but her strident voice frightened him, and he began to run.

"All right, that's enough fellows," Mr. Fowler said as he rushed toward R.

The next day, the Roche household was once again in a flurry of activity. The grounds were crawling with FBI agents and, inside, the campaign staff were busy monitoring the election returns. Meanwhile, R., who had been secretly captured during the commotion the night before, was being interrogated in the living room which was still in a state of disarray. Mr. Fowler looked on impatiently while Mrs. Roche, armed with a can of insecticide, fired her weapon at the least sign of movement.

"Can you at least tell us what they looked like?" the FBI inspector asked, pulling his mustache in frustration.

"Naked."

The inspector threw his hands up in the air.

"It's no use," he exclaimed.

He had used every technique in the book but had not been able to get one bit of coherent information out of R.

"Jesus Christ, David, what are you doing?" Mr. Fowler shouted. "Do you know what they're saying about you?"

He picked up the paper and shoved it in R.'s face.

R. grabbed the newspaper, examined it curiously, then stuffed it into his mouth.

"This is not funny. Are you out of your mind?"

He ripped the newspaper out of R's teeth.

"Listen to this. 'Before Roche once again disappeared, he told reporters that, if elected, he would fight for additional money for jobs, schools, and housing. Previous to last night's statement, in a bizarre appearance in a street demonstration, he demanded money for food.'"

"Food."

"David, what're you doing? Don't you realize you're going to alienate all your backers? How do you expect me to justify this?"

"Money for food."

"I give up!"

Mrs. Roche approached R. cautiously and sat next to him, her can of spray poised for action.

"Really, Davy. Haven't you gone too far? Have you forgotten your friends? I mean what will they say when they hear you publicly promoting charity?"

R. looked at her with a big smile.

"Charity."

Mrs. Roche's lips quivered, and her face reddened in shame.

"My poor Davy. What have they done to you?"

She wiped the tears from her eyes.

"Really, Mr. Fowler. You're responsible for all of this. I should've never listened to you. You've got to do something."

"Perhaps we ought to let your husband rest, Mrs. Roche," the inspector interjected.

"Excuse me, inspector," Mr. Fowler burst out, "but there's an election going on. We've got to do something."

"Mr. Fowler, I'm very well aware of the circumstances. But as you yourself can see, Mr. Roche is not capable at this moment of giving us any useful information."

This was quite observant of the good inspector, for R. was, at that moment, crawling on his hands and knees.

"Really, Davy. What's become of you?"

R. stood up and held out his clenched fists.

"Roaches," he said, opening his hands.

Mrs. Roche, espying the little brown beasts he offered her, quickly fired, letting out a steady stream of insecticide that filled the room. R. dropped to the floor and immediately began shaking.

"Take him upstairs," the inspector said to the two agents who were standing by the door. "Lock the room and make sure he doesn't get away. I'm sorry, Mrs. Roche. I have my orders. The president is counting on him. Your husband will need to be completely debriefed."

"Mr. Fowler," a campaign aide said, entering the room. "We're ahead by twenty percent."

Upstairs, the room spun around quickly and R. could feel his body beginning to change again. His legs started to grow back, his soft, white skin became hard and brown, and his tentacles, which he had dearly missed, slowly reappeared. And soon, he shrunk down to a size he was more accustomed to.

When the metamorphosis was complete, R. scrambled off the bed and up the dresser and looked in the mirror. He examined himself, crawling up and down the shiny surface to get a better view. Then he scurried joyously back down and crawled all over Mrs. Roche's toiletries, investigating their smells and textures. When he had had his fill of these, he rushed down to the carpet, traversed a pair of Mrs. Roche's expensive shoes, then darted up the wall and across the ceiling, stopping to hang upside down, happy at last to be back to normal. He remained that way for quite a while, perhaps five minutes or so (for cockroaches have no sense of time as we know it), then scuttered down the wall, onto the bed and burrowed himself comfortably between the pillow and the sheets.

THE HERDS ARE CHARGING THROUGH THE ROOM

Mother is crying.

They have sensed something sinister, some danger perhaps: the snarl of a lion, the lurk of a predator on the prowl. Or maybe they have detected some force we cannot discern, some signal portending events more apocalyptic: the trembling of the Earth, the violent belching of a not-too-distant volcano.

They could not explain it to you. It's something they know, something they must absolutely do.

The grasslands are a strange place: wild, unpredictable. Too many things can happen, too many things can go wrong. Not a place for civilized men, not a place to build a house, raise a family.

So mother has said. So she points out, even now.

The front door is gone. It has been pounded into nothingness, it has shattered into millions of minuscule pieces which scatter throughout the room from the thrash and sway of the animals. The house rumbles, trembles from the constant striking of hooves against the bare wooden floor.

We try to ignore the disorder, pretend it is not happening, we try to reach out to mother and ease the pain, but the din is more than we can bear.

Mother stops crying. She looks at us from behind glazed eyes, mumbles something we cannot comprehend. Her voice is low, almost inaudible against the stampede she has fostered. Her face is frozen with guilt as if she knows we too have suffered. She looks on from the head of the stairs, helpless, because she wishes to stop the chaos. She is distant and frightened, enwrapped in an eerie silence that helps her confront what she cannot control.

We try to comfort her—we, her sons, who have inherited this land, who have had to cope with the wilderness ever since we were born—we shout at her over the deafening clamor.

"Mother," we beg, "can't you forget what has happened? Can't you put the herds to rest?"

Maybe this is wrong because she tears violently at her hair and sounds a high-pitched wail which blends with the roar of the herds—rhinoceros, she says, zebra, gnu—and becomes indistinguishable.

The beasts enter so quickly, so helter-skelter they cannot be counted. They are like unwanted guests: they come and go with no consideration for others, their voices loud and gruff, their manners so ill you wish they would leave as quickly as they came.

But they don't. Or they do, but their friends keep arriving without warning.

And mother continues to watch with the eye of one who sees what others cannot.

We try to convince her it's not her fault, that the herds have come on their own, that just as they came, they will surely leave. Though nothing will ever be the same. We understand quite well, we tell her, we emphasize that fact in empathy with her dissonance and fear.

But she wails on, on and on, and no matter what we say, we cannot stop her.

Because the beasts keep coming, an endless stream of rolling flesh and muscle whose every thunderous step destroys a bit more of what has toppled over and broken: Mother's good china, which she inherited from Grandmother who died on Mother's wedding day (there is no relation between those two events, she would insist, no cause and effect, but we always knew better, given the nature of God and retribution, given the nature of the man she married and has lived without for all these years), the good crystal she pinched and saved for before things turned sour (how she would lie, she would say, how she would hide her savings and count them at night under the light of the moon when he was fast asleep, after he had had his filthy fill of her), the silver he bought her early on, beaten and flattened now into a shapeless pulp, before he unwillingly sired us, after she hounded him, way way before the day he up and left.

That was when she started crying, that was when the world took a nasty turn and barreled ahead out of control.

And we wonder if we have had some part in all of this. And we wonder if our very presence, our unwillingness to confront the wilderness head-on has caused a disturbance that has forced the herds to suddenly run.

But you can never tell why things happen the way they do. That's what mother has always told us. You can never know what horrible things will take place in the wilderness where men and beasts are bound to clash, she still warns us, where men slaughter men and women sit helpless against the violence they must endure, where any move, sudden or not—the flash of lightning, perhaps, the swift clap of thunder—is apt to spark a stampede you will surely be unable to reverse.

Mother stares across the room, past the charging herds, past the walls, it seems, past a place only she can see. We wonder if she can tell, if she can hear what is taking place around her. Her eyes sparkle like glass, like rich blue crystal gleaming in the sunlight, the blue of a flame about to rage out of control, the blue of a calm sky awaiting the outbreak of storm. It's as if her life rushes by like angry clouds she watches from the shelter of her room, safe behind the glass, from the rain, from the murderous lightning, the awful, vengeful thunder—God's certain retribution for something terrible she thinks she has done—and every now and then her girlhood dreams flash by like bright rainbows that appear and dissolve instantaneously from the swift movement of the black, billowing masses. Wondrous dreams, white fluffy fantasies bouncing gently before her eyes like balls of cotton.

Then suddenly they fall, tumble down the stairs like sacrificial sheep, down to the threshing floor where everything snaps and shatters, Mother's radiant dreams snuffed out under the hooves of beasts who lurch forward with no concern except for themselves.

And Mother screams, darts down the stairs to chase them with no thought of herself. She wants to snatch them back before they are trampled forever, and before we can grab her, stop her from her madness, she is down with the beasts, down among the rumbling clamor. She grapples on the floor, struggles to get up. She rises, goes down again, rises once more, glances momentarily at us with a gleam in her jaded eye, as if that's where she belongs, as if this is the culmination of a life in the wilderness where men and beasts cannot mingle, except for one glorious moment.

For now she is dancing, it seems, waltzing on the living room floor, hand in hand, beast and woman, executing a graceful minuet in that split second before she disappears, falls forever under the raging hooves as we watch and wonder if the stampeding will ever ever stop.

THE OLD OLIVE TREE

Suddenly, the approaching truck could be heard from down the road, and the quiet village began to stir. Abu Jamal quickly emptied his ovens of round, flat bread and ran outside. Abu Yazid rushed to the dilapidated entrance of his cluttered grocery. Abu Ali and Abu Ahmed abandoned their game of backgammon and stood up from their rickety chairs.

The villagers had been waiting anxiously for Saleh's return, and the children rushed through the streets to spread the news. The women dropped their housework at the sound of the commotion below and leaned over their small wooden balconies, chattering incessantly.

The shepherd, who was grazing his sheep in an empty grass lot, quickly herded his flock into the street and joined the crowd that followed behind as the truck chugged up the hill, spitting exhaust into the air, struggling as it wound through the crowded narrow road.

"*Mubruk, mubruk*," they congratulated Saleh as the truck passed by.

Not since the last time the traveling peddler had arrived,

dragging his overloaded donkey from house to house, up and down the steps that lined the hillside in the old city—not since then had the village been so alive.

"Big man, that Saleh," Aziza scowled, adjusting the hijab that covered her head as she rushed out of her broken-down building. "No one else here has a refrigerator. Who does he think he is?"

"Where does he get the money anyhow?" Um Hassan replied, wiping the sweat from her brow with the long sleeves that hid her arms. "He's just a waiter. How much money could he possibly make?"

"Of course, it's used," Aziza insisted. "It's a used refrigerator. That'll be the day when Saleh can afford a new one. When that happens, he can marry my daughter. *Mubruk*, Saleh."

The truck pulled up before the steep, narrow concrete steps that led down to Saleh's house, and the long procession of neighbors crowded around to inspect the big, white refrigerator perched on top. Saleh stepped out and smiled at everyone through his thick black beard.

"It's General Electric," he said proudly as the children climbed up on the flatbed and peered inside the refrigerator door.

"American," Abu Mohammed said approvingly, leaning on his walking stick. "Allah bless. They make good things in America. *Mubruk*, Saleh."

"Does it make ice?"

"Yes, Hassan, it makes ice. We can have cold drinks now, just like in the restaurants."

"Mama, Mama, Saleh can make ice now," Hassan yelled, running off into the crowd.

"Now we'll have all the ice we want," Saleh announced, his dishdasha blowing in the hot breeze. "And we can keep our meat fresh so we don't have to go to the market every day."

"Allah bless him," Um Ayman, the widow, said as all the neighbors began to speak at once. "He's a wonderful boy."

"And so he should be," Aziza replied. "An orphan, that boy. Who took care of him after his parents were killed in the war?"

"Saleh's refrigerator will make things around here a little easier," Abu Jamal commented.

"Allah willing," Abu Hassan the carpenter responded.

But not everyone was pleased about Saleh's refrigerator, and the old-timers insisted that they preferred to go to the market every day, just like they had always done, just like their fathers had before them. It was better, they said, and they would continue to do so.

"It's good," Abu Mohammed assured them. "We will try Saleh's refrigerator, Allah willing, and see. Remember when we had no electric lights? Everyone complained when they came. Now, thank Allah, we have electric lights, and who complains?"

Abu Mohammed laughed. He was the eldest in the village, and his opinion was always respected. They had to at least give Saleh's refrigerator a try, the villagers agreed, and surely they could not do without electric lights.

"But Saleh," Khalid asked, "how are you going to get it down to your apartment?"

Everyone stared at the steep narrow stairway that overlooked the city. This was a question no one had thought of, and even Saleh seemed perplexed as he inspected the broken-down stone steps.

"It's too wide," Aziza said. "You'll never get it down there. It's impossible."

"They make things big in America," Abu Mohammed chuckled.

"We'll manage, Allah willing," Saleh assured everyone. "Let's get it down off the truck first."

Saleh enlisted the help of three friends. They jumped on the truck and zig-zagged the heavy refrigerator to the edge of the flatbed where four men below grabbed hold of it and lowered it gently to the ground.

"Take the door off," someone suggested. "That'll make it lighter."

"Yes, that's a good idea," Abu Hassan said. "Hassan, run to the shop and get the screwdriver."

"We'll manage, Allah willing," Saleh repeated.

Hassan returned with the screwdriver, and Saleh quickly removed the screws and lifted off the door. The four young men positioned themselves around the refrigerator, lifted it up and edged it toward the landing.

"They'll hurt themselves, those boys," Aziza exclaimed. "Allah be with them."

"They're young," Abu Mohammed said, smiling.

Saleh and his friends carefully felt each step with their sandaled feet, the heavy refrigerator weighing them down, the sweat dripping from their faces. They pushed the large appliance through the overhanging branches, maneuvered it through the narrow mud walls that framed the stairway, until they came to the old olive tree which jutted out into the path. Here, they lowered, raised, twisted and turned it, trying to ease it through the small passageway.

"No way," Khalid shouted.

Saleh wiped his face with the back of his black and white checkered kuffiyya and thought for a moment.

"The old olive tree," he explained to the crowd above.

"I knew it," Aziza said. "I told you it was too wide."

"We'll have to cut it down."

The villagers reacted at once to Saleh's words, and the old olive tree, for so many years an almost unnoticed fixture in the village, now suddenly became the center of heated discussion.

"Cut it down? Allah forbid," Aziza burst out.

"Um Nizar," Saleh said respectfully, "we have no choice."

"That tree has been there since before I can remember and you want to cut it down?"

Aziza nervously tucked her hair under her hijab.

"I will plant another one," Saleh said.

"And how long will that take? How long will it take before it bears fruit?"

"There are other olive trees in the area," Um Hassan broke in. "What's one olive tree when we can have a little convenience for a change?"

Um Hassan was not the only one who felt this way, and the villagers slowly became divided.

"Convenience? Allah forgive you. I say the tree stays."

"Let's ask Abu Mohammed what he thinks," Abu Hassan suggested, trying to diffuse the tension.

The crowd turned to Abu Mohammed who had always resolved the disputes that arose in the village. He stroked his long, gray beard for several minutes as he thought about the problem.

"As far as I remember, the olive tree belongs to no one. It's on no one's property. Isn't that so Abu Hassan?"

"It's outside my house," Abu Ahmed interrupted angrily.

"But it's not on your property," Abu Hassan quickly responded.

"No one here planted that tree," Abu Mohammed continued. "Isn't that so?"

He scanned the crowd and waited for a reply.

"The tree belongs to the village. Now Saleh says he will replace it, Allah willing. The Prophet Mohammed, peace and blessings be upon him, once advised that in such situations the majority should rule. We should take a count. We should see how many are for cutting down the tree and how many are against it. Then we can make a decision."

The villagers agreed with Abu Mohammed, and a vote was held. The women abstained, as was the custom, and by a mere majority of one, it was decided to cut down the old olive tree.

"We will have a new refrigerator and a new tree," Abu Hassan commented, delighted at the outcome. "Hassan, run and get the saw."

The men argued noisily as they headed down the steps. When Hassan returned, Saleh and Khalid set the rusty saw against the tree and began to cut it down.

"It was planted after the partition," Abu Ali insisted.

"It's too old to have been planted then," Abu Hassan said. "Look at it. I'm sure it was planted before the Great War, before the British came."

"Yes," Abu Yazid said, "by Abu Mohammed's father. That's what I heard."

Saleh and Khalid slowly worked the blade through the thick trunk of the tree. The green leaves shaded them from the hot sun and shook gently in the afternoon air from the rough motion of the saw.

"It was planted after the partition," Abu Ali repeated impatiently. "I swear by my mother. I remember. I was a little boy then. I was there. An old man from Jerusalem planted it. He escaped. He brought the seed from there."

"Oh. You're talking about the tree near Um Ayman's house," Abu Farid said.

"No, it was this one. I can't remember his name, but he said he wanted to remember his home. If he could not live in Palestine, he said, he would at least have a tree from there. He said it would do until he returned. You were there, Abu Farid. Don't you remember?"

"Yes. I'm telling you you're talking about the tree near Um Ayman's house."

"I still say it was before the partition," Abu Hassan insisted.

"It doesn't matter now," Abu Yazid broke in. "It was a good tree. It always bore fruit, thank Allah. That's what counts."

"And there will be another one," Saleh assured them.

He removed the saw and gave a strong shove, and the old olive tree tumbled to the ground as the children clapped and jumped in excitement.

Up on the street, the women were still quarreling about the decision to cut down the tree.

"What will they do next? No wonder we lost our land to the Israelis," Aziza shouted in disgust.

"Um Nizar, don't get so upset. They're men. We have no choice."

Abu Mohammed listened silently to the women from the comfortable place where he sat.

"We have done this according to the holy Koran," he said, at last, speaking quietly.

"Praise be to Allah," they mumbled.

The men lumbered up the steps, carrying the newly felled tree.

"Allah," Aziza exclaimed, as they threw it into the street.

"Ok," Saleh said. "Let's try again."

Now that the old olive tree was gone, it was easier to make progress, and the four men eased the refrigerator through the narrow passageway, past the spot where the tree had stood. The children ran happily ahead of them, while the older neighbors followed reluctantly behind.

The crowd slowly broke up as the sound of the afternoon azzan drifted through the village. The women, still complaining about the fate of the old olive tree, made their way back to their apartments to prepare dinner. The children, having lost all curiosity, ran off to resume their street games, and the men began their trek down to the mosque.

"Aren't you coming to prayer," Abu Ali called to Saleh and his friends who were trying to get the refrigerator up the narrow staircase in front of Saleh's second-floor apartment.

"We'll pray when we're finished, Allah willing," Saleh answered. "We won't be long. We're almost there."

The village men disappeared into the quiet maze of passageways that had survived for generations, while Saleh and his friends continued their struggle.

By nightfall, the refrigerator was at last installed in Saleh's tiny kitchen. It took up a great deal of space, and it stuck out against the bare plumbing and shelves that lined the crudely painted walls. Saleh inserted the plug into the socket and smiled at the humming of the motor.

His friends relaxed in the small living room, drinking glasses of strong, sweet tea, and hungrily waiting for the dinner he was now preparing. The sound of the azzan drifted in from the mosque loudspeaker.

"I think we should pray," Khalid called out. "We've already missed two prayers."

"We will," Saleh answered from the kitchen. "Allah willing."

Aziza sat alone outside her house in the cool evening air. She thought about her son who had gone to the city to look for work, about her daughter who would soon finish high school, about the sewing she had promised would be ready tomorrow.

Abu Mohammed walked up the street, returning from the evening prayer.

"*Salaam aleikum.*"

"*Wa aleikum salaam.*"

He eased his old limbs down onto the ground beside her.

"You are still upset, Um Nizar."

"Many people are upset."

"It was a fine tree, Um Nizar."

"A blessing. A blessing that tree was. I used to play by that tree when I was a child. My husband, Allah rest his soul, asked me for my hand by that tree."

"He was a good man."

Um Nizar stared off into the starry night and remembered the days when life had been simpler.

"We must think of the future, Um Nizar. Allah is generous."

"Yes," she answered bitterly. "Allah is generous."

ATELIER

She goes with him. He is very nice, it seems. His face is finely chiseled. His eyes, deep and dark, are intense and penetrating. What you'd expect, she thinks, though his hands are big and strong, too big, it seems, for such fine, delicate work. Though there are still traces of paint on his fingers, under his nails where he has tried very hard to remove the streaks of yellow, red, and magenta.

She goes with him to his atelier. Even though they have only met. Even though she knows she must be careful in this city where no one is safe. You could be mugged or raped, or even worse, in this city where she lives and works.

But he has made her laugh, and she has not laughed for some time now, not since she became alone again, some six months ago, when her last lover took suddenly to the wind. Things became too restrictive, it seems, and he had to go. At least, that's what he said.

She goes with him because he, her new lover, was so kind when she tripped so clumsily at the bar—was it on purpose? She wonders, she had noticed him, hadn't she? Was there some unconscious wish that things would take a turn to where they are leading now?—and he so politely, ever so gently helped her to her feet and smiled.

He smiled.

And then he introduced himself: "Collin. Collin Spears."

And it was a shock to her, really, like when you accidentally touch a faulty appliance and you quickly pull back, only her reaction wasn't nearly so abrupt, for it had been so long since she had had to decide how to respond to someone who had smiled at her like that.

"Collin," he said. "Collin Spears.

"Are you all right?" he said.

But she was too busy standing up to reply, coordinating each muscle, each movement—it's not easy, you know—trying to manage her embarrassment, trying to coordinate her reaction to his kindness, that she could not answer, she could not even think to respond as the words penetrated the layers of her awareness: "Collin. Collin Spears."

It was as if a dream had overcome her, and the words were strange, evasive sounds that disassociated themselves from their source and took on a life of their own. She saw fields of snow bundled cozily into a picture-perfect scene, children snug in hats and muffs playing merrily, and there were bells jingling as a horse and sleigh slid quietly by carrying two lovers in a warm embrace.

Collin Spears. It was a cool, refreshing sound, a sprig of spearmint on a hot, humid day, anything but a man who had at once decided to look upon her with kindness. And then:

"Are you all right?"

Now she is with him. Catherine Whittaker. Legal secretary by day. Seeker of the heart by night. Walking through the broken, deserted streets in a part of town she has never been to. Her heart is pounding. She is anxious about her encounter with this man, this Collin Spears, she is somewhat frightened even, but her hand is in his, brings her back, ever so slightly, to reality, and she glances at his tender face, silhouetted against the harsh streetlight, his handsome, well-trimmed beard, and she decides his kindness is something she needs to risk at this very critical juncture in her life.

Happiness is a difficult state to assess, she decides as she flips through the paintings—all of the same woman, she notes, his last lover, no doubt—that lie stacked against the walls of his atelier. Like trying to define a color, like trying to determine, for example, the very nature of blue which, through all its shades and manifestations—cobalt, azure, indigo—can never truly be blue no matter how hard it strives to be.

Nevertheless, she appears to feel something akin to happiness— a light, floating feeling, a feeling she could flit through his atelier like Tinkerbell, a feeling the figurines that line the walls could somehow whisper secret madrigals from their frozen faces— something as close to blue as one can possibly get, she thinks.

Catherine Whittaker, who has not known love for an eternity, it seems, who, having now been made love to, having been taken to the very moon which beams down through the skylight and rests serene across her new lover's face, examines Collin Spears with a jeweler's eye as he sleeps naked on the bed, and she wonders if this could be a hint of the truest blue ever imagined.

Soon she is modeling for him. Soon he convinces her to quit her job and remove her clothes—the very strait-laced receptionist now with her hair untied and flowing, posing this way and that.

Soon she comes to realize how remarkable he truly is with his gentle hands which shape her very existence on the canvas by day, which probe the very depths of her passion by night. His kindness is unending, his dark, mysterious temperament captures her soul and absorbs her slowly and completely into his.

Catherine Whittaker—girl from the farm, who left her family for a life far away in the city, who, against all odds, made it big of a fashion, did it all on her own, now after fifteen years, reaching news heights at this low point in her life—bares her body and her soul to Collin Spears, a successful, urban artist whose dexterous fingers redefine her on canvas and off.

Never afraid to take risks, never afraid to use his subjects to the utmost as the instruments of his genius, Collin Spears strips her bare, Catherine Whittaker, innocent country girl, goes to the very heart of her, transforms her into lines and colors, planes and shapes until the canvas becomes her—that spot a tear, that angle a heartbreak, that splash of red a deep deep passion that longs to rise up. Until Catherine Whittaker becomes the canvas, her body capsulized into the two-dimensional space, her personality deconstructed, interpreted, transformed, her soul diffused into light and shadow.

Then, soon after, the initial days of blind wonderment end, soon she becomes just another fixture in his atelier—a painting, a figurine, an object frozen in space. Soon his atelier becomes filled with her—the canvasses abound, the figurines he has made of her multiply, until she begins to lose all sense of herself, until she can no longer distinguish between image and reality. Catherine Whittaker the woman and Catherine Whittaker the subject merge into one, here in his atelier where Collin Spears manipulates her desires, where light and shadow play havoc with her senses, and eventually the initial joy fades into the background like an inexpensive poster whose colors wane under the unrelenting rays of the sun.

One day, he says to her: "I have finished my work."

It's a casual remark, over a cup of coffee, in a mug he has fashioned in her likeness.

He has painted all he can of her, he explains, he has sculpted every possible variation. He must move on to his next subject.

"You understand, of course."

"Of course," she answers, feeling rather numb, though she is not sure she really does, though she is sure she has heard something like this somewhere before.

He will never forget her, he continues, as if pressed. How could he? he asks. She has become a permanent fixture in his atelier, has earned a permanent place within his heart.

Catherine Whittaker responds with a blank expression. She is not surprised, not upset, not anything really, for he has left her with nothing except the bare minimum of who she once was.

She surveys his atelier. Her image hangs in every corner, the three-dimensional figurines he has made of her sit in every nook and cranny. They are strange and foreign, nothing like what she thinks she remembers of herself; they are like flakes of skin she has unwillingly shed.

She carefully examines each one. She wants to find a clue, some fragment that will indicate who she might be.

She dismisses the paintings. She has grown tired of the garish colors, the harsh thick brush strokes he used on her face, the complicated planes of light he constructed where her body should have been.

She goes instead to the figurines, each with a different expression, each a window to a moment of her past. She hopes they will speak to her, hopes she will discover a sneer or a grimace that will help her understand how she is feeling at this very moment.

But they stare back at her, glum and silent, like ghosts that are unable even to haunt her. Their faces are blank, though they seem to wish, to sing, to speak, to scream something secret to her that she must now absolutely know.

Then it comes to her, a tiny glimpse of the past, a vague echo that rises up within.

She raises her head, looks at the man sitting before her, sipping his coffee in a cup shaped in her likeness. Her eyes sparkle momentarily as she recollects.

"I knew a man once," she says at last. "His skin was warm like fresh cow's milk. His touch was like goose down. His voice was the gentle cooing of a dove. He used to paint dreams," she says. "I could get lost in them if I let myself. I believe I am lost in one now."

She puts her hands to her face, her arms, her body, as if she is not quite sure whether she is awake.

She smiles.

"Collin," she says. "His name was Collin Spears."

"I am he," he says.

"Oh," she says, and she wakes up. "I must go now."

"Yes," he says, his face suddenly gone sad. "You must go. Can you find your way out?" he asks.

Catherine Whittaker collects herself from about the room like a school girl collecting leaves. She gathers her clothes, the trinkets she brought with her when she first moved in, all the possessions she has accumulated and saved since the day she came to the city.

"Yes," she answers. "I believe I have been here before. I believe I will never be here again," she says.

She smiles, a kind, simple, tranquil smile.

Collin Spears turns his face away. He gets up. One by one, he removes her paintings, stacks them up, against the wall. It is a ritual he has practiced, to mark the end of each project.

Catherine Whittaker watches him as she walks toward the doorway. His hands tremble as he lifts each canvas. His face, long and worn, appears old in the harsh sunlight that filters through the skylight in his atelier.

"Are you all right?" she asks, as she turns the doorknob, as if that is the only thing left to say.

SUDDENLY, THERE WAS HAROLD

Henry was a flower. Or at least he thought he was. A tall tulip with long, slender green leaves, broad speckled white petals, and a soft brown sticky patch in the middle for a nose.

One of the things he liked best about being a flower was that he could listen in freely to conversations without being detected. He thought of himself as a sort of spy. A kind of undercover man, lying about, incognito, watching and listening and taking in what he could otherwise not.

Like today. He was perched in a creamy white vase and could overhear Mrs. Hutchins telling her nextdoor neighbor about how unfaithful her husband had been.

"He's so insufferable," she was saying, wiping away a tear, to Mrs. Broome who gave her a look comprised of both pity and shock.

They were sitting on the couch—an embroidered sofa imported all the way from Belgium—sipping freshly-brewed tea and eating strawberry scones. He could have been eating strawberry scones as well but instead he was sitting surreptitiously in a vase of freshly decanted water.

"You would think he was still single the way he behaves. Still sowing his oats. Still trying to figure out where to park his bike. Still anything but a man with a wife and marital responsibilities."

Yes, Henry thought. I can listen and I can see. Providing I am in the right position at the right time.

Which, of course, he was at that particular moment, because he could see Mrs. Hutchins fold over in despair on the couch, could witness Mrs. Broome take her hand and pat it ever so gently as she tried, unsuccessfully, with a disconcerted look and a subdued sigh, to comfort her, as she waited anxiously for the first opportunity to take her leave without seeming too unfashionably rushed.

Henry was sad for a moment. Then he smiled, brightened really, under the soft sunlight that slanted through the slatted blinds and warmed him ever so gently. Which, for a flower, amounted to a giant grin. What better way, he thought to himself, to gather the deepest secrets, to hear the details of Mrs. Hutchins's life, to be with her always, than to be a bright, sunny flower, standing ever so innocent, erect in a white porcelain vase, set prominently in the center of a fine walnut table in a room with an expensive Persian carpet, a portrait and a still-life hanging on opposite ends of the room, and a large, crystal chandelier that cascaded down from the medallioned ceiling and hung suspended magically in the air above him. What better way, indeed, than to listen in to Mrs. Hutchins's conversations without her ever even suspecting.

Except that Henry, whose name was Albert, or could have been, had always wanted to be a dog. Or a furry little cat. Or a bird in a cage where he could flit around all day and then, if he wanted, when Mrs. Hutchins opened the cage door to feed him or to fill his water cup, he could quickly make his escape and fly off, out and up, swiftly and smoothly, straight through an open door or a window left carelessly ajar, out into the wide open air where she could never catch him. Then he could move about freely from yard to yard, soar up high into the sky and swoop back down, flutter from roof to roof, from window to window, as he pleased, and listen in, or peak through lacy bedroom curtains and watch the goings on in the very privates of people's lives. In the very privates of Mrs. Hutchins's deeply deprived life.

So one morning, bright and early, while Mrs. Hutchins was still asleep or, at least, still in bed, awake and wondering about the whereabouts of her unpredictable, incomprehensible husband, Henry, or Albert, up and transformed himself, gently pivoted himself against the edge of the porcelain vase that had been his home for an eternity it seemed (for being a flower had its draw-backs, seeing as one could not move about) and turned into a fine-looking butterfly—for despite his desire to be a dog or a cat or a fluttering bird, he had wanted to maintain his startlingly good looks, and so this was the perfect compromise—knocking over the vase at the very last minute as he catapulted himself up into the air, at the very moment Mrs. Hutchins entered the room, having been awakened by a certain something—an odd feeling she had, by an uncertain sound she thought she heard—and then, just as suddenly, being startled by the crash of the vase breaking against the ceramic tiles which had been imported all the way from Italy and had been arranged, ever so skillfully, by the Korean artisan who had come all the way from the other side of town to carefully arrange them around Mrs. Hutchins's dining room table, to please Mrs. Hutchins so she could boast boisterously to her friends and acquaintances.

"Harold?" she called out, rushing into the room in her silken nightgown.

But there was no answer. Only the odd silence of a missing flower and the glittery scattering of broken porcelain on the Italianate floor which she had now to tiptoe around in her red Chinese slippers to avoid getting cut.

The trouble was that Albert, now that he was free, now that he was a big butterfly with handsome yellow wings edged with the boldest black, missed Mrs. Hutchins. Though he would never admit to it. Though he would never tell her that, not directly, if ever a butterfly could tell a woman what he feels. For he had been with Mrs. Hutchins for many a year. Had watched her change from a beautiful bashful bride into the stunningly jaded woman she had now become. He had done this first as a wallboard when, stiff and silent, he would watch her dress and undress, then as a plush linen sheet—one hundred percent Egyptian cotton—on which she would repose like a portrait with her naked, perfumed body, then finally as a fine-toothed comb when, unbeknownst to her, he was able to inhale her scent, to secretly caress her smooth, silky, long, black hair.

But as the years meandered on, things began to go flat, and Mrs. Hutchins's easy smile gradually became pursed. Her gentle laugh, which had always come spontaneously, especially when she was surprised by an unexpected gift or delighted by a certain way Harold (who did he think he was, anyway?) came up from behind and kissed her on the head—this effortless laugh eventually became silenced. Or, rather, strained and edgy, like the sound of a taut string on an old, neglected violin when being tuned by a not quite so skilled musician.

Perhaps it was because she soon discovered she could not have children. Or maybe because Harold (damn that Harold, always messing about, always doing something to upset poor Mrs. Hutchins) eventually stopped paying her much mind as happens when marriages begin to unwind and then fade like paint under the hot bright sun. For eventually, Harold could no longer make her out, at least not as crystal clear as he once could, could no longer see himself even, hidden behind all that lather as he shaved each morning, could no longer detect the contour of her fine lips, the tone of her fair skin or the shape of her silhouette against the moonlight as his feelings shifted, then disappeared, and he could no more distinguish between day and night, between white and black, between what was real in his life and what wasn't than he could between the particular manifestation he had become and the one that had just preceded. It was as if he had developed an emotional myopia, as if all the things around him, including Mrs. Hutchins, had slowly lost their crisp, fine-edged outlines and gradually morphed into a milky murkiness.

And there wasn't much he could do about it (he being Albert who soon decided to call himself Ralph). After all, for all intents and purposes, he was not alive. After all, he was just an inanimate object. Lying about in her room. Watching her adoringly. Wishing he could break out of his hard-waxen shell. Riding stiffly through her thick, black hair. Wanting more than anything to love her the way she was meant to be loved. The way he himself wanted to be loved.

That's when he took to getting anxious. That's when things began to break up, to crumble like dried bread, to disintegrate like fine splinters of rosewood accumulating on the floor from a carpenter's lathe or tiny fragments left over from the workings of a leatherman's awl.

So one morning, years after he had been a worn panel on the fading wall, later, when he had given up his life as a flower, when being a butterfly no longer held any appeal, when his desire to be a dog or a cat or an exotic bird had lost its elusive, evanescent grip, Oliver—for he had decided to assume this wonderful name, this broad, rich moniker, imbued with a rich sense of staid stability and tried tradition—decided to divide himself up. It was a strategy meant to maximize his presence, a way of guaranteeing that he would always be in the right place at the right time. So he could watch Mrs. Hutchins no matter where she went. So he could always be with her. Only, he would be like an invisible angel, and she would never know.

It started when she decided to renovate the house. The interior decorator, a suave woman with wire-rimmed glasses and a thick notepad she carried around with her as she surveyed the house, taking notes and making sketches—mere doodling, Oliver noted jealously, mere scribble-scrabble limned on a crisp pad of paper and meant to take Mrs. Hutchins's mind off of him—as she talked to Mrs. Hutchins about this idea and that—leveraging her skills and imposing her views—an artist herself who had flown in clear across the country from San Francisco for the occasion, suddenly suggested geometrics. True, she told Mrs. Hutchins, it was the latest craze. True, like all fads, it would most definitely fade. But it had its basis in the natural world, was buttressed by history, by the long line of artists and artisans who had come before, whose work was backed up by circles and squares, triangles and trapezoids, octagons and spheres.

Ms. Hutchins had no idea what she was talking about—feigned interest, really, and a bit of knowledge—but she immediately agreed, for she needed a radical change in her life, desired, more than anything else, to rid herself of any vestige of her husband (her former husband, she had wanted to say, for she had not seen nor heard from him in years and assumed he had just gone by the wayside, had disappeared like a bubble in the air or like a thin scrim of smoke dissipating into the vast, vast universe).

"Yes," she said, her smile bursting into an arc. "Geometrics. We will go with geometrics."

And so geometrics it was. And Oliver, who now became Lawrence—now there was a name, he thought, he wished ever so much that his name had been Lawrence, could imagine himself more as Lawrence than anyone else—became a series of circles on a modern specimen of a rug, a rectangular black and white polka-dot carpet which now completely covered the Italianate floor. And his eye transformed into a sphere of a chandelier that hung suspiciously over a parallelogram of a table. And his arms, long and fluted, turned into slender cylindrical lamps set precariously on the floor on either side of a cubic couch.

"Lovely," the interior decorator exclaimed in her vague voice as she collected her handsome fee (though it was not quite as handsome as Henry or Albert or Ralph or even Oliver, not nearly as handsome as even Harold himself, Lawrence thought) and closed the door behind her, leaving Mrs. Hutchins in a house that seemed as strange to her as the husband she could not seem to shake from her system.

And she sat down on the quadrilateral armchair and surveyed her new landscape, burst suddenly into tears, tears that drizzled down like a sudden shower onto the rim of shapes Lawrence had become. And he was delirious with sorrow, and he soon became entangled in the very weight of Mrs. Hutchins's woeful weeping.

Then, one day, something changed. Something subtle and indefinable. Something Lawrence—who woke up David that day, who was now so convoluted he could barely flounder—something he could not quite put his finger on. Something Mrs. Hutchins detected through a small window in her life and an ancient glow that slowly filtered in. Something soft and elusive like a brief snowflake or a chink of light caught up in the chance twist of a crystalline kaleidoscope.

Perhaps it was the way the sun had risen that day. Or the fact that Mrs. Hutchins had decided, on a wishful whim, to arrange a vase full of cut flowers from her well-kept garden, flowers which stood now in tall, wispy silhouettes and which she tried desperately to variegate. And as she did so, there was a dreamy look in her eye, a distant wistfulness that beckoned back to bolder beginnings.

Mrs. Hutchins surrendered to the moment she had become, submitted herself to the moment that really had become her. Draped in despair on the triangular kitchen chair, she surveyed the squares and circles that made up her room, tragically traced the trapezoid her life had assumed.

"Harold," she called into the vacuum that encircled her. "Harold. Are you there?"

"Harold," she cried, raising her voice and clutching her tears. "Why don't you answer?"

"Harold," she wept, surveying the room from the corner of her eye, taking stock of each nook and cranny, of each fascicle that constituted the texture of her very convex life.

Then, peering into nothingness, she said, "I wish you had talked to me, Harold."

"Harold," she said, wiping the nervousness from her brow, "I wish you had told me that you loved me. Or didn't. Or something to that effect."

And she leaned her round face into the square of her open palm, and a tear fell from her eye like a burst of aching amber burnished under the opulence of the oval sun.

Then, suddenly, there was Harold. Suddenly, through all the circles and squares, David appeared, and then Lawrence and then Oliver, and, gradually, Ralph became Albert became Henry, and Harold had an inkling, and Mrs. Hutchins looked around and vaguely perceived him, distinguished his imprecise presence through the sharp compass of her jeweler's eye, through all the manifestations he had assumed throughout his long, lonesome life as an object. And she measured his imperfections against the geometry of her soul, calculated the distance from his obtuse love to the very radius of her diametric need.

"Harold," she cried. "Why didn't you tell me?"

Slowly, she bent down. Slowly, she gathered Harold up, or tried, tentatively collected the ambiguous fragments of him—the squares, the circles, the trembling triangles—slipped them over her uncertain hand like forbidden jewels, snaked them up her outstretched arm like a diamond bracelet that slithered all the way to the acute angle her slender elbow made.

Then, all at once, Harold decided that enough was enough. He had had his fill of all these changes. He had had enough of being circuitousness, of assuming the rigid crook of a right angle, of being a solid circle with no hole in the middle through which to fall. He wanted to be more fluid, more relaxed, more anything than the changeling he had so desperately become.

And he stood there before his wife like an ancient statue, salvaged from the brittle ruins of time, fragile and naked, stark as life and vague as death, as if the chrysalis of his being had suddenly shed its comforting cocoon, as if time had suddenly stopped and he was now living in that one intense second that made all the difference in the world.

Mrs. Hutchins waded through a jumble of tears and broken breaths, calmed her quaking nerves and quietly said: "You've been—" stopping herself and looking longingly at him.

"Yes," he answered.

"All along," she said, in a puff of hope and a burst of shame. "You've been filled with me."

"Yes," he replied. "I've been filled with you."

And his voice trembled with silence. And his brow wrinkled into a Gordian knot. And he stared quietly at the ground, hunched in an arch of guilt, consumed by a hollow of sorrow that only the lone crow cawing in the distant distance could fully comprehend.

"Harold," she sighed.

She was staring at the carpet, gaping at the raging lamps.

"I don't know what to say."

She picked up a fragile ornament from the coffee table—a glass elephant she had purchased once on an imaginary trip to Africa—and let it crash silently to the ground.

Harold peered through the brim of his eye, shuffled through the fragments of his convoluted life, and let the pieces sliver all around him.

That day, all the tears in the world tumbled from the sky.

That day, all the leaves that die in autumn, all the snowflakes that melt from the wintry heavens, all the sunlight that trickles down and bathes the world with its gentle sallow light accumulated in the spot where they now stood—a man and a woman—on a geometric carpet, which covered completely an Italianate floor, which stood in a house designed by a German architect, constructed of stone brought over all the way from Bruges.

Harold and Mrs. Hutchins lived verily ever after that. After that, that is, they lived as validly as could be expected, as two people could eventually live after surviving a love of such myriad proportions, a love which imbued the very nooks and crannies of the venerable house where they managed to virtually live.

THE LAST LAUGH

When Raven Willis woke up that day, to the muffled whoosh of traffic outside his bedroom window, he opened his bleary eyes and immediately sensed that he was not feeling all that up to par. Propping himself up on his elbow and leaning his heavy head against the leather headboard, he tapped his wife on the shoulder and announced casually, in his usual sardonic way:

"I'm feeling rather swinish today."

No "honey" or "dear." No "good morning" or "hey, guess what?" Just: "I'm feeling rather swinish today." Abrupt and to the point. Laced with unemotional humor.

Except that his voice was rather harsh and gritty and the smirk on his face, which was lost to the early morning darkness, quickly transformed to a grimace.

He was, in fact, feeling rather heavily under the weather: his throat somewhat sore, his nose a bit stuffy, his body a touch tired and achy. And it was more of a way to cheer himself up that he said these words, more anything than even a brief belief that he had suddenly contracted the latest fatal disease he had been hearing about in the media over the past several months.

"Mere claptrap," he would say whenever a breaking news bulletin announced yet another school closing or alerted the nation to the fact that the pharmaceutical companies had still not been able to produce enough vaccine to satisfy an already anxious population. "Mere drivel meant to scare the masses into buying yet another dose of miracle medicine which they have not even thoroughly tested."

And so to complete his early morning bout of humor—to cheer himself up and to ward off the fear that maybe he did have something that could cozy up to fatal—and to keep his worrisome wife from working herself up into her typical tizzy, he opened his eyes wide, tautened the skin on his face, and snorted like a pig, though this final act did have a rather negative impact on his rough, scratchy throat.

His wife, Ruth, who knew him well enough after seven years of marriage, who understood, after listening to him day in and day out, that his odd sense of humor was, as she liked to put it, deviously demented, who recognized his absolute, uncompromising need for absurdity to get him through the drudgeries of the day, quickly turned over on her side, leaned on her elbow, and, with her back facing him, murmured with just a touch of concern in her voice:

"It's just a little cold, Raven. Nothing to get worried about. Just a seasonal thing that will pass just as quickly as it came."

Yet she immediately jumped out of bed, rushed into the bathroom and closed the door behind her, pretended to be late, as she brushed her teeth and put on her make-up, then hurried out of the apartment without even as much as a kiss or goodbye.

Left on his own, Raven coughed and sniveled, blew his nose what seemed a hundred times, went to the bathroom and gargled, took his temperature—approaching 103 on his digital thermometer—and took some aspirin, then picked up his cell phone and called in sick, announcing offhandedly to his manager that he did not yet have the swine flu, as far as he knew, but could be fast approaching it, snapped the phone closed and snorted, then stared fearsomely at his bleary image in the bedroom mirror.

If it was just the regular flu, he reasoned—the garden variety that came each year which he refused to get vaccinated against—then he could simply ride it out and would be better in a day or two. If it was the swine flu, on the other hand, then he had better do something about it, given the fact that he was in the high-risk group (the supposed high-risk group, he added sarcastically, making two invisible quotation marks in the air) for complications and even death. And the last thing he wanted was for his tombstone to announce to posterity: "Death by Swine" or some other cutesy phrase they might see fit to engrave. Though now that he thought of it, it would be a fitting epitaph for an incorrigible jokester like him.

"Raven Willis," he said out loud, through the raspy strains of his laryngitic voice, "whose name was avian in nature, died instead of the swine flu."

Raven laughed feebly at this little bit of wit but his head pounded even more and the body aches seemed to intensify and he withered onto the bed and lay there sweating and shivering all at once.

An hour or so later, Raven awoke to the jarring sound of the ringtone on his cell phone. His head was pounding and his body seemed on fire and, as he opened his eyes, he felt as if he were looking through a thick wad of shriveled-up cellophane.

"Raven," Ruth said, "are you feeling better? Have you called the doctor?"

But Raven could not answer, though he tried. His voice was weak and it hurt too much to move his mouth.

"Raven? Raven, I'm calling an ambulance."

And though he tried to protest—who, he wanted to ask, is going to pay for that ambulance?—it was all for naught for Ruth had already hung up, and he was faced with the hollow sound of the cold cell phone flat against his burning ear.

Soon, the ambulance arrived with its piercing siren, alerting the reclusive stay-at-homes to the emergency that was unfolding in their quiet building, and Raven crawled out of bed and staggered to the door, collapsing just as he opened up for the paramedics, just as he was about to greet them with a friendly snort and a silly grin. And as they lifted him up and placed him on the gurney, as they took his vital signs and wrapped him snug in blankets, as they secured him to the stretcher with straps that they tightened firmly around his body, his mind seemed to fade and he could barely grasp the words that were being said over his precarious condition.

The last thing he remembered was the neighbors peeking furtively through bent-up blinds and darkened windows, covering their faces and their fright with their bare hands, as if that were enough to shield them from contamination, then the sound of the ambulance door being shut tight against their stunned stares and the whirring siren which seemed to soothe him and draw him ever deeper into stupor.

When he awoke—half awoke, really, for his fever was so high that he felt as if he were in a trance—he saw that he was in a dark room: the door closed, the curtains drawn, the lights set to dim. In the background, he could hear the quiet hum of machines and the constant staccato of beeps from the monitors that were tethered to his body. And all he could smell was the sterility in the room, an acute, stringent odor that he wished would quickly go away.

He tried moving his head, but it was heavy with pain. His eyes ached, his body felt clammy, and the throbbing on his forehead made him feel as if he would explode at any minute.

Soon, a nurse came in, wearing a white mask and latex gloves. She checked the machines, noted the readings on a PDA, and mumbled something inaudible under her breath. Raven peered at her through half-opened eyes, strained himself to give her a friendly snort—just for the fun of it, just to annoy her, to show her that he did not really subscribe to the industry she was a part of or to convince himself that it was not all that serious—and dropped his head back onto the pillow. The nurse ignored him—or perhaps his gesture was so weak that she had not noticed—tsk-tsked disapprovingly as she reviewed her entries on the PDA and left the room, removing her gloves and dropping them into a wastebasket marked "Medical Waste." Then she rubbed her hands with sanitizer from a dispenser that was conspicuously hung near the exit on the wall and closed the door with a solid click.

Now all throughout his life, Raven Willis had never been alone. At least, not for extended periods of time. Not truly alone, at any rate. While he was growing up, his mother would always be nearby, especially when he was sick. When he got older and left for college, he lived in the dorm and was surrounded by fellow students and, later, as he moved here and there, had always had roommates who came and went at all hours of the day and night but remained, somehow, inevitably around. Even throughout his marriage, his wife would leave only for short periods of time and then just to go shopping or to visit an old friend for an hour perhaps, at maximum two.

So now, as he lay in this strange hospital bed, in a room that seemed even stranger—sinister, he wanted to say, though he could not say why—he experienced, for the first time in his life, a true sense of solitude, a depth of loneliness he had never known throughout his thirty-six years, and he wondered if perhaps he had died or if everyone had abandoned him for fear of contracting whatever it was he had.

The silence, punctuated only by blips and beeps from the machines that monitored him, was frightening, and Raven wanted to cry out, but his voice was weak and his throat hurt too much and it was not worth the pain or trouble since he knew there was no one nearby to hear. So instead, he rested his head on its side, stared blankly off into the dusky room, and waited for time to pass, waited for this illness, whatever it was, to get itself over with or for his life to end if that's what it came to.

"Raven Willis," he noted to himself in a short fit of lucidity, "died in his hospital bed, died of a flu named after pigs though he had never been piggish at any time during his life."

A while later (no telling how much later, for Raven no longer had any sense of time, just lay there as if his entire life were now inert), a doctor arrived (and it was about time, Raven noted as his glazed eyes registered a white coat appearing at the door like a ghost and he unwittingly felt a tinge of relief), entered the room with quiet steps, his face and hands hidden behind protective coverings, walked over to Raven's bed, sat down on a chair beside him, and silently began his examination.

"Mr. Willis," he said quietly, as he moved his cold stethoscope silently against Raven's burning skin, "can you hear me?"

His voice was calm, emotionless, worn from years of counsel. Raven responded with a weak nod.

"It seems you've caught something rather nasty. Something much more than we had at first planned for, eh?"

"Swine flu?" Raven responded weakly through parched lips.

"H1N1. That's what we've been told to call it now. Don't want to upset the farming industry, you know. Nothing to fool around with, regardless of the name. Though, truthfully, it seems like some sort of mutation."

He checked Raven's eyes, examined his nose and ears with an otoscope, then noted his temperature and said, matter-of-factly: "Your temperature is nearly 104."

His face was old and leathery, as far as Raven could tell,

given the mask and surgical cap that covered him, and his voice betrayed a man who was tired and burned out, perhaps from the many years he had put in, perhaps from the tedious hours and days he spent tending to patients. He peered at Raven through the slit in his mask, like an eagle perched commandingly above, his eyes beady and piercing.

"We've tried the usual medications to no avail. We've tried ice and cold compacts. Yet you continue to burn up."

Raven looked up at him, helpless and in need, firm in his conviction about the medical industry yet aware that, at least for now, he needed them more than they needed him.

The doctor paused as if to think. Though he had spoken like anyone else, his voice seemed lifeless—mechanical, Raven thought—as if he had said these same words thousands of times, as if they were recorded inside of him and someone had simply pushed a button to allow them to play. Now, as he stood their silent, looking off into nowhere, it seemed as if he were waiting for someone to tell him what to do, waiting, like a blank computer, for a command that would set off a series of processes that would lead to a conclusion about how to proceed. Setting his cold dark eyes suddenly on Raven, he broke the silence and continued.

"Frankly, Mr. Willis, we're not really sure what you have or what to do."

He was standing now, hovering over Raven like a drone, his arms akimbo, his thoughts lost in contemplation.

"With your permission, we'd like to run more tests, try a few things—well, frankly, they're experimental but we have no alternative, you see."

He stopped and waited for Raven's response.

Raven could not think—he was, after all, delirious, could barely distinguish the doctor's dim silhouette from the darkness of the room, could hardly make out the words that he was hearing. And he could not, no matter how he tried, get his voice to reply. What he wanted most right now was for his wife to be beside him, for her to take his hand in hers, to comfort him in his last hours, to take responsibility for his life, to respond to this mysterious doctor who could not seem to get it right. Instead, he took a deep, painful breath, tried to hoist himself up on his elbows and fell back onto the pillow on his bed in a gesture that could have resembled approval given the context and the situation.

"I understand," the doctor responded. "We'll do everything we can. And we'll note your consent in our records."

The doctor pushed a call button, turned punctiliously on his heals and left.

Raven could no longer determine if he was awake or asleep, alive or in a state somewhere between life and death. A heavy silence settled in, punctuated only by the sound of the monitors which surrounded him and beeped with menacing repetition. The room seemed to swallow him with its pernicious presence or, rather, with its shadowy lack of life, like a black hole which had trapped him in its grip and now forcefully drew him in.

Raven thrashed back and forth on the bed. He tried to lift his hands, to stretch his aching legs, but his limbs were tied down to the bedding and he could not move them. He tried to call out, but his voice failed him, and the only response was a soft hissing, as of heat emanating from an antique radiator or of a snake slithering slowly nearby, stealthy and sinister.

Raven tried to calm himself down. When he was a child, awakened from a bad dream or when, in the middle of the night, he lay sick in bed, dizzy and nauseous, unable to call out for help, he would close his eyes, try to imagine something pleasant: a purling stream in a quiet forest or a bright sunny day in the park where he would play in the sandbox or monkey around on a swing.

Desperate now, he tried the same, but his mind wandered and the hissing summoned him, sonorous and sinister, and he felt himself being drawn further and further into the ominous arms of darkness which surrounded him, like a choking fog enveloped him in its fearsome arms and pulled him deeper and deeper into an endless black well from which there was no possibility of return.

Then there was a jolt, and Raven opened his glazed eyes to the glaring ceiling lights that floated quickly by and made him dizzy, to the faint sound of voices, distant and indecipherable, echoing indistinctly through the hollow hallways. Through his blurred vision, he could tell that his bed was being moved by two figures covered in white, and the walls—the cold, tile walls that glared like brass and made his head hurt even more—flashed by brashly, one by one.

Soon the movement stopped and the figures disappeared, and he felt himself being lifted, conveyed. Then, the loud grinding of a machine jolted him, and he was slowly sucked inside. Darkness enfolded him, interrupted only by intermittent flashes and the deafening sound which grew and grew until the platform he was on stopped dead.

The only thing he could remember after that—later, when the world was no longer the same—was a small opening above him and a pointed instrument descending slowly towards his face, its shiny, silvery tip spinning shrilly like a dental drill. Then light turned to black, sound ceased and, for all he knew, he could have died and gone to hell.

When Raven awoke, there was total silence. He opened his eyes, but all he could perceive was a fuzzy whiteness through which a faint light filtered softly. And though he could breathe well enough, he felt as if he would suffocate. Then he noticed an odd feeling: a feeling he had not had for days now, maybe weeks, for he had lost all sense of time. All of his symptoms had vanished. His lungs seemed clear, his head no longer pounded, and his body no longer ached.

Raven took a deep breath and let it out slowly. He felt changed, renewed, different from when he had been taken from his apartment, though he still felt as if he were in a dream—felt a certain shift in consciousness—as if whatever medication they had given him, whatever procedure they had performed on him had wrapped its arms inextricably around him and transported him to another realm.

The sound of a door opening caught his attention, and he turned his head though he could not see through the bandage that covered his face.

"Good morning, Mr. Willis."

It was a man's voice, small and high-pitched, friendly and cheery yet somehow removed, and Raven knew immediately that it was not the doctor who had first attended to him.

"We trust you're feeling better this morning."

Raven tried to answer but the most he could manage through the bandages was an indecipherable grunt.

"It's ok," the man sang. "These things take time. But before you know it, you'll be as good as new. The miracle of modern medicine, you know. And don't let anyone tell you any different."

Raven could hear him move about, could feel his hand against his skin as he took his pulse and checked all the other statistics he needed to note about his existence.

"Yes," the man continued, "it may cost, and in the end, you always have to pay, but that's why we have insurance. You do have health insurance, don't you, Mr. Willis?"

The man's voice became suddenly serious when Raven did not respond.

"I see," he said. "Well. That explains it. It always happens to those who refuse to buy insurance."

Raven felt put on the spot. He had spent all these years railing and raving against the medical system, especially the insurance companies who, as far as he was concerned, were only interested in profit, and here he was, brought back from the brink of death thanks to that very system. It was truly, as the man with the tiny voice had said, a miracle of modern medicine. And the fact that he had no insurance—had refused to participate at his job and had forced his wife to forego her benefit as well—made things even worse. Now, like a child caught with his pants down, he felt ashamed. And what weighed on his mind even more was the cost which he knew would be exorbitant. How many thousands? he thought. And how would he possibly pay for it?

"Not to worry," the man said, as if he were reading his mind. "These things get resolved. One way or another. They always get resolved. The blessings of democracy and all that."

Raven turned his head to its side and closed his eyes. He felt suddenly sick to his soul, humiliated, weighed down by guilt and fear. What would happen now? What would they do to him if he could not pay up?

"Somewhere else you'd still be waiting for your surgery. But here there is no waiting. 'Ask and you shall receive,' as they say."

Raven smiled at the irony of this last statement. He had, after all, never asked for anything. It was his wife who had asked. And then, suddenly, the word surgery registered itself in his brain. Surgery? he thought. What surgery? He had come here with the flu. Certainly that didn't warrant surgery. Had they somehow mixed him up with someone else? Given him the wrong procedure?

"Ah, the blessings of liberty," the man sang in his little voice, like a song he had learned from his childhood. "Only in America. This is indeed a great country."

Well, Raven thought, he was feeling better, there was no denying that. Maybe he was being just a little too skeptical. As he had always been. Cynical. Untrusting. Unwilling to believe in the system. Maybe it was time for him to put away his feelings of contempt and submit himself to the good that it offered. For no matter what one said, it did have its benefits.

"You rest now," the man said. "I'll be back later to remove those bandages. Just as soon as they say so. Just lay back and relax. That will help the healing process. You're going to feel remarkable when we're through with you. Transformed. Not at all like you expected."

The sound of the man's footsteps faded, followed by the squirt of hand sanitizer and the short snap of the door.

Raven lay back in bed and wondered, how long had he been here? Where was Ruth? Was she not allowed to see him for fear she might contract whatever it was he had? How long had it been since he'd eaten? And why didn't he feel even a pang of hunger? Or the need to go to the bathroom? Or the urge for a glass of water? The only thing he did feel was an unmistakable desire to get up and leave this place. He wanted to be at home, in his room, with his wife. He wanted to be at work with his friends. He wanted to be free of these surroundings, of the smell of sterility, of the utter silence that was so devoid of life, he felt as if he had gone deaf or, even worse, had died.

He tried moving his hands and legs but they felt odd and heavy and did not respond as they should have. Then, he attempted to sit up, but somehow the muscles would not cooperate. Out of frustration, he tried to scream, but nothing akin to what his voice used to sound like would come out. Instead, he thrashed about the bed making indistinguishable sounds which squealed through the room and caused him to panic.

Then the door opened and he could hear footsteps rushing into the room.

"Mr. Willis," a woman's voice said, "what's wrong?" Then, in a voice that differed in tone, she said: "We'll need to sedate him. Mr. Weisel!" she ordered.

Raven struggled as he was restrained on all four limbs, grunted as the needle pricked through his skin and he felt the medication make its way through his body. He imagined the liquid traveling through his veins like tiny cars on a metal track, dispersing themselves here and there at random interchanges like a million mindless drones. "Raven Willis," he thought to himself as his mind began to fade, "came to the hospital against his will, came defiant, came with the swine flu, and was finally subdued by a pack of pigs."

When Raven felt that he had awakened at last that day, he knew at once he was in a different place. There was bright sunlight and clean air and the smell of sterility was markedly gone. In its place was a smell of freshness—of grass and hay—a scent so unmistakable and acute, it made him breathe in deeply out of curiosity. What was more was the fact that the bandages had been removed from his face and he could see clearly that he was in a pleasant room—cheery and cozy, with a pleasant sense of warmth that enveloped him like an imperceptible blanket. He took another deep breath, noted how remarkably well he felt, and slowly breathed out.

"Raven Willis," he thought, "who had approached the brink of death—" But his thoughts stopped here, and his mind went blank, so blank, it felt as if he had no mind at all.

Soon the door opened and someone entered, though, from the slant of light that eclipsed the figure, he could not tell who it was. Silence ensued, followed by the quiet sounds of sobbing.

Raven looked up as the figure approached him, as the image slowly emerged from the silhouette created by the bright wash of sunlight. A woman stood over him, stared silently down at him, then covered her face with her hands as her sobs turned into uncontrollable hysterics. Soon, she turned around and left the room without saying a word, as if she had not noticed how well he had become.

Raven tried to call out to her, but he could not remember if she had a name, could not recall—or perhaps did not know—who this person might be. But he felt an urgent need to communicate with her, to touch her milky skin, to shout out "I'm alive," because it seemed she did not know, because somehow, he felt that this would make her feel better.

A while later, the orderly came back.

"Good morning, Mr. Willis," he sang in his tiny voice. "I trust you're feeling well today."

Raven looked up at him and noted how tall he suddenly seemed.

"We'll be moving you out of here permanently," the orderly said. "Don't want to create any unnecessary expenses, you know. Especially seeing as you have no insurance."

He looked at Raven crossly, as if to make him feel guilty.

"Not to worry," he said. "In the end, everything gets paid. Things always get paid, Mr. Willis. If not by you, then by someone else. That's the way the system works. You may need to rob Peter to pay Paul, as they say, but in the end, things always get paid."

Raven felt suddenly angry, and he stomped his feet against the ground. Who did this guy think he was, talking to him like that?

The first chance he got, he would complain. Then he remembered that the orderly was right, and he curled back down onto the floor and rested his head sullenly between his arms. No, he thought, he did not have insurance and, yes, someone had to pay. And he looked down at the ground and felt humiliated.

"It's all right, Mr. Willis," the orderly said consolingly. "Society understands these things and accounts for them. And in the end," he added, bending down and whispering, "it all comes back to you anyhow. The last laugh, as they say."

He stood back up, walked across the room, and uncovered a tray that was sitting on a cart he had rolled in with him. Humming quietly to himself, he lifted a shiny, metal bowl and placed it on the ground.

"In the meantime, Mr. Willis," he said. "Here's your breakfast. And here," he added, setting down another aluminum basin, "is some water in case you get thirsty."

Raven looked across the room at the two bowls but remained stubbornly in his place.

"Come now, Mr. Willis, it's not so bad. Now the truck will be here soon to pick you up and take you to your new quarters. So eat up. You're just going to love it out there in the country. Nice and quiet. Just you and the other animals. And the caretakers, of course. You see how you're contributing to society? Helping to create jobs?"

Raven Willis observed the orderly with a quizzical look on his face. Here was someone who perhaps understood him, who, at least, seemed forgiving of his trespasses against society.

"Come, now."

Raven stood slowly up on all fours, waddled across the room, sniffed curiously at the two bowls, then grunted several times and set to chomping at his oats.

A MAN AND A FISH

When Joseph Small awoke one curious morning, to the heavy sound of emptiness that swaddled the room like a thick blanket, he sat down alone at his breakfast table, in his customary way, having gone through his usual morning rituals, and knew it was not going to be an ordinary day.

It had nothing to do with the fact that, instead of the usual eggs and potatoes that appeared each day on his kitchen table, there turned up, instead, a whole, uncooked fish, sitting on his plate, partially wrapped up in parchment paper as if it had just arrived from the fishmonger, though its head remained uncovered and its tail lay flat and flaccid, and its dull, lifeless eyes stared at him menacingly as if it were his fault that the poor creature's life had suddenly come to an end. Nor did it have anything to do with the slow, steady ticking of the grandfather clock which stood commandingly in the next room—a hand-crafted heirloom brought over from the old world that had been passed down for several generations and had ended up in his possession as the sole surviving member of his family—whose uninterrupted rhythm suddenly, and for no particular reason, reminded him of his own heartbeat which, he feared, did not seem to be beating at all.

No, it had to do with a certain something he was now feeling—a distinct sense of loss which manifested itself deep inside, a black hole that had been with him all his life and had been slowly growing, bigger and bigger, and seemed at once ready to swallow him up whole like a snake about to devour its prey.

"Anna!" he called out to the housemaid, though, as he thought about it, he had not seen her since the day before and was not quite sure what he wanted to ask in the first place. But there was no answer and, after two more attempts, he simply gave up.

Joseph Small stared at the mysterious fish with his dull, brown eyes and sighed. He waited, though for what, he could not say. He slowly tapped his finger against the hard surface of the table and, with each dull response, contemplated his inconsequential life. He lifted his fork, then placed it carefully back on the table—how, after all, was he to eat this preposterous fish? He heaved a breath—a breath that did not seem all that substantial as he did so—and released it as he contemplated the meaning of the deceased creature's inexplicable appearance.

Joseph Alexander Small—son of Alexander William Small, whose father, Viljem Bartolomej Smolinski, had immigrated from Europe and whose name had been transformed by the officious folks at Ellis Island in a half-hearted effort to assist with the assimilation process and who had settled in what was then just a burgeoning metropolis—Joseph Small, having recently turned an age that made him think about the finite nature of life, having no known existing relatives, who had never married, nor had had any desire to, whose life revolved around waking up, having breakfast, going to work, and then returning to the same house he had lived in all his life—Joseph Small stared into the eyes of the angry dead fish as if he were staring into his own lifeless soul.

Not that he didn't have his own sense of anger. Growing up, he had been scolded and scorned—beaten and berated by the nuns at the Catholic school he had attended as a child and made to feel insignificant and useless by his mother who, though born in America, still had shades of the old ways and believed that, to better serve her son, it was best to instill a sense of guilt and dread into his otherwise capricious head.

"The fear of God," she would warn, staring sternly at him when he had done something mischievous or not to her liking, "is what will get you from this life to the next."

"And," she would add emphatically, just when he thought she had completed her merciless lesson, a severe smile vaguely appearing on her colorless, thin lips, "the fear of happiness will ensure your success."

Joseph would go to his room, when she had completely finished—go to the room he shared with no one (for there had never been anyone to share it with)—would go and sulk and cry and wish, wish that he were dead, as dead as the door he had just closed to shut himself off from God's inevitable retribution. Success, it appeared, as he tried to console himself under the comforting covers, was very much in his future because happiness was something that managed to avoid him on a daily basis.

So Joseph grew up with few friends, belittled by those he came in contact with, ridiculed and badgered and made to feel as small and inconsequential as the name he bore. Even when he reached that age when childhood innocence begins to slip away and interest and appetite start to take hold, the girls he knew began to express their disdain for him. Disdain or ridicule, for Joseph could never tell what their intentions were or what it was they really felt for him.

Like Lucy O'Reilly with whom he would laugh and joke each day, before school and after, even risking the ire of the nuns during class. Lucy, with her pretty brown curls and plain cotton dress, who, after he had mustered up the strength to politely request an after-school get-together at the neighborhood ice cream parlor, decided, quite immediately and without any explanation, to never speak with him again. Or like those neighborhood girls he would try to avoid, who strutted down the street with their impudent smiles and mocking voices, pushing their curious baby carriage around as if it were a toy—why, he wondered, feeling always intimidated, feeling always as if he were being belittled, were they always wheeling it about and whose baby was it anyway?—who laughed at him as he passed and made him feel as if his lot in life was to simply be taunted and teased—"Hey Rocky," they would shout, with just a touch of derision in their voices, "Rocky baby"—so much so that he wished there were some other way he could take to get to where he was going.

Or at least that's what it seemed—life was filled with cruel people who somehow seemed to set their sights on him, and girls, it appeared, were the worst of all, so that what had been his last hope at forming relationships vanished like a wisp of vapor on the distant horizon.

Joseph remembered. He closed his eyes and watched his life go by, like a faded film, like a long, drawn-out melodrama whose end never seemed to come. Then, he looked straight at the lifeless fish and said:

"Well, my friend. It seems our destinies have crossed. What lessons do you have for me? And what words of condolence can I possibly conjure for you?"

And with that, Joseph Small smiled. And the dead fish smiled back, or so it seemed, to a man who had never really known a smile, had never really understood what it was like to stare into the depths of another's soul and come back fully content, like someone dipping a bucket into a deep well and retrieving it as it overflowed with clear, pure water.

And then something extraordinary happened. Something even more astonishing than the sudden appearance of a freshly dead fish on his kitchen table, for the creature he had just spoken to and who, it seemed, had responded back, suddenly moved, wiggled its tail and twisted its head in a spasm of life, jumped up and out of the parchment paper it was shrouded in, and floated gracefully into the air.

Joseph Small blinked his eyes. He leaned forward towards the empty plate that stared back blankly at him and then looked at the fish hovering over the table and asked himself if, perhaps, it was all just a dream. A figment of his imagination. A fantasy he had fabricated like he had done so many times throughout his lonely days as he tried to fill the void in his life with hope.

Joseph thought about this as he pondered the meaning of fish and life, of waking up each morning and going about one's business, of this peculiar thing known as existence which, for so many years, he had experienced as if he were nonexistent at all, like a flimsy mesh or like a translucent film whose ghostly images came and went haphazardly. For there had been nothing meaningful in his life, nothing special in going to work each day, spending eight hours with his fellow workers—people he passed most of his time with but with whom he would never otherwise have a relationship—punching in cryptic commands on his keyboard and examining data that meant nothing, at least to him—nothing charming like he imagined his life might have been had he never been born in this particular time and place, had his ancestors decided to stay where they were, in a part of the world he had never been to but which seemed to him mysterious and magical, filled with legend and lore, unlike the mundane, monotonous metropolis he had somehow found himself in.

And then, just as suddenly, the fish looked briefly at him and said out loud in a voice that sounded all too familiar: "Hey Rocky." And having uttered those words, it swiftly swam away.

Joseph jumped up from his chair. He rushed into the next room where he found the fish floating silently in still air, light and graceful, coyly observing him as if inviting him to follow, suspended gently beside the ancient grandfather clock whose ponderous ticking syncopated the all too familiar silence. And then, just as quickly, it turned its head and sped off, passed magically through the splintered walls, out, out to a place where Joseph imagined it might find a place to thrive—a lush lake, perhaps, or an ocean filled with other fishes.

Joseph grabbed his jacket and followed, instinctively adjusting his clothes to make sure they were just right ("appearance is everything," his mother would say, "appearance makes a man or destroys him, if it is not just right") and ran after the elusive fish, passing just as mysteriously through the walls and entering a maelstrom of muted light and muffled sound, coming at last to a dark, quiet place where nothing seemed to exist at all—not even the fish he had been pursuing.

Joseph looked around and asked himself: if life had been dull and meaningless where he had just come from, what could he possibly find different here in this void which seemed as colorless and drab?

Then, he tried to move, and each movement, it seemed, had a consequence that appeared to be beyond his control: when he wiggled his fingers, light pulsed in the void where he stood, and when he shifted his feet, the loud echoing of his footsteps permeated the quiet like thunderbolts from the sky.

This, he thought, must be what it means to impact the world. This, he concluded, must be the secret that had been missing all along, the magic answer to the question he had been asking all these years—what more could there possibly be to life? To his life? If the nuns from his childhood had insisted there was nothing beyond what was already there ("everything in God's world," they would say, "has already been determined, there is nothing new that man can possibly do or create"), he now saw that there were things that went beyond one's cognition.

And so Joseph stood there in the dark, wiggling his fingers and stretching his toes, moving in all sorts of contortions to see what effect he could have on this new world he had just entered, never once asking himself where he was or how he had gotten there or even where the angry dead fish had gone to now that it had led him to this incomprehensible place.

Sometime later—and there was no telling how long, for time seemed to stand still in this strange, indeterminable world, revealed itself merely in the thoughts that toggled tentatively in his head and emerged gradually into the air, echoing like distant bells in an ancient bell tower, like little ducks quacking in the midst of the night, whose every iteration interrupted the steep silence like the grandfather clock he had left behind—later, after he had wiggled and jumped, sat and sprang, bent and twirled, Joseph decided it was time to explore, to seek out the dead fish which had been responsible for his coming here and which had spoken to him in words he had not heard since the odd days of his late childhood.

"Hello?" he called out, tentatively, with just enough force to light up the darkness. "Hello? Are you there?"

Silence ensued, but then he heard it, soft yet distinct—the words he had heard just prior to his departure—"Rocky, Rocky baby"—tender and inviting, not at all derisive like what he recalled from his early youth—and the blackness lit up briefly and a gleaming tunnel of light emerged and, through it, he could see the fish with its bright flashy tail and its shimmering gills, hovering in nothingness and looking at him coyly as the words it spoke repeated themselves incessantly and fell all around him like gentle raindrops in a lush English garden.

Joseph began to tremble. He wanted to run, to hide, to escape back to the comfort of his familiar house. His heart started to pound and his being seemed to collapse upon itself but he did not know the way back and, even if he could find it, was not quite sure how he would pass from this realm back to the one he had emerged from. So instead, he stood and waited—waited for what, he could not say, only that something significant surely would happen, just as his coming here had suddenly happened and eventually, when it did, he was certain he would be able to proceed.

And then it did. The darkness suddenly filled with a soft glow, with just enough radiance for him to see ahead, and he slowly moved forward, inched his way toward the fish which was no longer in sight and arrived at last at the banks of a secret lake.

Joseph looked around, noticed an odd stillness in the air, a calm that resounded with tranquility such as he had never before heard: the trees swayed silently above him, and the lake water lapped noiselessly against the shallow shore. Birds flew quietly up in the sky. Not a sound did they make, not a twit nor a tweet emerged from their sullen mouths nor even a soft fluttering from the flapping of their beating wings. Then, looking down, he saw his reflection shimmering in the water, a likeness which did not seem to be all that substantial and which gleamed elusively on the surface of the rippling lake.

"Hello?" he cried out once again, as he stared at himself, but the only answer was the deep, still quiet and the stark, lonely image of his likeness floating on the water like a flimsy veil.

Joseph Small waited, at the edge of the lake, waited silently as he stared at his reflection wavering in the water, for waiting had been the only thing he had ever known, waiting had been the constant companion to his long, negligible life. He waited for a sign. He waited for an indication of what he should do. He waited for the strange, little fish, which had, after all, been responsible for his being here, waited for it to reappear, to come back and reveal itself, tell him what he was supposed to do, tell him where he was and what the meaning of all this could be. Yet for all his waiting, he was left merely with his fragile reflection which stared back at him reproachfully from the deep, black water ("never depend on others," his mother would say, "you have nothing but you and yourself to depend on in this world or you will only be disappointed"), accusing him, it seemed, of indifference and indecision, forcing him to confront a reality he had not wished to deal with since the day his mother had suddenly died.

Soon, he felt his heart sink. Soon, he felt his being shrink and curl, and he reached out angrily at his lifeless reflection, floating evasively on the water's rim, sank to his knees and tried desperately to gather it up, gather it into something he could touch and feel—a ball of anger, or any emotion he could muster that would make him sense, for once, that he was truly alive. But the reflection eluded him, stubbornly remained floating on the face of the water, furrowed and vague and utterly insensitive to his intangible feelings.

This must be what it's like to be dead to the world, he thought. This must be what it's like to wake up and find that you have never been awake at all.

Joseph stood up, calmly, slowly dried his hands against the nap of his pants, observed himself rippling in the cool, clear water, staring back still and emotionless as if he were the reflection and it the reality looking up and beyond towards the vast, vast universe.

Eventfully, the sun rose. Eventually, it climbed up from the depths of the glassy lake, scaled the wispy strands of clouds like the rungs of a rickety ladder, up up into the clear, azure realm of nothingness, searching for a place to rest, revealing itself in all its golden splendor, stopping merely to warm the world, to assure that its clarity had reached every nook and cranny of this dark, quiet place.

Joseph watched silently, stood and waited for the dead fish to return, wondered at the meaning of it all, at the purity of the lake water from which his reflection had suddenly vanished, at the distant occlusion of the elusive horizon, at the sound of the birds whose noisy chattering filled the air with silence, at the whereabouts of the little dead fish which had disappeared, at the meaning of trees which imbued the landscape with their hushed existence.

And Joseph wondered. He sat on a large rock at the side of the lake and pondered these things, until his mind was filled with peace, until his fingers and limbs relaxed, until the essence of his being became at last silent and still.

Then, in the far distance, on the vast, blue lake, appeared a speck, a tiny dot which gradually grew, bigger and bigger, approaching, at last, silent and slow. Joseph watched as the silent boat approached, gliding gently on the surface of the lake, and stopped quietly before him.

And Joseph knew instinctively what to do. Joseph Small, who had doubted everything throughout his meager life, who had always been guided by his well-intentioned mother, who had been told by the stringent nuns of his childhood exactly what to do in such circumstances, whose very existence had been defined by those around him—Joseph Small knew for once what was required at this very juncture of time and space, knew that the difference between being told and merely understanding was like that slender sliver of sunlight which determines the difference between night and day.

Joseph stepped onto the boat and sailed away. He watched the shore diminish in the distance, felt himself surrounded by nothingness, embraced its cool touch as it lightly caressed his skin and, looking down into the clear, still water, caught a brief glimpse of the fish which swam happily away.

"Rocky," it called out. "Goodbye Rocky."

And the trees became trees, and the birds flew like birds and filled the air with their birdlike song, and the lake remained still and calm and blue as lapis.

Joseph Small stood at the bow of the boat and waited and waited to awake.

A SORT OF SANTA CLAUS

Alexander Pipple was a toymaker. In his workshop, which was separated from his toy store by a glass wall, he used his saw and lathe to shape raw, lifeless wood into playthings that brought joy to all. He made dolls and boats and trains. He fashioned animals of all shapes and sizes. And he built circus wagons and racing cars and futuristic spaceships. Whatever Alexander could imagine, he made, and he did it with such precision and devotion that everyone who patronized his shop admired his skill and talent.

Alexander loved his work, and he loved the children who flocked to his store with smiles on their faces and joy in their hearts. Every day, they would come and eagerly gaze as Alexander proudly worked his craft. They would watch him carefully sand a soldier's leg or put the final touches of color on the shutters of a miniature dollhouse, and though he never said a word to them, they felt as though he had told them a long, wondrous tale by the time he had finished and it was time for them to leave.

And every day, he would let one lucky child choose a special toy to take home just for being there. It might be because she had glanced at him in a certain way or because she had a sad countenance that penetrated through the dreamy smile that graced her face when she was in his toy shop. Or it might be that he noticed, among the crowd of children, a young boy whose tattered clothes and soup-bowl haircut indicated that he was from that part of town where parents struggled just to keep food on the table. The children he chose might be from poor families or they might be orphans, and Alexander, who had no children of his own and whose heart was as big as the world he lived in, would take pity on them and offer them the finest of his toys.

Now Alexander's wife, Greta, was a stingy fishwife who had no patience for her husband's naïve behavior. She would constantly scold him for wasting his time and giving away his work and, when he refused to see the error of his ways, would come down to his shop, which was just below their humble apartment, and chase the children away with her high-pitched voice and her long, wooden broom.

"Alexander," she would yell, all flustered, laying her broom down in the corner and fixing her hard stare on him. "How many times do I have to tell you not to give in to that vermin?"

Most days, Alexander would ignore his wife and continue pouring his love into his toy making. Other times, he would put down his tools, look briefly at her as she ranted and raved, and simply smile. This was usually enough to quiet her down and, after one or more harsh sentences about how ignorant he was about the ways of the world, she would turn around and march angrily back up to their apartment where the sound of her stomping feet and the occasional riffs of fury that came drifting down the stairs and through the closed door seemed far less abrasive.

One day, however, Greta's manner seemed even meaner than usual as she chased away the children like someone shooing away mice, and her voice seemed even shriller as she chastised him with no concern for his feelings or the fact that there were still a few customers in the shop. That day, when Alexander could no longer disregard her sharp voice and her harsh comments, he put aside his work, wiped his dusty hands on his faded apron, looked firmly at her severe eyes and calmly said: "They are only children, dear. What harm can they do?"

"Harm? I'll tell you what harm. They come here every day and distract you. They charm you with their little smiles. And then, when it's time to close down, you give away your work. We can't go on paying the bills if this keeps up. We're losing money and all because you're a weakling who falls for the shenanigans of children. You've got to stop giving away your toys and start selling them instead. Otherwise, you'll just have to close up shop and find yourself a real job."

And with that, Greta opened the door that led to their apartment and stormed up the stairs, huffing and puffing invectives against her poor husband.

Alexander Pipple sighed. His wife had never threatened him like this before. He could not imagine doing anything else and still remaining happy. And he could not envision life without seeing the joy on a child's face when presented with one of his wonderful creations. And while he realized he was giving away some of his work, he was still selling enough to enable them to lead an acceptable life.

Alexander looked sadly at his watch. It was almost time to close for the day and, now that the children were gone, there was no reason to remain open. He closed all the shutters and locked the front door. Returning to his workshop, he looked at the wooden figure that he was just about finished with, a figure of a young boy with a serious expression on his rosy face and a sparkle of joy in his clear, blue eyes.

Alexander took his paint brush and lovingly touched up a spot on the boy's eyebrow, fixed his eyes so that they shone brilliantly, and added a few freckles to his handsome face. He reached for his sander and polished a rough spot on the boy's left arm and another on one of his legs. Then, he inspected the figure from top to bottom and, happy at last with his creation, he dressed him in a warm shirt and a pair of woolen pants and placed a little cap on his head. Satisfied, he looked tenderly at him and said:

"I wish I had a son like you. Then, I would be truly happy and all my troubles would go away."

A tear fell from Alexander's eye and landed gently on the boy's forehead. He carefully rubbed it off with a soft cloth, placed the figure on a shelf with a "for sale" sign in front, turned off the lights and headed up the stairs to his apartment with slow, heavy steps.

The next morning, Alexander sat at the breakfast table and silently ate the eggs his wife had prepared and the bread she had baked. He took a sip of the strong, dark coffee, placed his cup down on the worn, wooden table, wiped his hands on the frayed napkin and, with a sigh, said, "Well, my dear. I'd best get to work now."

Greta fixed her mean eyes on him and, in a stern voice, said,

"Now you remember what I told you, Alexander Pipple. I don't want to see any children down there today. Is that clear? No children. And don't give away any toys!"

Alexander closed the door behind him without answering and lumbered down to his shop. He opened the shutters, unlocked the front door, and then made his way to his workshop, stooping to pick up a "for sale" sign that had fallen to the floor. Turning toward the shelves to replace it, he suddenly noticed that the figure he had finished the night before was missing. He looked around, scratched his head, then tried to recall if his wife had noticed him working on it for, if she had, she would surely think he had given it away.

"Ah, well," he sighed, with a sad look in his eyes. "He was such a beautiful one. I don't think I could make another like him."

Alexander stepped into his workshop, picked up a piece of raw wood, and stared blankly at the flat yellowish material, seeking inspiration. This was the way he always started new projects, but today, no matter how he tried, he could not come up with any ideas, and his mind kept wandering back to the wooden figure which had gone missing.

Just then, he heard the door to his shop open and the little bell his wife had placed above the aperture jingle. Alexander glanced through the glass as a young, handsome boy strode nervously into the shop.

Heeding his wife's words, Alexander put down his tools and stepped into the store as the boy walked up to the counter and looked straight up at him.

"Good day, sir."

"Good day, young man."

He was about eight years old with a rosy complexion that seemed flawless except for a small faded blemish on his forehead. He had a serious demeanor, with just a touch of humor shining through his bright, blue eyes, and he was dressed in clothes that appeared to be hand-me-downs, for they seemed much too small for him. Alexander guessed he was an orphan, or a child whose parents abandoned him by day so they could earn enough to feed him at night.

Holding his hat in his hand and smiling as he mustered enough courage to spit out the sentence he had apparently memorized, the boy said:

"I'd like a job, sir."

"A job?" Alexander replied with a kind smile on his face.

"Yes, sir. A job. In your toy shop."

"I see," Alexander replied. "And what kind of job did you have in mind?"

The boy thought for a minute, as if trying to remember the answer he had previously prepared, then said:

"I could sweep the floors, sir. I could arrange all the toys. I could dust the shelves and keep everything tidy. I could even keep the children away while you work so your wife doesn't get angry."

Alexander looked curiously at the boy and tried to remember if he had ever seen him before. This was no ordinary child, he thought. It was apparent from the way he talked. He seemed to know what went on in the shop and even, perhaps, what went on between him and his wife. He wondered how the boy knew what he knew and if this was one of those tricks his wife insisted the children would play on him.

"And how much would you get paid for your work?" Alexander asked.

The boy thought a minute before answering.

"Nothing much, sir. Just something to eat," he said, and he bowed his head sadly.

Alexander was moved by the young boy and his courage in coming into his shop as he had.

"What's your name?" he asked.

The boy hesitated. Then, looking down at his feet to hide his embarrassment, he said in a barely audible voice:

"Boy."

"Boy?" Alexander repeated in surprise.

"Yes, sir. That's what everyone calls me."

"And your parents?"

Again, the boy bowed his head sadly, and Alexander understood what he had suspected upon first seeing him. His heart suddenly felt heavy and his eyes welled up with love and sympathy. Just then he heard his wife's steps storming down the stairs and the back door open, and he looked in panic toward the boy who was suddenly no longer there.

"Alexander," she bellowed, "I heard the door. Somebody here?"

"No, dear," he answered, scratching his head curiously. "It was just the wind."

"Very well," she responded with a look of disbelief on her small face. "Then get to work. And mind those kids."

With that, Greta stormed up the stairs, slamming the door to their apartment with the force of a thunderbolt.

"You mustn't let her treat you like that."

Alexander turned around and saw the boy standing where he had been just before his wife came down.

"If I had someone who cared for me, I wouldn't behave like she does."

Alexander stared at the boy in wonder, his eyes flat on the blemish on the boy's forehead.

"I mean," the boy continued, "I'd at least show respect."

The boy bowed his head again and looked down at the floor, lifting his right foot up on its toes and twisting it back and forth.

"You seem quite bright," Alexander said. "You'd make a fine shop boy. But I don't know if I could afford you."

"I don't eat much, sir. And I'd be quiet as a mouse. Even your wife might get to like me after a while."

Alexander scratched his head, intrigued by the boy and his request.

"You seem familiar," he said. "As if I've seen you somewhere. As if you know me."

"Sir?"

The boy eyed Alexander coyly, twisting his foot back and forth on the floor and glancing up at him from beneath his bowed head.

"Very well," Alexander said, at last. "You're hired. For room and board. But you must sleep down here in the shop. And, at least for the time being, we must keep this a secret between you and me."

The boy's eyes opened widely at Alexander's words and a big smile spread across his face.

"Thank you, sir," he said. "You won't regret it. I promise you."

So the young orphan started working in Alexander's toy shop. He swept the floors and dusted the shelves and made sure everything was arranged neatly. And when the children gathered in the shop to watch Alexander at his work, he allowed them to stay, but just for a short time, after which he politely asked them to leave, promising they could return the next day as long as they remained quiet. And when nighttime came, he locked and shuttered the front door, turned out the lights, and then went to sleep in a little niche Alexander had made for him in the back room where he stored his supplies.

Alexander continued his work, feeling more inspired than ever, creating even more wondrous toys just in time for the Christmas holidays. He watched the boy proudly through the glass wall of his workshop and felt joyful that he had taken him under his wing. Business started to pick up and Greta, who became quite pleased with what she saw were the results of the stern talk she had had with her husband, stopped coming down to the shop as frequently as she had.

Alexander would sneak meals down to the boy, whom he had started calling Son and, when his wife went on her weekly shopping trips, he would take him upstairs so he could bathe and wash his clothes.

Then, one day, when the shop was filled with children, quietly watching Alexander fashioning a Santa Claus and fixing the wooden reindeer onto a red sleigh, and the young boy was busy helping customers choose their purchases, Greta unexpectedly walked in through the front door. With a look of exasperation that made her chubby red face seem like it would explode, she gazed all around and shouted in a shrill voice: "Alexander! What's going on here?"

Unsure of what to say in front of all the customers, Alexander put down his work and stepped into the shop. Everyone went silent and watched in anticipation as Alexander approached his wife.

"What is this, Alexander Pipple?" Greta shouted. "Didn't we have an agreement? What are all these street urchins doing here?"

Alexander was about to answer when the young boy stepped in front of him and said: "Mrs. Pipple. I was just about to ask the children to leave."

"And who are you?" Greta roared.

"Greta, dear," Alexander said. "He's just a boy who's been helping me out. Can't you see how busy we are?" And Alexander indicated with his head the line of customers waiting to pay for their toys.

"A boy? Helping you out? What does he know about business? I won't have it, Alexander. I simply won't have it."

"He's been doing a very good job," a woman standing in line said.

"Yes," agreed another.

"A good job at swindling my husband, no doubt. No, Alexander," Greta continued, turning back to her husband, "I want him out along with all the others. Right now!"

"But Greta—" Alexander began.

"Right now!"

And Greta crossed her arms and began tapping her foot impatiently.

"Mr. Pipple," the boy said. "I will leave now. And I will take all the children with me."

Alexander looked sadly as the young boy gathered the children.

"Mrs. Pipple," the boy said, as he approached the shop entrance. "I apologize for any inconvenience I may have caused you."

And with that, he left, and the other children followed sullenly behind.

The store remained quiet for a few seconds, all eyes on the door that had just quietly shut. Then, one of the customers looked Greta squarely in the eye and said:

"I have never seen anything so disgusting in all my life. If that's the way you treat children, then you can keep your toys."

And the woman took the merchandise she had planned to purchase, slammed it down on the front counter, and stomped angrily out of the toy shop. Then, a man standing at the back of the line walked up to the counter, placed his selections there, and left. And soon everyone in the line had done the same and the shop became empty except for Alexander and Greta.

Alexander looked at his wife as calmly as he could and said:

"I think it's time to close up for the day."

Alexander and his wife did not speak to each other for several days. Alexander would get up earlier than usual, fix his own breakfast and then slip silently downstairs to his workshop where he would spend the day, quietly making toys and anxiously waiting for his little helper to return. Greta, meanwhile, made it a point not to disturb her husband, though she would sneak softly down to the shop several times a day to make sure he was still working and to see if there were any children loitering around.

Meanwhile, business had come to a standstill. Since the day Greta had scolded her husband in front of all the customers, not one toy had been sold. Word of Greta's attitude towards children had quickly gotten around town, and no one would shop at Alexander's toy store. Even the local newspaper had gotten wind of what had happened and ran a story on "Mrs. Scrooge, The Woman Who Chased Away the Joy of Christmas." Greta took one look at the story, felt a slight pang run through her heart, then tossed the paper aside with a humph.

Then, several days later, with the wind blowing hard and the snow coming down heavy, Greta ran down to the toy shop as quickly as her stubby feet would allow, holding a letter in her hand and calling out her husband's name in panic.

"Alexander," she hollered, opening the door at the foot of the stairs, and holding her hand to her chest as she huffed and puffed from exertion.

"What is it my dear," Alexander answered, quickly putting down his work and rushing out of his workshop.

"Alexander," she said, trembling all over and holding out a letter to him. "What are we going to do?"

Alexander had never seen his wife in such a state and immediately escorted her over to a chair and helped her sit down. Then he took the letter from her and read:

Dear Mr. and Mrs. Pipple,

It has come to our attention that your rent for the last two months has not yet been paid. We are hereby serving notice that payment must be received by the end of next week or you will be promptly evicted from the premises.

With our sincerest regrets,
The Management

Alexander quietly folded the letter and placed it back in the envelope in which it had arrived.

"Alexander," Greta cried, wailing and beating her hands against her breast. "Where will we go? This is our home. They can't just take it away from us like that, can they?"

Though the answer was obvious, Alexander Pipple did not respond, and for the first time in his life, he felt totally helpless. Throughout his years, he had encountered many obstacles, but he had always managed to overcome them. Once, when he was in elementary school, he had been told by one of his teachers that he would never make it past eighth grade. Determined to prove her wrong, he studied day and night, in between the odd jobs he kept in order to help his large family make ends meet, and finished the year with the highest grades in his class. Later, after he had married Greta and they discovered that they could not have children, he overcame his deep despair by pouring his emotions into his work. There were times they could not afford meat, but they survived on bread and eggs. And one year, when the bitter winter came and they could not find money to put coal in the stove, Alexander took the scraps of wood that he always saved and used them to heat the house. But now, when they could no longer afford the rent and they were being told to pay or get out, he could see no practical solution in front of him. They had nowhere to go and very little money saved in the bank. All they had were the clothes on their backs, the furniture in their home, and the toys in his toy shop which were now worthlessly piling up.

Alexander looked angrily at his wife. He wanted to scold her. He wanted to tell her that this was all the result of her mistrust and intransigence towards children, he wanted to raise his voice for once and take command, but the sad look on her face as her tears fell to the ground softened his heart and he said not a word, just took her hand in his and patted it comfortingly.

"Everything will be ok," he said, though even he did not believe it. "Everything will be ok."

And Alexander Pipple walked slowly back to his workshop. He picked up his tools and continued work on the circus wagon he was building. Greta followed him, stopping at the doorway to watch her husband's deft hands shape the firm wood. He had always been good to her and now, as she saw him bury his sadness in his toy making, she began to realize just how talented he was. She looked on silently as he hewed the wood and marveled at the way his hands seemed to dance as the raw material slowly took shape.

Alexander stopped his work suddenly and looked up at his wife.

"Don't disturb me," he said in a firm, loud voice. "Don't disturb me."

Greta was stunned by her husband's tone. She turned her miserable face and opened the door to go up to their apartment. Then she heard the little bell above the front door jingle, and she turned to see a strange looking man enter the shop. He was dressed rather shoddily, in a coat so old and tattered she wondered how it kept him warm. In one hand, he held an old plastic bag which seemed to hold everything he owned and, in the other, a worn wooden cane he used for walking and which he now leaned on as he looked around the shop.

"Good day," the man called out.

Greta closed the door behind her and returned to the shop.

"Good day," the man repeated as she approached him without answering. "I'm looking for a toy."

Greta eyed him with a look of disgust. His hair was grimy and matted, his shoes were worn and mismatched, and his pants were so filthy she wondered how he could possibly wear them. Were she not worried about provoking him, she would have immediately asked him to leave.

"We have lots of toys," she said curtly.

"I need something special," the man continued, moving slowly around the shop with the aid of his cane. "For someone very special to me."

Greta followed him closely and watched him like a hawk so she could catch him just in case he tried filching any toys and slipping them into his plastic bag.

"This is quite nice," he said, stopping beside a wooden train set whose tracks meandered through an old-fashioned village.

"And what makes you think you can afford that?" Greta asked, unable to hold her tongue. "From the looks of you, I wonder if you can afford anything at all."

The man stopped and turned his dull eyes towards hers. His face was haggard and unshaven and the stony look he answered her with indicated that he was used to people taunting him.

"Madam," he said. "I will pay the price. I always pay the price."
The man paused and swallowed hard.

"I'm looking for something for my son," he continued. "Yes, even someone as wretched looking as me can have a child. I haven't seen him since he was born. But every year, I buy him something special and leave it in front of the door where he lives. I'm a sort of Santa Claus, you see. A secret Santa Claus."

He stopped and smiled, leaning heavily on his cane, his eyes resting firmly on Greta's as if to say that she would have to deal with him whether she liked it or not.

"I see," Greta said, nervously turning her glance and wishing that he would just go away.

"Ah," the strange man said, hobbling with his cane to the opposite end of the store. "This is it." And he picked up the wooden figure with the blemish on its brow, the one that Alexander thought had been lost for good. "Yes, this is the perfect toy," the man continued, closely examining the figure. "The perfect toy for my son."

"Yes. That is the perfect toy."

Greta and the strange man turned at the sound of Alexander's voice.

"But I'm afraid it's not for sale."

Alexander gently took the wooden figure from the man and looked at it as if he had just found a lost child.

"And why not," said the old man, "when it's here on display like all the other toys?"

"Because," Alexander answered quietly. "Just because."

The man scrutinized the old toy maker. Then, lifting his cane into the air and pointing it at him, he said:

"I can see you're a man who drives a hard bargain. I'm prepared to give you everything I own," he said, indicating the old plastic bag with his cane.

"Ha," Greta said with a look of derision on her face. "God knows what kind of junk you've got in there? You think you can fool us like that? We don't need your rags, mister."

"Looks can be deceiving," the old man replied. "What I have here may seem worthless from the outside. But from the inside, it might be worth more than you can imagine."

And the old man grinned cunningly, revealing half a mouth of uneven teeth and a gold crown that sat prominently in the front and seemed to glimmer right into Greta's eyes.

"It's not for sale," Alexander said. "You can have anything else in the shop. For free. Anything except—"

"Alexander!" Greta shouted.

"It's that or nothing," the man said. "I don't want any hand-outs. I offer what I have and want nothing except that figure."

"I'm sorry. It's not for sale," Alexander repeated.

The strange man looked from Alexander to Greta and back to Alexander. His face softened revealing a layer of sadness and disappointment.

"Very well," he said. "Then I will take my business elsewhere."

The old man picked up his bag and turned to leave when Greta suddenly said, "Alexander. Let the man have what he wants."

"No, Greta," Alexander answered.

"And why not? You always give your toys away. At least he's willing to pay."

Alexander looked tenderly at the wooden figure in his hands

and remembered the boy who had been his helper. For a few short weeks, his wish for a son had come true, and though he saw no connection between the figure and the boy, he felt as if they were somehow linked. He struggled to hold back his tears and wondered if the boy would ever return.

"No, Greta," he said to his wife. "Not this time."

"Alexander Pipple," Greta said, in that voice that made her husband know she meant business. "Give the man what he wants."

Alexander held the figure closely to his face. He nervously straightened the little cap on the doll's head, like a father seeking to delay his child from a long, unexpected trip, and fixed the shirt and pants so they were just so. Then, he handed the wooden figure to the man and said, "Ok. You can have him. But you must promise to take good care of him."

The man took the figure, placed it under his arm, and held out the old plastic bag. Greta reached out to grab it but Alexander pushed her hand away and said, "Keep what you have."

"Alexander!" Greta shouted.

"Greta," Alexander shouted back. "For once in your life, just be quiet." Then, turning back to the man, he said, "May your son one day know the man who loves him so much."

"Thank you," the man said Then, turning to leave, he said: "Thank you. And God bless you."

The little bell above the door jingled as the man left the warm shop and disappeared into the snow.

Greta and Alexander stood silently looking at each other in the empty shop; Alexander with a gentle smile on his face and Greta with a mixture of hurt and anger.

"It's time to close up," Alexander said. "And then, my dear, we must start packing our things."

Greta was about to let her husband have it but the reminder that they were about to be evicted suddenly struck her and she was unable to say anything.

Just then, the sun started to shine through the front window and the shop seemed to light up brightly. Greta turned her head and noticed that the snow had stopped falling and the weather had cleared up. The streets had become alive again and she could see people taking advantage of the break in the snow to finish their last-minute shopping. She looked around the shop, filled with toys in every nook and cranny, and she looked at the crowds of people trudging through the snow. Then, as if a bell had just gone off in her thick, little head, she turned to her husband and said, "No, Alexander. We're not going to close up shop. We're not going to give up. We're going to sell toys."

And with that, Greta rushed out into the cold and in a loud, sonorous voice announced: "Toys for sale. Hand-made, hand-painted toys. Get the best toys in town."

At first, the people stared at her as if she were crazy, standing outside with no coat to shield her from the cold, flapping her arms in the air like a giant bird and shouting like a madwoman. But soon, one passerby stopped to look in the window and Greta ushered him in, and then another, and before long people were flocking into the shop, and Alexander was rushing around trying to keep up with them.

And then Greta saw the street children, shivering in the snow with one eye on the warm toy store they had always come to in order to watch her husband. Perhaps it was the fact that, like them, she was beginning to tremble from the cold, or maybe it was the spirit of the moment that caught her off guard, but Greta's heart suddenly melted and she called out to them.

"Come on, children. Come on in and get warm. I'll make you all some hot chocolate."

The children looked at each other in astonishment. Then, one by one, they slowly approached her.

"Come on, now. Hurry up. You'll freeze to death out here."

So the children gathered inside the store which was soon filled to the brim, and Greta made hot chocolate for everyone, and the warmth of the soothing beverage, as she at last had a chance to drink, spread through Greta's body like a calming salve and she beamed with joy as she watched her husband's talent at last bear fruit.

And when it was time to close up, Greta looked at the children and said, "Now I want each of you to choose a special toy for Christmas. Any one you want. And remember to spread the word about your Uncle Alexander's toy shop."

So the children eagerly chose their toys and at last left the shop to go home, and Alexander and Greta, feeling exhausted and relieved, closed up shop and went up to their apartment to retire after a very long day.

"Now Alexander," Greta said, as they sat at the kitchen table, drinking another cup of hot chocolate before retiring for the evening. "About those children."

"Yes, dear," he answered, wearily. "I know."

"You don't know a thing, Alexander Pipple" she said. "Always letting people pull the wool over your eyes like the dreamy dolt that you are."

And she smiled at him in such a way that made him wonder whether or not she was serious this time. So Alexander Pipple let his wife continue her prattle into the middle of the night, giving her a "yes, dear" everyone once in a while just to let her know he was listening. And before he knew it, the sun was starting to rise on a brand new day and he gave his wife a long, warm look and said to her, "Good morning, Greta, my dear." And taking a deep breath, he gave her a kiss on the check and said, once again, "Good morning." And though he never came to know what had become of the young boy who had brought so much joy to him in such a short period of time, he knew deep inside as his wife responded in kind that life would never again be the same.

THE KEEPERS

They're up there. I hear them clamoring in panic. The rush of their footsteps resounds, as they scurry wildly through the garret, dash past ancient eaves, press against broken planks that ache from years of settling—that groan from the flames.

Searching for escape! As the fire leaps and rises! As their startled voices cry out!

For fifty years I have listened to them, when the full moon gapes through the clouds, when they lurk about in the middle of the night—speaking softly now, now quarreling, their unhallowed voices echoing through the house.

"No," howls one, "it's not so."

"Yes," the other shouts, making all who hear tremble as if the harsh wind of winter had just blustered through the house. "It 'tis," she says. "And you shall see. I will make you see. And every last living thing in this wretched house shall see. Even she."

"You will do no such thing. Not now. Not until the time is right."

Then the squabbling. The hissing. The unbearable yowling that would drive even the sturdiest insane. And the fearsome forays from the attic: silently, down the dark stairs, creaking with fear, through the hollow hallways, past the keep where they stop and listen, stop and breathe, stop and stare with eyes that flash in the darkness—eyes now glowing, now suddenly black not even the hungriest owl, perched patiently outside the shuttered window, could detect.

The breathing swells, possesses the house, ceases as the children, cowering in their beds, cringe under their covers or hide futilely in the darkest corner of their fear, the recent arrivals crying futilely out for help. Then the silence. Then the slow steps as the creatures lurk back up with the chosen child clutched between their claws.

Then, at last, the silent dawn. And I? I?

I have seen them as clearly as I hear them bellowing helplessly now. Have witnessed them, come face to face with them when they appear, mesmerize siren-like, as they stare, sneer, transform into black, slinky beasts, snarling, ready to pounce on the unsuspecting, on those who know no better than to look into their eyes and become possessed.

And then the screams. And then the sudden silence. And I?

But let me start from the beginning. The beginning of what has now become my inevitable end.

I came to this haunted house a young boy. An orphan. Abandoned by the death of my mother and father in the early years of their conjugal lives. Of my then innocent existence on this Earth. An accident in the countryside that spared my life, but claimed theirs, as God claims His due or as the devil hastens to claim what is not rightfully his.

I survived. A freak happenstance, I would later realize, that was to shape the rest of what would become my long, abject life—that would shape my very soul.

With no known relatives, I was left to wander, for the life of an orphan proceeds from one abandonment to another, leaving him to languish in the place that at last deigns to harbor him—in my case, a church orphanage tucked far off into the nethers of the countryside.

Until, one day, an old man and woman appeared, an odd looking pair dressed somberly, their faces lifeless and sallow, the woman covetously clasping papers in her black-gloved fist, the man standing limp and silent beside her like an ancient, gnarled tree, dressed in what was meant to be his Sunday best — a pair of worn, black trousers, not quite pressed, a faded jacket with long tattered tails and a ragged black cravat set precariously against a faintly yellowed shirt. Distant relations they claimed, in their strange, whispery voices, though none I had ever heard of. But the woman held out the crumpled papers she clutched onto as if they were her very life, thrust them into the head mistress's face—a stringent woman, a nun who had never been known to smile, though that morning I thought I detected a slight curl of what might have been nothing more than contempt.

But what did I know then? Of smiling or malice? Or greed or worse? Of what the world had in store for unwanted children like me? How was I to understand what the import of all this might be? I was a mere child, not yet aware of the ways of the world, knowing only that I wanted to escape that heartless orphanage at any cost.

So I pretended to know them. Addressed them as Auntie and Uncle, in my as yet childish ways, kissed the man's wizened hand, his long fingers, wan and thin, and held my gaze down, in fear, and feigned respect.

The nun set her hard, glassy eyes on me, in that small, dark room, glanced at the odd-looking couple then back at me cowered humbly before them, and, for just one insubstantial second, I detected a flicker of compassion on her long, stern face. Or was it perhaps concern? Either way, she knew that my destiny was in her hands, that whatever decision she made at that fateful moment would rest eternally on her soul till the end of time.

"Very well," she said at last, pushing the papers back across the table as if she were rejecting something unholy, clutching the crucifix that hung down her side as she rose from her chair. "You may take the boy."

And she turned and hastened from the room, the swishing of her black, serge habit like the hissing of a serpent as she rushed out the door.

All I remember, after that, was packing my clothes into a small, brown satchel, getting into a carriage—an old, dilapidated wagon with worn wooden wheels—and watching the black clouds in the sky gather as the clomping of the horses' hooves drowned out my past and thundered toward my uncertain future. And the driver, who I only remember as a mere shadow. And the odd look on the ashen faces of what would be my keepers as they eyed me every now and then, then stared emotionlessly out the rain-speckled window.

When we arrived at the manor house, in the early evening, after having ridden in utter silence, stopping only when necessary, resting briefly to eat a morsel of stale bread and a bit of dried-up cheese, or to drink a draught of water before resuming our hard, uncertain journey, we were greeted at the door by Mattie, a short, stout woman with thin, pale lips and the look of one whose soul has confronted the very vales of hell. As I soon came to find, she ran the household, looked after the children as best she could and, as I later learned, prayed and cried and trembled in the privacy of her quarters.

Mattie took one long, sullen look at me, dropped her eyes to the ground and said, in a low, stern voice, "You will follow me. And you will do exactly as I say."

Then she turned and proceeded through a long, dark hallway, up a spiral of stairs that groaned with age and wound their way up to the next floor, down a cold, drafty passageway and stopped before a room where the slightest ray of the setting sun was just able to escape through the crevice at the foot of the door.

"You will stay here," she said, turning for a moment with a look of pity that made my blood chill. "With the rest."

As she unlocked the door with the large skeleton key she pulled from her pocket and swung it open, I could see, through the dusky light, a room full of children, tucked fearfully into their beds, their frightened eyes wide open, staring silently up at the ceiling, and not one of them turned to greet me or even recognize my presence. Mattie stopped beside an empty cot, the covers ruffled as if someone had recently slept there, and looked down at me to indicate it would be mine. Then she turned and, without a word, left, closing the door with a sharp echo and a loud clanking of the key as she locked it.

That night, I lay apprehensive in my new quarters, wondering whether my rush for freedom had led me to even worse circumstances, and listened as the other children quietly whimpered in their anxious sleep and as strange elusive echoes emanated from the walls, sounds I would later come to dread.

The morning arrived at last, cold and bleak, though, as I write this, it comes to me that every day was such: rain or shine, spring or winter, each dawn brought with it a distinct chill that left you wondering how anything could possibly survive here.

One by one, the other children arose, murmured what sounded to me like a semi-silent sigh, then looked fitfully around as if searching for something they had somehow lost during their sleep. Then the sound of the key in the lock—a sound I soon came to both fear and welcome—and Mattie appeared with a worn look on her face, as if she hadn't slept the entire night. Carefully surveying the room, she counted each one of us, then led us down the dim hallway to a room where we washed and dressed and prepared for our day.

Breakfast was a bowl of raw milk and a sliver of cold bread, sometimes accompanied by a wedge of hardened cheese, and was always preceded by a reading from the Bible by the old man, a Mister Aloysius Blackstone, as I came to find out, while his wife Lucinda looked on with her long, drawn face, her lips quivering as her eyes swept the room and fell momentarily on each one of us, as if noting who was there and who wasn't.

"God is your savior," she would utter at the end of the recitation, in her hard, hoarse voice. "You may trust no one but Him."

Then silence as her eyes hovered over us, before uttering, at last, "Amen."

Then, with a dull clap of the Bible, as Blackstone snapped it closed, we ate in stark silence, each of us careful not to lift our eyes for fear they would be met by Lucinda's cold stare or that of her husband whose palsied hands would tremble as he lifted the stale bread to his mouth.

Our days were just as joyless. Staring out the windows, unshuttered as soon as the sun rose, tightly boarded up at the very moment darkness set. Idling silently, each to ourselves, for we were not allowed to speak or smile or laugh. Wondering who would be next and what price we would pay to maintain our tenuous existence.

Except for Sundays when, following services in a small, unadorned chapel where we would kneel on the jagged stone floor and pray until our knees ached and we were allowed to leave. With fear in our hearts, we would be led silently from the chapel door down the unpaved path to the tombs where we would trim the wild brush that fronted the mausoleum, guarded by ancient gargoyles whose hollow eyes followed you whichever way you went, or sweep the cold stone steps that led down to the cobwebbed crypts or tamp down the loosened earth in the cemetery that each time seemed to have come freshly undone.

On one of these weekly sojourns, I made the innocent mistake (for I was still new and did not yet know the ways of the manor) of speaking to one of my fellow orphans when I stumbled upon a strange-looking object—a hand of sorts, it seemed, or perhaps the paw of some wild animal that had fallen prey—which I pointed to with a sense of both awe and fear. It was a childlike venture, blameless in nature, for no human being wants to remain silent and insulated without some contact with his fellow creatures. The boy, whose name I did not know, tried to warn me with a sudden twitch of his face, but it was too late, for Lucinda Blackstone rushed over, yanked me by the arm, and gaped into my eyes with a look that chilled my innards.

"You must never speak, child," she whispered in her deep, raspy voice. "Not now. Not ever. Lest you wish to conjure the devil!"

She shoved her grim face into mine, her fetid breath stirring the hairs that covered my forehead, then pushed me away violently.

Later, after we returned to the manor, I was sent upstairs, locked in a closet for the rest of the day with no light, no food, no drink, only the baneful creaking of the boards and the silent whisperings of the air. That night, after I was sent to bed, I opened my eyes to find the boy I had spoken to that day standing beside my cot, his body bent as if in pain, his face contorted in unfettered fear. He did not speak, but his face conveyed his terror. I stared back silently at him, but the tears in my eyes could not convey the depth of my sorrow nor the tenor of my regrets.

The next day, he was gone. And, except for a brief, elusive look on Mattie's face, as she counted the children remaining in the room, and an undefined glance of recognition on Lucinda's countenance as we quietly gathered around our breakfast, his absence went unnoted.

One day, it rained—rained more than usual. An infinite deluge that matted the tangled shrubs and bushes, a downpour so hellish it deafened the senses with its constant clash against stone and wood, against the ancient house, against the already dank earth and the wormy paths that wound through the cursed grounds and lead to the ancient tombs on the far side of the manor. The thunder clashed and the wind whipped the weeping willows already battered by the incessant storm.

I had been there for several months, maybe more, for when you are captive, you lose track of time. Learn how to behave. Know what to do and, most importantly, what not to.

Looking through the window from the darkened room where I spent the majority of my days, I watched Mattie rush out, wrapped up against the weather, splashing madly through puddles and mud, pushing through hanging branches and broken briers, stopping erratically to look back towards the manor house, staring coldly at the east turret, scowling, then continuing quickly down the long, stony path to the crypts where only she would dare to go alone.

I closed my eyes, coverd my ears as she pulled open the iron gates, as the grated creaking echoed through the thunderous rain, as the lightning, sharp and sporadic, illuminated her form, then left her lost in the misty shadows.

And then the howls, a piercing scream muted only by the storm, and I shuddered to watch, shuttered my window and cowered in the darkness and hoped and prayed for an escape from this tortured life.

Later, she returned. Made her way somberly to her room. Shut and locked her door. Secretly, I stood outside and listened as I heard her crumble onto her bed, whimper and moan, mumble words I had not yet learned to comprehend.

That night, I came to understand the hidden horrors of this house when it suddenly shook as if an earthquake had abruptly taken hold. Strange, incomprehensible sounds arose, as muffled footsteps made their way towards the keep where we lay trembling. As the lock creaked, a rapid chill filled the air. Then, the door suddenly rattled open, and all sound vanished, replaced only by a deep, heavy breathing which slowly traversed the length and breadth of the room.

Peeking through my covers, I spied the glowing eyes slowly floating through the keep and quivered as the horrid creatures slowly crept past me. Then, the chosen child was whisked away, and I covered my ears in horror to shield them from the desperate shrieking.

Then, silence, except for the fading footsteps, the weakening whimpering of the child held firmly in their grip and the quick uneasy breathing of my fellow inmates which gradually calmed to a less rapid pace.

Later—much later it seemed—the cries of the sacrificial child— the very last we would ever hear from him—and the horrid howls as only the devil, I imagine, could conjure.

And in the morning, the nervous rattling of the keys as Mattie opened the door and surveyed the room, her swollen eyes falling at once on the empty cot as if she knew instinctively who it was who had been taken.

That morning, I vowed I would escape. Gazing around the nursery through the dusty dawn light and trying to make sense of what had happened—of what kind of hell I had come to live in—I swore I would organize my fellow inmates into rebellion. Surely, I reasoned, we outnumbered them. Surely ten or fifteen children could overpower two aging, feeble adults. Surely we could make a dash for it, outrun them, until we stumbled upon a nearby house where we could, without doubt, take refuge.

As for Mattie, I was certain she would be on our side. That she wanted to flee just as much as we did.

How foolish we are at that tender age! How invincible we envision ourselves! How utterly fearless we can be in our imaginations until faced with a reality we cannot possibly conceive! But I had convinced myself I could find a way. I was sure the others would follow me. That Mattie would protect us. For certainly none of them wanted to spend the rest of their lives imprisoned in this horrid place, wandering around lifelessly and wondering each day whether they would survive to see the next.

So I spent the following weeks scheming. Thinking of ways to flee. Of how to organize a band of abandoned children who were so deluded that they believed this was the only way life could be. As I plotted, I realized that communication would be the most stubborn obstacle, for even if I could come up with a plan, it would be nearly impossible to convey its substance to the others without arousing suspicion. Who could I trust? Who would agree and who might betray? And how could I contend with Lucinda's unrelenting watch over us?

Until, one day, it came to me. It was a Wednesday, the day our monthly supplies were delivered to us by the same shadowy figure that had first brought me here.

I watched through the window as the carriage pulled up and Mattie rushed out the front door, pulling her cloak around her, and directed a few of the children who listlessly obeyed, unloading the provisions—sacks of flour, tubs loaded with butter, blocks of cured cheese, drums filled with milk and cooking oil—around the side of the manor where they carried it all down into the dairy cellar.

As the driver fastened the hatches and the last of the supplies were carried into the manor, I noticed a small space at the back of the carriage, obscured under an old tarp, where at least one person my size could safely hide. Surely, I thought, I could conceal myself within those confines. Surely, I could make my escape in that small compartment, hide until we came to a town where I would find someone to come and free the rest.

As the carriage pulled away that late afternoon, drawn by its two ghostly black horses who succumbed to the sting of their master's whip, I resolved to take this chance. It was my only hope. The only hope for all of us. And since there was no safe way of speaking with the others—since there was no trust among any of us—I decided I would go it alone.

The next couple of weeks passed by slowly. The days dragged on as I tried to cope with the anxiety and the solitude, as I reinforced my resolve to make my escape from this wretched place. The nights were even more tortuous as I lay totally still, hidden beneath my covers, listening fearfully for the arrival of the creatures and, whenever they appeared, praying that they would bypass me as they slinked about the room, selecting their victims and returning with their prey to their secret den.

Then, one evening, at dusk, as the clouds gathered, as the sky darkened and the winds began to stir, the carriage arrived unexpectedly, delivering, this time, three children who, no doubt, had been taken in the same manner as I had. Looking from my window, I watched as Lucinda and Aloysius exited like stealthy felines followed by the unsuspecting boys who gingerly hopped down. As the door to the manor opened and Mattie came out to escort them to their certain doom, I realized that this was the chance I had been waiting for, for I could use the darkness to conceal myself.

Quietly, so as not to arouse suspicion among the other children, I stood up and snuck my way out of the keep, gently closing the door behind me, and proceeded down the hallway. Using a hidden passageway I had recently discovered, I rushed down the stairs and slipped out the back door, staying as close to the stone walls of the manor as I could, sneaking around the far side closest to the carriageway and my means of escape.

Looking around to make sure no one was in sight, I made a quick dash, tripping, as I did, over a rock in the roadway and leaping under the coach as the sudden sound caused the jittery horses to stir. The odd-looking coachman immediately came around to find out what had set the animals off, and I held my breath and stiffened my body at the sight of his old, beat up boots approaching the very spot where I lay hidden.

Several moments passed as my heart pounded madly. Then, the driver's feet were gone, and I breathed a sigh of relief until suddenly, as I turned around beneath the belly of that carriage, I came face to face with the brute countenance of that frightening individual, his red puffy cheeks and scruffy beard just visible beneath the dim light of the rising moon.

"Well, laddie," he said. "Got some place to go this time of night?"

"Please sir," I pleaded.

He stared at me and, for just a moment, I thought he might relent, but then he called out and, before I knew it, I was yanked from beneath that carriage and held firmly within Lucinda's unyielding grip.

"Going somewhere?" she bellowed, shoving her haggard face into mine.

I stared back fearfully at her, not knowing what to say.

"Cat got your tongue?" she asked, laughing mockingly and turning to the driver who responded in kind.

A moment later, Mattie rushed over, clutching her cloak around her neck and staring angrily at me as if I had broken some unspoken rule.

"Take him to the attic," Lucinda shouted. "We'll show him what happens to little boys who try to escape."

Mattie's countenance immediately transformed—the kind, burdened face that had greeted me the day of my arrival suddenly turned into a monstrous grimace which mirrored the sorry soul

Yet, when Mattie did not appear for her morning duties, and when her absence at breakfast was conspicuously palpable, I knew for certain that what had transpired in that garret had been no nightmare.

As I ate my cheese and drank my milk, I noticed Lucinda staring at me, her mouth snarled into a bitter smile, and the old man set his jaundiced eyes upon me each time his trembling fingers reached for the stale bread which he tore into menacingly. It was as if they knew exactly what had happened in that attic, as if they had been there.

That Sunday, following services in the chapel, as we performed our morbid duties down by the tombs, I was pulled aside by Lucinda, led down the jagged stone steps and into the dark, dank realm of the mausoleum. Holding me firmly between her two hands, she looked at me with a flash of impish affection which quickly vanished and said, "Now you see, don't you?"

I stared back at her silently, not quite sure what she meant, though something inside me acknowledged what I feared the most.

"Now," she said, "you are one of us. And you shall never escape."

She mumbled something I could not comprehend—an incantation of some sort—then looked back at me, laughing like one who had moved beyond fear.

"And your fate," she said, pointing to the daylight coming through the entrance, "shall be worse than theirs."

Lucinda laughed again, the hollow sound of her voice reverberating off the hard cold stone of the tombs, her gaunt face marbled by the shadowy light of that dank mausoleum.

I soon learned my fate, soon learned what it was that had kept Mattie trapped inside her morbid sorrow. For it was she, I quickly understood, who had chosen each victim, she who saw to it that the creatures were satisfied, she who understood the reality of this wretched house. She was their slave, just as I had now become, their minion who, having encountered their evil existence, was only allowed to live so that they could survive. For when you look into their eyes, you become ensnared in their world. In order to live, you pay with more than your soul, knowing that each day will be worse than the previous one, that in choosing the next victim, you will be pounding yet another nail into your own craven heart. Burdened with sorrow, heavy with the execution of the deed, Mattie had spent each day in her own secret hell. A hell that had now become mine.

Life—if you can call it that—went on, only now it was I who held the keys.

I have spent these many years inhabiting this nightmare, greeting the new arrivals with as much kindness as one can muster, wielding the keys to the keep with tremulous heart, keeping a vigilant eye on the children, whose fate was now in my hands, and another on Aloysius and Lucida whose lives go on and on, despite their feebleness, their secret concealed beneath their frigid hearts.

Whenever commanded, I select the next victim, unlock the

door in the midst of the night so the creatures can enter, and watch as they lurk about the room seeking out their next meal.

And so this horrid house, possessed by the possessed, haunted by the very haunted, cursed by history, by ancestors who torched and burned, raped and killed, who skewered sleeping children on their swords, then cleared it all away, like chaff, like the bones of mice and other vermin, making way for a wooden shell that would exist only to seal the fate of their own offspring for generations to come. And so it shall remain. And so those who are cursed to occupy it, who have no power to escape, who must exist until the house is destroyed and the beasts are slaughtered, put to rest forever.

For fifty years, I have lived here, have watched the old man and woman fastidious in their work, rounding up unsuspecting orphans and bringing them here for sacrifice. For fifty years, I have carefully selected each victim, savoring each offering, watching with strange wanton pleasure as the creatures clutch them between their claws and drag them away to feed upon only to wake the next morning with a heavy sense of regret like a drunkard who must face the consequences of the previous night's intoxication. For fifty years, I have lived knowing that, but for one mistake, I would end up like Mattie. A fate, perhaps, better than the one I am living, yet one no one wants to face. For fifty years, I have secretly plotted, searched for a way to free the Earth from this evil, to find a way to put an end, once and for all, to this noxious curse.

Until tonight. Under this moonless night. With the lonesome owl as my witness. After having schemed and suffered for so long, I watch as the house bursts into flames. After having waited for a night when every depraved culprit—from the wicked creatures to the old jaded couple to the coachman to the ghostly horses themselves—have been unlucky enough to find themselves in the confines of this sorry manor.

On this stormy night, when wind and rain make it impossible to travel, they are all inside, the horses secure in a makeshift stable, the creatures ready for their latest victim.

I have planned it carefully, have doused each and every exit, for there can be no escape from this conflagration, not even for the children inside who, I hope, will be the last to suffer.

In the distance, the unholy owl watches, hoots, then takes flight to the deep refuge of the dark, forbidding forest, as the flames ascend, cling to the sides of the manor, reach up to the shuttered keep where the children succumb to the smoke and fire, up to the east turret where eyes glow from within the darkness. I can hear their muffled cries, their voices rising, their screams begging for mercy, for it is the fire that they fear the most, the fire that will destroy them once and for all.

Soon I will join them. Soon I will dive into the conflagration to cleanse my soul and rid this world from the last vestige of evil that has occupied this house for ages.

And so I write these final words, as the howls continue and the far-off owl hoots and I prepare to enter the flames.

ABOUT BEING CASPAR CRUMP

Caspar Crump—that was his real name and he hated it—was puzzled. Totally confused. Even, one might say, stupefied.

It was his name again, staring back at him silently, taunting him, ridiculing him, mutely, remotely, from a place in cyberspace where he could not fight back even if he wanted to (and he always wanted to but felt incapable), reminding him of how he could just not get away from it, reminding him now of all the times he had tried so desperately to escape it.

"My name is Caspar," he would mutter, when required, with a pained look on his face, because he knew that eventually they would require his full name. "Crump," he would add finally, inaudibly, but of course the inevitable would happen because when they asked him to speak up—and he was always being accused of mumbling, which bothered him, which made him want to cower in the corner even more—he would have to repeat it out loud several times so that everyone around, as his voice crescendoed, could hear: "Crump! Caspar Crump!"

And he'd look about, self-consciously, glance uncomfortably at the people who were in line behind him, stare crossly at the teller or the clerk or whoever it was that was demanding his name, and wonder what they were thinking, wonder if, deep inside, they were laughing at him or saying to themselves "what an odd name" or, worse, mocking him like the kids in school used to do when he was a child or the little girls as they skipped down the street—"Caspar Crump, Caspar Crump, your name is weird and you belong in a dump," or "Caspar, Caspar, what a disaster."

It wasn't so much his first name that bothered him. Caspar was all right, though it was rather cartoonish, though, in truth, he would have rather been called Carl or James or even something as mundane as John. But it was easy, had a nice ring to it and, he imagined, as he got older, an air of sophistication. It was Crump that annoyed him—sounded like bump or grump or, even worse, chump—and, for the longest time, he hated his father for giving it to him, for passing on a name like that, though it was no fault of his own, though he too, Casper imagined, had had to endure it as much as he now did. Surely his father could not have been satisfied being a Crump!

And then, of course, he found out what it meant, looked it up one day and was horrified to find that, at its very origin, it referred to someone with a crooked back. It was then that he started looking more in the mirror, began straightening up every now and then, pushing back his shoulders and stiffening his spine, as if the name itself were indicative of some curse he would never be able to escape.

Or perhaps it was just the combination he disliked—Caspar Crump—its perfect rhythm, its hard repetitive sounds, its alliterativeness as if his parents were trying to be poetic when they were struggling to come up with a name. No, Casper Crump just didn't make it, was almost anachronistic in a world of Johns and Jims or Robinsons and Whites.

But now, as he sat at his desk and looked incongruously at his computer, he was more in shock than angry, more bewildered than irritated, for he was taken by surprise by a message, sitting plainly in his inbox, from an individual it seemed with the very same name—Caspar Crump.

Caspar stared oddly at the computer screen. Perhaps, he thought, he had emailed himself by mistake. Perhaps he was still half asleep. Or maybe he was just dreaming, for there certainly could not be another individual in this world with such an impossible name.

Casper hesitated, as he always did in times of uncertainty. Was this some trick that someone was playing on him? Should he read the email and then respond to whoever it was that was contacting him? Or should he just ignore it? Was it spam, perhaps? Had his email been hacked? Would he get some nasty virus on his computer if he opened it? After all, why would one Casper Crump contact another? Could this person, perhaps, be as obsessed about his name—their name—as he was and, having discovered another with the same onerous appellation, had a need to communicate? Commiserate? Perhaps, even, bellyache?

So Casper sat at his desk, baffled and stunned, staring silently for the longest while at the computer screen, biting his lip and scrunching his face, as he tried to figure out how—or even if—to respond. He felt as if he were having an out-of-body experience, as if his spirit had left him momentarily and he was looking at himself from across the room, as if he were looking at himself as another, looking at a total stranger whose name happened to be Casper Crump—an odd name, he thought for a moment, but rather interesting—who existed somewhere else yet whose presence was felt in the room, until he finally came back down to Earth, reattached himself to his body, and stared numbly at the cursor blinking indifferently on the computer monitor.

Some time later—an hour or two, perhaps—after Casper had had enough time to contemplate this jarring event—one which firmly interfered with his regular morning routine—after he had confirmed that it was indeed someone else with a totally different email address, after he had gotten himself to finally open the file, after he had fully digested its contents ("My name is Casper Crump," it read, innocently, "and I came across your name online and wondered—" etc. etc.), Casper decided that there had been some kind of mistake, an unfortunate mix-up which made his heart pace and his gut drop and the palms of his hands begin to sweat. It was hard to describe the feelings he felt—angry, but he could not figure out why, violated, perhaps, as if someone had broken into his room and intruded on his life, even, at one point, panic, as if his identity had been stolen, as if who he was—an individual with an odd name, a name he detested but his name nonetheless—was suddenly no longer simply who he was. He was suddenly someone else, or someone else had suddenly become him, he wasn't sure. How could there possibly be another Casper Crump? Who was this person and what did he look like? Where did he live and what did he do on a daily basis? And, more importantly, how did he feel about being Casper Crump?

Casper nervously pushed the keyboard aside, stood up, and paced madly about the room. Then he went into the bathroom and stared at himself in the mirror, tracing the outline of his face with his finger, looking closely at this blemish here and that mole there, smiling, frowning, examining each facial expression, each muscle movement, just to make sure that everything was still in order, to make sure that he—Casper Crump—was still the same Caspar Crump he had been the night before when he had gone to sleep, that he was still Casper Crump and no one else, and that no one else had suddenly become him.

Satisfied, he went into the kitchen and made himself a pot of coffee. He examined the scoop, as he lifted it in his hand, noted its cool presence, felt its smooth surface against his rough skin, listened carefully to the click of the beans, the whiz of the motor, watched, through the little plastic window, as the beans became pulverized, smelled the earthy aroma that was instantly released, waited patiently, his eye on the pot, as the hot brown liquid slowly trickled down. He was not normally so observant, but today—the day his name had been stolen, appropriated by some individual who had no right to it—he felt suddenly aware of his surroundings, aware of every movement he made, of every sound he heard, even of his voice as he suddenly shouted, to no one in particular: "Who the hell is Caspar Crump!?" And as he did so, he felt a sudden burst of strength as the words formed in his mouth, as they released themselves, one by one, loud and clear, words he would not have uttered so loudly in public had he been required to do so, not in the way he had now done with such precision and power.

And he sat down and drank his coffee, felt its soothing warmth spread through his body, felt the hot liquid swish against his lips, against his tongue, drank in loud sumptuous sips and stared out across the room, at nothing in particular, feeling content that he was here in his own space, his own apartment, a singular individual with a suddenly not so singular name.

Then the phone rang. Jolted him out of his chair and his reverie, brought him back down to Earth, back to reality, and he put his cup down and paced across the room, searched frantically for his cell phone, followed the sound of the ring tone, fumbled through a pile of papers and clothes, picked it up and answered.

"Hello," he said. "Yes," he continued, "This is Caspar." And then: "No, I'm sorry, you have the wrong number." And finally: "Yes, this is Caspar Crump but I do not live in Kalamazoo."

And with that, he hung up and placed the phone back on the table where he had found it, sat down, and stared off into space and wondered just how many Caspar Crumps there could possibly be. Surely, there had to be some kind of mistake. Surely, someone was playing a joke on him, someone who knew how much he detested his name, how self-conscious he felt about being who he was. But who could that possibly be? For he had certainly not told anyone about his feelings—no one except Ceci, that is—had not confided in anyone, not even his own mother and father who had assumed nothing unusual as he was growing up, who had assumed that he was just a normal kid with a name that they liked, a name, they assumed, that he just accepted.

So Caspar sat back down on the couch and wondered what was happening to him on this day that had started out like any other day, a day where he had awoken just before the alarm went off, as he normally did, had taken a shower and gotten dressed as usual, had followed his routine as unconsciously and naturally as he did every day, except that now something was not right, something was somehow off kilter, some kink in the normal rhythm of his life had suddenly appeared.

Caspar switched on the TV to calm himself, to numb his mind, to get his thoughts off the disconcerting events that were taking place that morning. He stared blankly at the screen, half listened to the newscaster as she spoke and smiled and followed her teleprompter, as she attempted to assure everyone that everything was all right, despite the traffic, despite the weather, despite all the tragedies that were happening all around the city, when suddenly she disappeared, and a man came on—a rather striking man with a neatly trimmed moustache and beard and a carefully combed head of hair—stared straight into the camera and said, "Hi, my name is Caspar Crump," or at least that's what Caspar thought he heard, and he suddenly perked up, leaned toward the TV and listened as the man talked about a product he had recently discovered, how it had changed his life dramatically, how he, Caspar Crump—for he was looking straight at him it seemed—might benefit from it as well if only he would pay $29.95 plus shipping and handling.

Caspar watched impatiently as the man spoke, waited to see if he would repeat his name again, examined him as carefully as he could to see if there was any resemblance, to see if, perhaps, there was a crook in his back or any other imperfection that would indicate he was a true Crump, to see if, perhaps, he was some sort of distant relation. It was possible, he reasoned, that in this vast universe, there was another who looked like him, felt like him or, even, acted like him. But the man never repeated his name—perhaps he was ashamed of it as well—just went on and on about this ridiculous product that no one needed, that, he insisted, would change your life forever, if only you would buy it in the next ten minutes, and if you did you would get a special bonus and free shipping, etc. etc.

Caspar began flipping channels, nervously, indiscriminately, looking for the same advertisement, looking for the man who had called himself Caspar Crump, wanting to reassure himself that he had heard the name correctly, but every time he came across the commercial it was half done and he never got to hear the man announce his name again.

Caspar angrily switched off the TV. Perhaps he had misheard the man! Perhaps he had said his name was Gasper! But Crump? How could he possibly mistake that name for another? Maybe he had imagined the whole thing—he had, after all, been thinking about that email, obsessing about that person with the same name who had had the temerity to contact him. Could there possibly be three of them now, out there in this world, three Caspar Crumps making their way through life, struggling to come to terms with their names and their lives and all the other associated insecurities? How likely was that? And what about that Caspar Crump in Kalamazoo?

So Caspar decided to call Ceci. Things were getting out of hand, and he needed someone to help him see clearly, to understand, to logically and rationally help him come to terms with what was going on, or at least with what he thought was going on. Surely, after all these years together, she would be able to help him sort it out, calm him down, help him find an explanation for this maddening dilemma.

Caspar picked up his cell phone and clicked on her name, let the line ring, wondered, when Ceci did not pick up, where she could possibly be on a Saturday morning, then listened, as the voicemail message came on and his heart slowly began to sink. "Hello, you have reached Caspar Crump. I'm not able to come to the phone right now," etc. etc.

Caspar stared at the cell phone, checked to make sure Ceci's name was really there, clicked on it again, and got the same results. Caspar Crump, it seemed, was beginning to haunt him, or maybe he was haunting himself. Whichever way, he was coming to his wit's end and he wasn't sure what to do, what path to take, for whichever one he followed, it seemed to lead to the same place.

Caspar put the phone down and went through each room in his apartment. He quickly closed the blinds, unplugged each and every device that communicated with the outside world, turned out all the lights, and sat in the dark trembling uncontrollably and wondering just what was beginning to become of him.

Later that day—or perhaps it was night, he couldn't tell—Caspar awoke to a loud knocking on his door and the sound of someone shouting out his name. Dazed with sleep, he made his way across the room and opened up to a man standing in the dull light of the darkened hallway, dressed in a beige trench coat with a matching cap in his left hand.

"Caspar Crump?" the man asked, in a tone as if he already knew.

"Yes," Caspar answered.

"You're under arrest."

Caspar gazed at the man standing in his doorway and finally managed to say "Arrest?" though the word came out rather weakly, though Caspar was so bewildered at that very moment that he was not even sure if he had spoken.

The man flashed a badge in Caspar's face, then, after a moment's silence, drew a piece of paper out from his briefcase and read, in a loud officious voice: "Caspar Crump: in the name of society, in the name of the laws by which we abide, in the name of everything we hold sacred, in the name of, in the name of," etc. etc.

As the inspector read his statement, hallway doors opened, and neighbors—people Caspar had never before seen—appeared, one by one, dressed in night shirts and dressing gowns, watched accusingly as they listened to the inspector, tsk-tsked and mumbled among themselves ("deserves it," one of them muttered), then slammed their doors tight, jangling their security chains which echoed loudly through the dark, hollow hallway.

The inspector continued to read and, when he finished, he handed Caspar a small package wrapped in brown paper.

"You are to remain here until further notice," he announced.

And with that, he donned his hat, turned, and marched away,

disappearing gradually into the darkness of the long, narrow passageway.

Caspar closed his door and stared glumly at the package. Could this be some sort of nightmare? he wondered. When would he wake up? Should he pinch himself like they did in the movies? Should he go to bed and hope that, at some point, he would actually wake up?

Caspar turned on the light and sat down on the couch. He slowly unwrapped the package, opened the box, undid the tissue paper and found, neatly folded inside, a black and white shirt and a matching pair of pants. Unconsciously, he took off his clothes, folded them neatly, and slowly assumed the striped garments he had been given to wear.

Caspar Crump soon discovered that he did not know how to be a prisoner. At first, he thought, he should confine himself to one place. So he locked himself in his bedroom, placed the key on his night table and sat stiffly in the wicker chair beside his bed. But after a while he needed the bathroom and, later, when he began to feel hungry, he found the need to go to the kitchen to make himself something to eat.

"Perhaps," he said to himself, "I should just lock myself in my apartment." Then it came to him: "Maybe I'm already locked in."

But Caspar tried the door and opened it, peered down the darkened hallway at neighbors who caught surreptitious glimpses of him through their narrowly cracked doors.

Was he allowed to go outside? he wondered. Move about freely?

Could he eat and drink as he pleased? Watch TV? Make telephone calls? And why was everyone looking at him as if he were a common criminal?

Caspar Crump wondered what he had done to deserve this. Couldn't he just go on with his life like other people did? When would he be released from this strange incarceration?

So Caspar sat down on his couch and pondered his dilemma. And as he pondered, taking into consideration all that had occurred, he waited in anticipation for something to happen. Something small or something significant, it really didn't matter. Days passed, weeks accumulated, one upon the other, turned into months, then years, and Caspar wondered what he should do, wondered when the inspector would return to release him, to pronounce him innocent or at least to tell him what his crime had been, wondered when the neighbors would stop staring at him, when Ceci would call and explain to him what he had done wrong. He pondered these things and then wondered some more, wondered what was expected of him, as he waited for someone to call, waited for a clue as to how he should be now that he was a prisoner. His life, it seemed, was at a standstill, on hold until someone informed him how he was supposed to be.

Caspar Crump sat in his apartment and waited. He waited and watched, watched and waited, as the seasons changed—winter became spring and the birds began to sing again, then the early summer winds gathered and swept through his life, flowers bloomed here and there in every corner of his apartment and trees spread their foliage, then fall came and went with its tumble of leaves, carpeting his room, gathering and accumulating in every nook and cranny, until winter returned with its purifying coat of white snow and a biting cold that blew right through him. And throughout it all, Caspar remained on his couch, a good citizen minding the authorities, getting up only to eat and drink and perform his routine functions. His hair soon silvered and his beard lengthened, and yet no one came to deliver his sentence, no one—not even a Caspar Crump—tried to make any further contact with him.

Caspar Crump—that was his name and though he hated it he knew very well it was his—sat and waited. Waited for his life. Waited for a clue. Waited for something to happen, though nothing consequential ever did.

THE OTHER

"What's it like for you?" he asked.

He was sitting alone, sitting, in the corner, listening to the quiet, to the shameful stillness that swallowed the moment in a fit of loneliness.

A cool draft filtered through the empty room, a slight waft of wind that brushed between the two of them and disappeared into the darkness. He tried to hold on to it, but it kept slipping through his fingers and he gave up. Somewhere, a light bulb flickered weakly, barely clinging to life, and through the fading glow, he found he was naked, and he wanted to cover himself from the chill of it all but all he could do was stare forbiddingly into the frightening rain that fell relentlessly against an open window.

The other sat still and silent, shifted slightly, wondered what it was the other was asking, what it was that might be wanting other than what he had already given, that made the world so hollow for him it might possibly implode. He examined himself, tentatively, found that he was whole, found that the difference between the two of them was like the difference between the two chairs across the room sitting vacant beside the bare table.

"It was all I ever wanted," he continued. "To open a door and see the same thing you did. Or she did. Or anyone."

He looked directly at him, looked hungrily upon him, looked through and around him, studied every bit of him, every joint and limb, every appendage, every freckle and follicle of hair, until he was satisfied, though he wanted more, though he wasn't sure if satisfaction was ever enough.

"Is that asking too much?"

Then, he was alone. Engulfed by the black chasm that always appeared at times like this, that seemed to have no precipice, no beginning and no end, that consumed and separated him unquenchably from the other.

And his vision faltered, tumbled to the ground, rolled out and about, like marbles spinning silently, disappeared down deep into the aching chasm, and he could not see for seeing what he thought he was supposed to see.

It was like that sometimes. Sometimes, his body would just rise and slip away. Sometimes, without warning, like flecks of dead skin, bits of him would shed, when he least expected. Sometimes, his life would splinter like wood shavings flaking onto the floor. Burst like glass. Drop like leaves, worn with age and weather, giving up, giving in to the forces over which he had no control.

And there was nothing he could do about it, nothing but watch from a distance and surrender, as he disintegrated into tiny crumbs of himself that accumulated all about.

And there were times there was nothing he could touch, or feel, or hear. Nothing but the sense of his skin and the chink of light that sometimes made the afternoon. In those moments he would reach out, folded in fear, grope for something tangible to put his mind around, and the first thing he came in contact with, he'd wonder if it was real or if it was just some particle of his fragile being that loomed before him, some element that even he could not comprehend.

Like the people he'd encounter. Like the ones he'd try to touch, try, in his way, to feel, to absorb, to be. Till the sensation tingled down to his soul, disappeared, resonated, somewhere, in the darkness, like a flicker of lightning, like a faint spark that stubbornly refused to linger. Then, he'd find himself alone again, naked and yearning from deep inside, from the very ridge of his impenetrable skin.

Sometimes, he would simply sense the objects all around him. The room. The emptiness. This chair here. That table there. Feel their aura as if they were alive, listen and see until nothing else existed, try to comprehend, try to figure it all out, wondering what it was that made them. Then he'd ask the questions one was not supposed to ask, the ones that one should know. Intuitively. Instinctively. Naturally.

Because that's the way it was with him. Because he wondered each time. Because otherwise he would be faced with the endless chasm and his weight would become so heavy he'd want to lie down, want to sleep, want to float away somewhere where things were light, where illumination might somehow caress his frightened body.

"I never knew how to be," he said one day.

It was a casual remark, uttered in a moment of uncontrolled thinking.

He was standing in a room, gripping the air all about him, listening to the rain that fell somewhere in the place he had come to be, that never seemed to touch him.

"Just—wanted to be."

That day, the other was watching him, from a distance, though sometimes he'd come close, though sometimes he'd approach so that the other felt like someone was there. And yet he wasn't. Or perhaps, he thought, he was, and he just didn't know.

"Perhaps I never tried," he continued. "Or could. Or couldn't."

He reached out for the other, closed his eyes, touched him, felt his warmth penetrate him with a life he had never come to know. And then it was gone.

"Sometimes I wonder."

"Sometimes, there's this image staring in the mirror."

"Sometimes," he said, "there is no mirror."

"I mean," he said, looking deep into the other's brown eyes, where his own were curiously rendered. "Can one ever confirm that?"

He held him close now, tried to absorb him, tried hard to be what the other easily seemed to be.

"Can you tell me that?"

His eyes were trembling.

"Please."

And he waited and waited but the only answer he received was the pattering of the rain that fell all about him, fell and consumed him and left him feeling parched and alone.

And so he wondered: when would he feel alive? He wondered when he would wake up and feel refreshed. Feel the sun penetrate his skin, reach down and warm the very depths of his being. He wondered if there was a secret formula he could replicate, that he could substitute for breathing, for the pulse he never seemed to sense, for the heartbeat that sometimes seemed to arise and deafen him into silence.

That was something he could not escape. The wondering and the feeling that, somewhere, there was an answer that eluded him, that eluded no other. That the other somehow could sense.

That's when he descended into himself. That's when the stars and the lights collapsed, when the moon and the sun eclipsed his soul and left him mired in a tunnel of uncertainty.

There were times he felt reduced to his own molecules. Times he would look around and think: this is a hand, that a foot. This, a man. That, a mere object. There were times he'd look all around him and conclude: that the tree before him really existed. That the light around him was a band of color he could wrap himself up in. That the street lamp was more than it simply was.

And he would feel their presence. Feel them as if they were alive. Feel their pulse. Their aura. Their existence.

There were times he thought he could rise up into the clouds, bathe in the nascent raindrops, return anew, shimmering with life.

But then he'd look around and see nothing. And then nothing became something, and that was something he would contemplate, until he realized that nothing could never be something and something could never be nothing. Nothing, he concluded, could never be other than itself.

At those times, he would discard his loneliness, like a wasted sheet of paper, watch it drift alone on a breeze, float away like fluff and dander.

At those times, he would say: "Yes."

And then a smile would materialize, like a brief butterfly, like a shimmer of light on the morning lake that would suddenly disappear.

Until one day, a woman arrived. She was wrapped in a cloud of uncertainty, sat across from him with her legs folded, her long face ensconced in waves of long silky hair.

"Are you something or nothing?" he asked of her.

Her face was vacant, her voice as evanescent as a gentle breeze, her kisses like a chimera, like the sun that warms the Earth with rays unseen.

And then she was gone. Instantly. Like a passing summer. Like a dandelion flecking into the air. And all he could remember was a particle of sand that stuck to his skin momentarily until he flicked it off, brushed it with the back of his hand until the skin on his leg was clean once again, dry and clean, the wavy strands of hair gently brushing against him in a passing breeze.

And the answer came to him like a moth, elusive, diaphanous on the wind.

One day, he found himself in the middle of the desert, in the midst of an oasis with a shimmering pool of water and a mirage of flowers and palm trees that rustled noisily in the barren breeze. He cried out to the immenseness and listened to the sound of his voice as it came back to him and then settled into a space of time that spanned the world around him.

But there was no answer.

Nor was it that he could simply respond. Nor take the sound and capture it, hold it against him. For, though it was a part of him, it had escaped into the universe, left him cold and flat in the midst of the sand dunes that surrounded him and no matter how he tried he could not retrieve it.

So he shed a tear.

And the other tried to comfort him, but he kept shedding tears, like the raindrops he had left behind, while the other tried to stop him, put his arms around him, engulfed him in his elusive presence. And nighttime came. And the stars appeared bright. And then a sudden darkness plunged him into its vast bosom and he was comforted by the emptiness of it all.

That's when he took to wandering. He journeyed from city to country, visited towns and villages, forged forests and navigated seas, made his way up rivers and down every empty highway. Until he had exhausted ever possibility. Until he reached the end of what could only be a very long and narrow road. Until it all shriveled up into a ball of air. Until he understood that he was meant to be nowhere. Or that nowhere was what he was meant to be.

"Where do I go now," he asked to no one in particular. "What shall I find that I have not found before?"

There, amidst it all, he sat upon a rock and pondered. And the men he had seen appeared before his vision, the women he had lain with came to him and whispered in his ear, whispered things he could not grasp, whispered things that made no sense and yet the sense of it all seemed to wash him in its simplicity.

And he lay down like a thimble, like a tiny stone on that very rock where he hoped water would somehow burst.

But it never did. The rock was always a rock and remained so.

And he wondered: "What have I missed?"

"What," he thought, "did I not do that the other has?"

And he continued on, drifting here and meandering there, crying the same phrases he had learned to cry, over and over, listening to the echo of his voice until his voice was the only sound he came to understand. Until he felt like the bottom would drop and he would be left hovering in nothingness, in an empty space that somehow refused to fill up.

Then one day, when there was still no answer, when the answer he sought continued to elude him like feathers in the air, he came to a place. Empty. Nondescript. A place where only he existed. For it was he who existed solely in the space that surrounded him.

Until suddenly, the other appeared in all his simple glory.

He was naked again, trying desperately to cover himself though there was nothing to grasp, no reason any longer to hide what he had hidden.

"Is this what it's like? he asked.

He was standing, surrounded by nothing, brimming with

nothing, surrounded by everything that refused to adhere to his skin.

"For you?" he added, tentatively.

"For you?" he shouted.

But there was no answer. For the other was no longer there. For the other had disappeared, suddenly, permanently, as if he were nothing, as if he had never existed.

And he was alone, utterly alone, contemplating alone, watching himself, alone. Breathing, at last. Alone.

"Is this how it's supposed to be?" he asked.

A ray of sun inched its way between his eyes, between the pores of his porous skin, between the very crevices that made up his life. And it warmed him with its warmth, lit him with its light, revealed him as the revelation he was always meant to be.

And he sat down and prayed, swaddled himself in his lucent arms and allowed the sunlight to at last embrace his unfilled soul.

THE BEASTS

The beasts are lurking outside the door.

The children are crying.

The mother is trying to calm them down.

"It's ok," she says.

It's not ok, but she says it anyhow. That's what a mother is supposed to do.

The beasts are growling. Their voices swell, gruff and ferocious. From the sounds of it, they are growing stronger and more vicious.

The mother looks nervously at the children.

"Just one more," she says, half-pleadingly.

It's been going on like this for two days now.

"One more."

She doesn't like this one bit, but she has no choice.

Her face is drawn. She hasn't slept since the beasts arrived on her doorstep. She is trembling, but she tries to appear calm in front of the children. This makes her tremble more.

The beasts heave themselves against the door. Their bodies thump heavily against the hard thick wood.

They want too much, she thinks. Just one more and they'll go away.

The oldest child is seven. The mother drags him by the arm. The child struggles to get loose, but the mother wins. The other children cringe in the corner.

The mother unbars the door and opens it just enough for the beasts to grab the child. Then the mother hurls the door shut, barring it again and breathing a deep sigh.

She covers her ears at the son's screams.

The other children start to cry again.

"It's all right," she says.

The son's screaming stops.

The mother tries once again to appear calm. It works for a few seconds, then the anxiety returns in brief, fitful waves.

Outside, she hears moist, indistinct sounds: chewing, slurping sounds. Then there is snarling. It's always like that: first the killing, then the feeding, then the violence begins. She has come to notice this.

"Oh God, let them kill each other," she exclaims.

Maybe they'll go away. Maybe they'll disappear.

The children are still crying.

She curls her arms around them. She wants to comfort them.

"Shall I tell you a story?" she asks.

The children shrink back.

"Once upon a time, there was a lady who had ten children..."

The fighting stops, and the beasts begin pounding their paws against the door.

"...and they all lived peacefully in the forest."

The beasts howl vehemently. They know what's inside, and they're getting impatient.

The children stare anxiously at the mother.

"One day," she continues, "her husband left on the annual hunt."

The door shakes violently at the hinges.

"Then the snows came, and soon everything was covered in a thick white blanket."

If only the blizzard hadn't trapped them inside. If only her husband would come back with help.

The mother grabs her son by the shoulders.

"You will save us," she says, putting on a brave face to encourage him. She carries him to the door. "Do it for me. Do it for your sister."

The son screams in terror. The mother unlatches the door and tosses him out.

Maybe they'll have pity on him. Maybe they're satisfied and will leave us alone.

Then the son's screams die out, and the mother trembles as she hears the feeding resume.

The mother snatches up her daughter and cradles her.

"I'll never let you go," she cries. "Never."

The daughter squirms in the mother's arms.

The beasts bellow full force now. She imagines them gathering the frozen wilderness into their lungs and releasing it in one hungry breath.

"I've given them everything and still they're not satisfied."

The daughter is whining. She tries to push the mother away, digs taut fingers into her skin.

The door shudders from the weight of the beasts. The mother wonders how long it will be before they break it down.

"What do you want from me?" she shouts.

She roams frantically about the room. She clutches the daughter to her breast.

"What do you want?"

She drops to the floor.

"Haven't I given you everything?"

The mother rocks back and forth. She cries hysterically.

"Haven't I given you everything?" she repeats, cradling the daughter between her arms.

Now she detects a rough grinding, a brittle, crunching sound, the snapping of wood.

She jumps up instinctively: she must do something or she will die.

She throws open the door and flings the daughter out to the beasts, quickly slamming it shut and securing it again. She has become an expert at this.

She covers her ears. She refuses to hear, but her daughter's screams come anyway. Her body shakes so hard she can hardly stand it.

The mother is crawling on the floor now. She is looking for a place to hide: in the closet (too risky), under the bed (they'd surely find her there).

If only she could remember how the story ends, she suddenly thinks.

She forces herself to concentrate.

"Soon after," she recites hesitantly, "some wild beasts arrived on her doorstep."

The beasts are breaking through the door.

The mother is shivering.

There are no more children left.

"At first, she tried to ignore them."

Her teeth chatter as she speaks, her voice quivers.

"Then she tried to befriend them by giving them scraps from the table."

The door breaks open, and the cold air penetrates her with its iciness.

"And they all lived happily ever after," she cries out.

And the beasts rushed in and strapped her down.

PRICK

How quickly it had happened: prick!

Just when she was starting to feel relaxed, just when everything was beginning to go smoothly.

Then: prick.

Like a streak of lightning.

The jolt of it, the sudden, instantaneous prick.

Such a common accident, one would hardly give it a second thought. Something to be brushed off like when, as a child, she would stick herself playing with her mother's sewing kit. "No big deal," her mother would say, "just a little prick, nothing to spill your pretty little tears about."

Prick.

And then there was blood.

Just a little. But she immediately put pressure on the wound—not a wound really, just a prick—how silly, so the bleeding would stop, she couldn't remember ever doing something so silly before.

But there was the patient, sitting, waiting. She didn't want anyone to think she was slow, to doubt her ability. She was new after all; she didn't want anyone to say she didn't know what she was doing. What would the patient think? What would her colleagues say? Not with all her experience. Not after waiting so long to get this job.

Prick.

And then blood.

How kind the patient had been, when the needle struck, how genuinely concerned. "Are you ok?" she asked, just like her mother ("It's just a prick, dear, nothing to worry about"), so kind, as she recalled, later when she got home, really kind, and she was ok, really she was, surely nothing would come of it.

Just an innocent little prick, that's all.

Nothing to worry about, certainly nothing to complain about.

Oh sure there was a little pain. Not pain really, more a sudden sting, more the shock of it all, but she would be all right, after all she was new and things like that didn't happen to her.

Prick.

Then the blood.

If she could only calm down, if she could only get it out of her mind, stop her thoughts from running wild, stop her heart from pounding.

Prick.

Then: blood.

How could she have been so careless! So the needle wouldn't release. She should've called someone. But there was the patient, the kind patient, really so kind, "Are you ok?" ("It's ok, dear"), sitting there with her arm bent, so cooperative—surely that said something about her, surely someone like her had to be clean— waiting for a Band-Aid, waiting to finish so she could go back to work or back home or wherever it was she needed to be to get on with her life.

Life: how striking that word sounded now, how loudly it rang in her head, how it seemed to slide off her tongue and slip away. Life: like the cereal she used to enjoy eating. Like the game she'd play when she was a child, far from the cares of all the things she was facing at this awful moment in time. Her life. Would it be taken from her so suddenly? Would she die? Just like that? From a simple little prick?

Of course, there would be pain, she understood that, of course it would linger, manifest itself in so many ways, she had read about it in magazines, she had seen it on TV, but why did she have to die now, why like this for God's sake?

But surely the patient was clean!

After all, she looked so healthy, dressed in that lovely print dress she was wearing, so properly groomed, her hair so smooth, so silky, she seemed so middle class (she had noticed her through the window, watched her getting out of her black BMW), so well-educated (didn't she have a ring? didn't she have that look about her?), but you can never tell in this day and age, nothing is guaranteed, nothing is clear when it comes to others. After all, who knows what she was like in her private life, who knows what she did when no one was looking, when no one was monitoring her activities, her health, her vital functions.

Her blood.

Prick.

If only she could forget the blood!

Such a routine procedure, such a routine test: to check the

hormone level, a test any healthy woman would have, surely she must be healthy!

If only she could get the image out of her mind: the syringe toppling over, jabbing her, then crashing to the ground.

What a silly mistake! All because the needle wouldn't detach, all because she was too proud to ask for help. She should've called someone, she should've left the syringe on the table, damn the rules, after all, it was only a job, why hadn't she thought of herself first? Why hadn't she thought of her baby, oh God, her baby, growing inside her. All because of a job, all because she was too ashamed to ask for help.

Prick. And then the blood.

Why hadn't she let it just bleed? How silly of her, pinched the wound to cleanse it instead of trying to stop it? But there was the patient, sitting, waiting, such a good patient, her arm bent, she needed to be attended to, surely she was clean, surely in four days the blood test would show she was clean.

What would she do for four days, worrying like this? And even then, after she got the results, she'd have to wait for a whole year to be absolutely sure. Couldn't they do something about this disease anyhow? Why wasn't there more research? Surely if they wanted they could find a cure!

A prick, that's all it was, a simple prick.

It had happened so many times before, it was part of the profession, the risk you took every day you stepped foot into the lab, you had to put it out of your mind, to laugh at it, pretend it didn't exist, the risk that is, the possibility you faced every day that you could contract it. In order to survive, to get on with the job, to get through the day, you stared at your patients, almost mockingly, wondering, hoping nothing like this would ever happen, and at night, when you were home, far from the danger, you heaved a sigh of relief, but not too loud, and only when you were alone, not so loud so no one would know how frightened you really were, not so loud certainly as she was doing now, only now she was really alone, now she was absolutely, frighteningly alone.

Such a small prick, how could anything so horrible enter her body through such a small, small prick?

But there was blood! Red, healthy looking blood. The kind she dealt with every day, except it wasn't always so healthy like hers, or like hers used to be, maybe that's what she had to say now, surely she couldn't say healthy, not for a whole year, not for a whole agonizing year, and the patient was waiting there, her arm bent to close the puncture, "Are you ok?" ("It's nothing to worry about dear, nothing to get your pretty little eyes all red and puffed up about"), staring at her curiously, "Are you ok?"

Of course she was ok!

Really!

At the time!

But then she thought of it, and she wanted to faint, she wanted to scream from way down inside. And everything started to close in on her, like a vortex, like the cartoons her daughter sometimes watched where the picture is suddenly sucked away into nothingness, like dirty bath water as it scowls away down the drain, taking the scum away with it. And her heart began to beat rapidly, like her first day on the job, just four days ago—four long days, but not as long as the next four would be—when she had felt like she was going to her death, how awful the feeling starting a new job, only this time she was right, this time death was waiting for her, this time it was hiding in a test tube, in the veins of the patients she came in contact with, and she was going to die, she was sure of it, even if the test turned out negative, she'd die from the waiting, from the fear that was eating at her, as the virus would eat at her if it turned out positive. God forbid, oh God please, she didn't deserve this, not after the life she had lived, such a good life, such a clean life, please God, she didn't want to die, not yet, not until her baby was born, not until her children grew up!

And what about her baby? What about her baby?

A small prick really, such a small, small prick.

But then there was blood, healthy looking, maybe not so healthy blood.

It's rare, they told her. You're not going to tell your husband, are you? These things happen all the time. It's rare someone gets ill.

Such a small prick. Such a stupid, silly mistake.

But she had to tell him. She wasn't that kind, she certainly couldn't hide something like this from him, though she wondered what he'd say, though she feared his reaction. Would he just avoid her? Would he treat her like some kind of leper, separate her totally from his life?

You'll just get tested, they said. It's voluntary you understand, and the patient's blood will be screened. It's very rare you know. In a few days you'll have the results. But you really won't know, not for a whole year, even if the patient's blood is negative, even if yours is negative, you really won't know for an entire year. And in that time you'll have to be careful: don't share knives and forks, no unprotected sex, for your husband's sake, you know. You're not really going to tell him, are you? But you'll feel better anyhow, even though you'll still have to wait for a whole year and by then you'll have given birth and—

And what about my baby?

What about my baby!?

Prick.

Blood. Healthy looking blood!

But she would have to calm down, she just had to calm down.

After all, it was rare, statistically rare.

Prick.

Such a fatal mistake, If only she hadn't—

Maybe she'd find the patient's number, call her up, ask her.

No matter how unprofessional it might be.

Prick.

If she had only—

If she could just stop breathing so heavily.

If she could just get some rest.

Prick.

Sleep, before her husband got home, sleep all night, a restful sleep.

That's all she wanted.

She deserved that didn't she?

At least that.

Prick.

She would wake up and see it all in a new light.

Surely she was clean.

("Everything'll be all right, dear.")

Prick.

Though she'd have to face it in the morning at work, though she'd have to face her husband eventually.

Maybe she'd wake up and it would all be a dream.

Prick.

A dream.

Prick.

("Just a dream, dear.")

Prick.

An awful, awful nightmare.

Prick.

Prick.

Prick.

And then there was blood!

CROSSING PACIFIC AVENUE

Mrs. Peck usually remained calm. She would listen to Magda's lilting divinations—a keen insight here, a notable clue there—then return to her modest little home on the outskirts of town where she carefully planned her every move until the next regularly scheduled appointment. Her life revolved around these sittings—whether it was auspicious to visit Sadie Greenfield, whose acerbic outbursts could lead to a nasty bout of bickering, or whether it was ominous to venture to the avenue to buy a new bonnet or that expensive pair of shoes she had long been promising herself. The coffee klatch, the bridge game, the occasional visit from her only son—all ranked second to her weekly appointment with Magda, and whether they even took place would depend on her expert clairvoyant counsel.

But today the stars were apparently crossed, for Mrs. Peck observed Magda's swarthy face turn suddenly sallow as she contemplated the spread of Tarot cards she had carefully dealt, pointing excitedly to this card and that and fitfully clutching at her sequined headdress with her long, tapered fingers. Sensing that something was amiss, Mrs. Peck took to tapping her knuckles against the hardness of her elbow, a habit she had not engaged in since the day she had buried her husband.

"This is not good," Magda moaned in her strong gypsy accent, tsk-tsking over the Two of Swords and thrashing her right hand rhythmically against her chest. "In all my years I have never seen such evil!"

"Magda, what is it?" Mrs. Peck asked, peeking apprehensively at the spread that had upset Magda so.

"Oh God, my God, why such evil? I cannot bear to gaze upon the likes of it," Magda lamented, staring off into the dimly lit room with a look that startled Mrs. Peck even further.

Mrs. Peck began to tremble, and a chill skipped down the slightly pronounced curvature of her spine. For six months she had been coming here—six comforting, reassuring months—and she had never seen Magda in such a state.

"Magda, please," she begged, "you've got to tell me."

"You must not leave here" Magda implored, emphasizing each word. "You. Will. Be. Killed."

Mrs. Peck clutched her bony, rheumatic hands together, as her head filled instantly with thoughts that spun direly around in tiny circles causing the wrinkles on her brow to twist in quick rhythmic waves.

"My God," she said at last, the words barely creaking out of her throat. "Why?"

"Why I cannot say. It is God's will."

"But how? Tell me. Maybe I can do something to stop it."

"You cannot change the future, Mrs. Peck. Nor can I. Oh such evil, such evil!" she wailed, beating her breast again as if seeking repentance.

"Magda please," Mrs. Peck pleaded. "I will pay you."

"It is not money I ask for."

Magda peered reproachfully at Mrs. Peck with her small coal-black eyes, shifting the bangles uneasily on her arm.

"Very well," she said finally with a sigh, as she turned to the table and pored once again over the cards.

"I see two streets," she began, pointing to the Two of Swords. "One is wide. Very wide. The other is not so. There is a vehicle. It is large. Perhaps it is a truck. Or a bus. Yes, a bus. And here," she continued, pointing to the Tower, "oh such disaster, such evil, I cannot bear to look upon it," she cried, sweeping the cards up with the swiftness of a vulture.

"That is all, Mrs. Peck. I cannot go on."

"But Magda, you haven't told me everything. You're hiding something."

"When you leave here," Magda whispered, "you must be careful. Very careful."

Mrs. Peck stared blankly, weaving her hands together in nervous amorphous patterns. "Then I will avoid buses," she declared.

"You cannot change the future," Magda repeated emphatically. "Only God can protect you now. That is all."

Mrs. Peck glanced at the table, hoping the cards would reappear in a more auspicious arrangement. Her wish unfulfilled, she fumbled absentmindedly in her purse and extracted a twenty-dollar bill.

"Thank you," Magda said quietly, stuffing the money down the front of her robe. "God be with you."

Mrs. Peck snapped her purse shut, her heart pounding rapidly, and gathered her things.

"I do not like to give my clients such news," Magda apologized before opening the door. "It is not good for business. You wish to see the future?" she intoned to a dark figure sitting in the corner of the waiting room.

A young woman emerged from the shadows and scanned Mrs. Peck's ashen face apprehensively.

"Step this way."

Now Eleanor Peck was by no means a decisive woman. Having been raised in a household where every decision, no matter how small, had been taken by her father, she had grown accustomed to seeking guidance from the men around her and succumbed to their judgment even when she instinctively knew that what they had resolved was not always in her best interests. Her marriage, to a man who just happened to come along after her father had decided that the time was right, had been arranged in this fashion, and her husband, who mysteriously fit into the same mold as her father, managed their family in the same way, so that by the time he died, she had become so settled into this pattern that it seemed she would never be able to get on alone.

So now, as she sat anxiously in Magda's gaudily furnished waiting room, trying unsuccessfully to distract herself by criticizing the decor—she really should get a decorator, tone down the colors, get rid of those sequined curtains—Mrs. Peck wondered just what she was going to do.

What if she walked home? she thought suddenly. It was eleven o'clock and traffic would be light. She could take the side streets.

Surely she wouldn't encounter any buses there. And she'd get to see all those lovely homes with their neatly trimmed gardens. Hadn't she always wanted to do that?

Better still, she could call a cab. She could instruct the driver to take the back route. That way, they'd avoid all the major roads.

Then she remembered Pacific Avenue. No matter how she went, she would have to cross Pacific Avenue.

Mrs. Peck considered all the ways she could possibly get home, but no matter how she tried, she was confronted with Pacific Avenue, and her heart sank with its customary heaviness, only it was deeper now, unlike anything she had known for years.

What if she just took the bus as usual? she thought. It couldn't possibly hit her if she were on it, she reasoned. Unless it happened as she waited, as she stood on the corner, an innocent bystander, distracted by the people going by—yes, she had always liked watching people, mothers walking leisurely with their children, middle-aged ladies taking a late morning stroll, old men cobbling along to pass the lonely hours, how lucky they must be, all of them, how at ease, if only she could be like them now. Maybe when she least expected it, it would strike her, viciously, as it pulled up into the bus stop.

No, she would stand way back, in that little garden on the corner, behind the stone embankment, and after the bus came to a full stop, only after would she begin to approach it. She'd get on through the back door, just in case the driver didn't notice her and the bus suddenly started to move. She'd make an excuse, who cares what the other passengers might think.

Mrs. Peck grabbed a magazine from the table and began to fan herself. She had grown suddenly hot, and sweat was appearing on her restive brow. She pulled a handkerchief from her purse and patted her face dry.

Then it suddenly struck her: perhaps Magda was wrong. Perhaps she had interpreted the cards incorrectly, missed an important clue. Perhaps that awful Tower was meant to fall in a different, less ominous position. It was possible, wasn't it? After all, wasn't it partly based on chance?

Mrs. Peck approached Magda's door. She would ask for another reading. It was her right, wasn't it? After all, she was a steady customer. Wasn't there some sort of rule about it? Wasn't she entitled to pursue a grievance?

She raised her hand to knock when she remembered the woman inside and backed away.

Perhaps the spread was meant for someone else, she said to herself, sinking back into her exasperation. She had been late, hadn't she? By at least ten minutes. God knows who had been there during her regularly scheduled appointment.

Just then, the door to the inner room opened, and the young woman emerged.

"Thank you, Magda," she said, her face beaming—how shallow she seemed, how absolutely gullible—trying to avoid Mrs. Peck's anxious gaze. "See you next week."

"God willing," Magda answered as the young woman left the premises. "Mrs. Peck, are you still here?"

"Magda," Mrs. Peck began hesitantly. "I was wondering. Maybe—do you think, perhaps, another—"

"Mrs. Peck, you must let the fates guide you. Now you go home and, God willing, I'll see you next week."

With that, Magda returned to her room, shutting the door firmly in Mrs. Peck's face.

Hours passed like days, it seemed, filled with uncertainty and anxiety. Mrs. Peck made several attempts to leave, each time hesitating, fearing the worst, ending up right back in Magda's broken-down armchair which had become her sole source of comfort. Each scenario she imagined was fatal, each conceivable means of returning home led to the same disastrous result—the taxi would crash, the bus would run off the bridge that overlooked the train yard, the electric trolley would have a sudden short and she would be instantly electrocuted. She even considered walking home through the old part of town where the streets were narrow and the buses didn't run, but there she would be attacked by wild dogs and confronted by violent gangs: she would be raped and left alone to die. No one would know, she lamented. They'd look everywhere but her body would never be found.

If only her husband were here. He would know what to do. Then she remembered her son. Surely he would help her, despite what he thought about Magda. Surely he would not ignore her pleas. She had no one else to turn to, no one to listen to her woes outside of Magda and Sadie Greenfield.

Sadie Greenfield, she repeated to herself, a weak smile emerging across her face. If anyone would know what to do in a situation like this, it had to be Sadie Greenfield. Still, one had to be careful with Sadie, you never knew how she was going to react. God knows how nasty she could be. That's why she always relied on

Magda's guidance, especially with regards to Sadie, but now she had no choice.

Hands trembling, Mrs. Peck searched her purse for a coin, then went out to the hallway and dialed Sadie's number, her heart thumping anxiously as the phone rang.

"Hello, Sadie. This is Eleanor ... Sadie, the most terrible thing has happened ... You remember Magda, the psychic I told you about? Sadie, she is not a quack ... She has helped me through many a crisis, and you know it ... Sadie, I never knew you felt that way ... Really, I don't know what to say ... You're too busy now? Oh, I see, well if that's the case ... No, no, don't bother calling me tonight. It won't be necessary ... Goodbye."

Mrs. Peck hung up the phone with a humph. Imagine the nerve of that woman! After all these years! Too busy? Busy gossiping, that was more like it. Well, she would show her, she would. It would be a snowy day in summer before she'd call her again. Busy, indeed. Now she would *have* to call her son.

Mrs. Peck rummaged through her purse. What had she done to deserve a day like this! First Magda's dreadful prediction, then Sadie's heartless outburst, and now she could not find change to call her son. A tear pressed its way through, but she forced it back and gathered up her things. She would have to find change, that was all, and that meant leaving the building. She'd show that Sadie! Just wait!

Mrs. Peck walked slowly down the narrow stairs, hesitating at each step. Her body shaking, she forced open the outside door.

It was dark, and the rush hour had reached its peak. Mrs. Peck scanned the street thoroughly. Satisfied, she walked slowly, faltering along among the crowds, veering as far as she could from the curb. She grimaced each time she heard the sound of a truck, at each indication of an approaching bus, holding her breath and bracing herself until the roar of its engine had died down.

All the stores were locked up for the evening. Perhaps that was a sign, she thought, an indication to walk. Besides, now that she couldn't get change to call her son, she had no other choice.

It began to rain: a thin drizzle which gradually increased in intensity. Mrs. Peck picked up her pace, running as fast as her short, stubby legs would allow, until she came to Pacific Avenue, the intersection packed with vehicles, the sidewalks teaming with pedestrians. Her body immediately went into a sweat; her heart beat wildly. She leaned up against the streetlight to support her trembling legs, the specter of Magda's prediction looming before her with all its clarity.

If she could just get lost in the crowd, walk between them!

"Are you all right, miss?" someone asked.

Mrs. Peck gazed at the stranger as if she were in a trance, her face gone white, filled with fear as if she had just seen a ghost.

"Yes," she said, finally, embarrassed at herself. "Yes, thank you."

The light turned green. She took a deep breath and pushed herself forward. Her steps were heavy, and her heart was beating so fast she thought it would take off and abandon her.

Then it happened, suddenly, just as she had reached the halfway point and she was beginning to feel she was going to make it. She was struck, from the right. She let out a cry, and she fell flat on her back in the middle of the street.

When she reached consciousness, she thought she had died, had reached that state she had read about, somewhere between life and death, and soon, very soon, she said to herself, she would be in the hands of the Almighty. Then she felt the pain in her right leg, and she opened her eyes and stared up at the crowd that had gathered around her.

"Am I alive?" she asked, lifting her hands to her face.

Before her stood a young man, his arm and face slightly bruised, his bicycle lying on its side, its wheels still spinning.

"It was an accident, miss," he said. "There were so many people around and ..."

Mrs. Peck smiled at him. Then she laughed quietly. How silly, she thought, remembering Sadie Greenfield's comment, how absolutely silly.

"I'm alive." A bus, Magda had said. She had assured her it would be a bus. "Please, help me up."

"Are you ok?" the young man asked, lifting her onto her feet. "Should I call a doctor?"

"No, I'm fine. Really. Thank you."

"Can I at least help you home?"

"No. I'll be just fine now."

She looked at him kindly, as if he had rescued her from the worst tragedy. "Thank you so very much."

She glanced at the crowd, standing in the rain, watching, wondering about her welfare. How curious, she thought, that they should care. She smiledat them and wanted to cry.

"Thank you so much," she said again, wiping a tear from her eye.

She started to walk. Her leg was painful and she limped slightly, but she was alive, she was so happy to be alive, and when she reached the other side of Pacific Avenue, she let out a shout of joy.

It was pouring now. Behind her, she could hear the cars proceeding, and she detected the groan of the bus as it crawled along in the traffic. She made her way to the bus stop, waited for it to pull up, and stepped on, handing the driver a five-dollar bill.

"Ma'am, you need exact fare."

"Keep the change," she said, her face dripping with rain and tears. "Just keep the change."

THE MEN HAVE COME TO FIX THE DRAIN

One of them is in the bathroom, the other is in the bedroom talking with Mommy.

The drain is full of hair. Mommy doesn't shave. I saw her once when she was taking a shower. Last week, I noticed a couple of hairs on me. Mommy says Daddy likes it that way. But Daddy doesn't like hair in the drain, so Mommy is getting it fixed today.

I like to watch men work. I could sit for hours and just look. It makes me feel kind of tingly all over. Like when Daddy sits and draws pictures for me. He traces the outline and then fills it in with pretty colors. I like to watch his big brown eyes as he works, his mouth, and his big fingers moving slowly along the page. Daddy never hits me. But he doesn't sit with me much anymore. Not like he used to before the changes started coming.

Mommy and the other man stop talking. The bedroom is quiet except for a sound like curtains blowing in the summer air. Then I hear Mommy suck in her breath like she does when I've done something wrong and she's angry, or when she wants to cry.

I try the bedroom door, but it's locked. I knock, and there is silence again.

"Maureen," Mommy calls. "Go play, honey. Mommy is busy."

A warm breeze puffs through the bathroom window. I watch the man take a long, slender object from his work chest. He sticks it in the drain and slides it down. A strange smell comes up on the breeze. Like something old and rotten. I can almost taste it.

I put my ear to the bedroom door and hear Mommy giggling. I wonder why she is so happy today. Then I go back to the bathroom.

The man is jiggling the long metal thing violently in the drain. He pulls and pushes, up and down, up and down with his big hairy arms. His face gets all red, and he begins to sweat. Maybe he's angry. That's how Daddy gets sometimes, with Mommy, when they have a fight. Only Daddy holds Mommy and shakes her. His face gets all puffed up like he's about to explode, and he stomps away. Sometimes Mommy holds me against her right after. She strokes my hair and mumbles to herself. Maybe she's done something wrong and Daddy's found out. Maybe she wants something Daddy won't give her. Either way, Mommy seems hurt.

I would ask the man if he's angry, but Mommy says never talk to strangers. Maybe that's why she decides not to talk anymore to the man in her room. Maybe that's why she lets the curtains and the breeze speak for her.

The man in the bathroom is making a big racket now. His snake—he told me it's called a snake—grates against the drain and makes a terrible sound. I want to cover my ears. I want to shout at him because he's blocking out everything, even the sound of Mommy crying again. Only I can't tell if she's crying. I can't tell what she's doing anymore because the man is making so much noise.

All of a sudden, I feel like screaming at him at the top of my lungs. I feel like telling him to stop what he's doing, to go away and take his friend with him. I don't care about the drain anymore. So what if the water goes down slow. So what if it leaves a dirty ring behind in the sink. I want Mommy. I want to tell her to stop crying. I want to hug her like she hugs me when I'm sad. If I've done something wrong, I will stop it. If only she won't cry anymore. If only Daddy will stop pounding his fist every night after he comes home, after he and Mommy have their usual fight. But the man in the bathroom is making so much noise, and Mommy has the door locked, and Mommy says when I talk to adults to be polite. And I don't feel like being polite right now.

The man in the bathroom turns the water on. Maybe he has read my face, maybe he feels sorry for me. He turns the water off and takes a plunger and begins to work it up and down. The water splashes me like when I've got the shower on too strong.

I strain my ears above the splashing. I can hear Mommy better now. Her voice rises and falls, gets fast, then slow. Like she's running and can't catch her breath. This happens to me sometimes when I'm outside with my friends, only I'm quiet about it and I know better when to stop. But Mommy is almost singing now, as if she's having fun, and I can hear the man too, as if they are both running through the grass and even though they are out of breath, they don't want to stop, and I wonder if Mommy and Daddy ever enjoy being together like this.

The man in the bathroom makes a big plunge, and there is a

huge gurgle as all the hair clears and the water drains. It's a nice sound, makes me feel better, and Mommy too because suddenly I hear her sigh in relief.

The man runs the water in the sink. I listen to it swirl away quickly and cleanly.

Maybe this is what we need, maybe now Daddy will be happy. Because he always complains about the hair in the drain and about the way the water doesn't go down, especially in the morning when he shaves.

Maybe when he gets home tonight and sees what Mommy has done for him, he will be glad.

ACKNOWLEDGEMENTS

Letters from Inside brings together stories I have written over the past 30 or so years. Many of these stories have appeared in literary journals and anthologies, including *Phoebe, The Northern Virginia Review* and *Blue Cathedral.* Some have also appeared in a previous collection, *Sifting Through the Madness* (Xlibris, 2000). Others, like "Key Bridge" and "The Last Laugh," appear here for the first time.

I am grateful to all the editors who have, over the years, read and commented on my work and who have given me encouragement throughout my long, meandering career. Comments like those of Katrina Gray who said that "Suddenly, There Was Harold" was "a brilliant exercise in creating surprise sympathy for a character, and the message—if we were flies on the wall; if love were steady; if we really *listened*—is conveyed so sweetly that the weight of it ends up feeling more like zero gravity" (Atticus Review November 15, 2011). We writers thrive on the currency of reassurance which inspires us to continue pushing forward.

There are many people to thank for allowing me to create stories that I somehow imagined – stories that pop into consciousness like a will-o'-the-wisp and somehow take hold and blossom into existence. First, and foremost, is my family, to whom this book is dedicated, for putting up with me and my creative idiosyncrasies. I also want to thank Susan Richards Shreve who encouraged me, a poet in a fiction class, to continue my storytelling pursuits. Norah

Vawter has also encouraged me throughout the years. And special thanks to Jessica Bell, publisher of Vine Leaves Press and cover designer extraordinaire who, when I told her I had a collection I wanted to publish, responded: "You have a short story collection?"

And to you, the reader, for picking up this volume and giving it a chance.

"The Herds Are Charging Through the Room" *Eratica*, Fall 1998

"Underneath the Griffin Tree" *Phoebe, Volume 28, Number 1,* Spring 1999

"Atelier" *OnCue Magazine*, April, 1999 and in *Creativity and Constraint*, Wising Up Press, Fall 2014

"Letters From Inside" *Blue Cathedral* (Red Hen Press), April 2000

"A Sort of Santa Clause" *Amazon Shorts*, January 2007

"Crossing Pacific Avenue" *Langugeandculture.net*, March 2010

"Suddenly, There Was Harold" *Atticus Review*, November 2011

"Letters From Inside" *Ginosko, #12*, Fall 2012

"A Man and a Fish" *The Hamilton Stone Review, Issue #27*, Fall 2012

"The Departure" *The Northern Virginia Review, Volume 32,* Spring 2018

"Metamorphosis II (or The Sudden and Inexplicable Disappearance of David C. Roche)" *Artlijo (http://www.arlijo.com/), Issue 118*, June 2019.

VINE LEAVES PRESS

Enjoyed this book?
Go to *vineleavespress.com* to find more.